Arsenic in the Azaleas

Lovely Lethal Gardens, Book 1

DALE MAYER

Books in This Series:

ARSENIC IN THE AZALEAS: LOVELY LETHAL GARDENS, BOOK 1
Dale Mayer
Valley Publishing

ISBN-13: 978-1-773361-08-6
Print Edition

About This Book

A new cozy mystery series from USA Today best-selling author Dale Mayer. Follow gardener and amateur sleuth Doreen Montgomery—and her amusing and mostly lovable cat, dog, and parrot—as they catch murderers and solve crimes in lovely Kelowna, British Columbia.

Riches to rags. ... Controlling to chaos. ... But murder ... seriously?

After her ex-husband leaves her high and dry, former socialite Doreen Montgomery's chance at a new life comes in the form of her grandmother, Nan's, dilapidated old house in picturesque Kelowna ... and the added job of caring for the animals Nan couldn't take into assisted living with her: Thaddeus, the loquacious African gray parrot with a ripe vocabulary, and his buddy, Goliath, a monster-size cat with an equally monstrous attitude.

It's the new start Doreen and her beloved basset hound, Mugs, desperately need. But, just as things start to look up for Doreen, Goliath the cat and Mugs the dog find a human finger in Nan's overrun garden.

And not just a finger. Once the police start digging, the rest of the body turns up and turns out to be connected to an old unsolved crime.

With her grandmother as the prime suspect, Doreen soon finds herself stumbling over clues and getting on Corporal Mack Moreau's last nerve, as she does her best to prove her beloved Nan innocent of murder.

Sign up to be notified of all Dale's releases here!

http://smarturl.it/dmnewsletter

Chapter 1

Day 1, Wednesday: The First Day of the Rest of Her Life...

THIS IS WHAT she'd come to? A thirty-five-year-old soon-to-be divorcée, penniless, living in her grandmother's dilapidated home? Doreen Merriweather—back to Doreen Montgomery now—parked her aging Honda Civic in the driveway of what was her new residence in the Lower Mission area of Kelowna, British Columbia. And stared.

Goodness. This was not how she remembered the house. It was just another lump to take in a long line of lumps she'd already taken.

She blew the errant curls of blond hair off her face. The warm spring sunshine highlighted the two-story house's ancient clapboard siding, windows in desperate need of cleaning. Shutters in need of paint or repair, and a roof more covered in moss than shingles. It had a lost-in-time and forgotten-by-the-world air to it.

She could relate.

For just a moment she allowed herself to wallow in self-pity. Her previous home had been an eight-thousand-square-foot mansion in West Vancouver with an in-ground pool and four staff to look after it and her soon-to-be ex-husband—and now Doreen's younger replacement. A smart Barbie doll of twenty-eight. A *very* smart Barbie doll, as Doreen had found out belatedly.

"Just be grateful you have a home at all," she reminded herself. "Without Nan giving this place to me, we'd be on the street at this point." Feeling better, she turned to her pedigreed basset hound, Mugford Horace III, but *Mugs* to her, and said, "Right, boy?"

He gave her a droopy-eyed look.

"I know. You're not impressed either. Still, it's what we have, and we're thankful for Nan's generosity." Just because Doreen's life had changed, didn't mean she wasn't up for the challenge. She knew there would be days when it would all seem to be too much. But she should be used to that as it described most of the last six years of her marriage anyway.

Doreen had signed the separation forms some two weeks after her husband had asked her to leave their house and their marriage. Right before Thanksgiving, in fact. On her lawyer's advice, Doreen signed the divorce settlement papers as well—to have it all over with, even though the divorce couldn't be filed until after she and her husband had been separated for a year. *This way offers minimal emotional pain for you, Doreen. You can move on without having to revisit the painful time in your life.*

Only, shortly after signing all those papers, Doreen had found out that her divorce lawyer was her husband's lover… Yeah, life's a bitch.

And so was her divorce lawyer.

She hadn't figured out what to do about it yet—if anything. Part of her wanted to walk away and leave him to his money—and new girlfriend. Another part of her wanted to fight him tooth and nail and take the house right out from under him.

But how?

She had no money. Or connections. And although her lawyer was as crooked as they came, how did she trust another one to help her right the wrongs done?

Money bought people. And apparently their loyalty too. She couldn't afford to lose any more of either.

Mugs nuzzled her hand. She shook her head, bringing herself back to the present, sitting in her car still parked outside her grandmother's house. Doreen's new reality. She pulled the keys from the ignition and exited her car.

She walked up to the front door. Her grandmother—*Nan* as she preferred to be called to avoid the old-age stigma surrounding "grandma" and all such other labels—had said the keys were atop the doorframe. Doreen reached up and found the key ring, and, with relief, she unlocked the door, pushing it wide open.

For better or for worse, this was the first day of the rest of her life.

Pulling her phone out of her suit pocket, she dialed Nan's number. "Nan, we're here. Just wanted to let you know."

"Thank you for calling, dear."

Doreen heard a rustle on the phone, like Nan covering up the speaker, then she called out as if to someone else in the room, "She's just arrived. A few minutes before noon. Write that down."

And that made no sense. While Doreen was still trying to figure out what her grandmother meant, Nan was talking to her again. "Glad you made it safely, dear. Now make a cup of tea and settle in. We'll talk tomorrow when you're rested." Just at Doreen went to hang up, Nan said, "It's lovely to have you close. I'll get Marge to stop by in a few days. She's gone on a holiday so perfect timing, dear."

Click.

Doreen hung up, shaking her head. Nan was still as quirky as ever. Who was Marge? She wracked her brain looking for a mention of that name and drew a blank. She'd find out later. She had more pressing problems right now. She headed back to the car, to her faithful pet. "Come on, Mugs." She opened the passenger door and waited for him to jump down. He raced across the lawn, his nose down, big floppy ears bouncing with every step.

"Mugs, over here."

He woofed and raced behind her toward the front door.

With him at her side, she stepped across the doorway. She was immediately hit with that *lovely* aged smell that came with the ancient house.

Knowing her circumstances, Nan had convinced Doreen to move into her house with her until a spot opened up at Rosemoor then she could have the house all to herself. Unexpectedly, a spot opened up and Nan had moved in before Doreen had time to adjust her plans. Doreen had been living with friends—or their empty apartments—since leaving her old home. The last place had belonged to a woman she'd been close to. Unfortunately she hadn't realized that without the husband, the prestige, the money... the woman no longer considered Doreen a friend. And her hope that this woman's brother, a lawyer, could help her fix her divorce mistake went out the window.

She'd overstayed her welcome waiting for him to get back into town. Only to realize he'd been in town the whole time and was waiting for her to leave... she'd left the next day.

As part of Nan's decision to live at Rosemoor, she had also decided to give the house to Doreen, Nan's only living relative, so she'd always have a home to live in.

And Doreen was incredibly grateful to have it. She walked to the nearest window in the living room and pushed it wide open, letting in some springtime air, then went to the next room, the formal dining room. It had been a long time since she'd been in the house, and her present reality warred with her past memories.

There was just something about the house of an older person who had lived in it for the last forty-odd years. The living room and dining room overflowed with furniture, all covered in brightly colored afghans. The walls were full of mementos, the shelves full of knickknacks. Decades of items that added joy to Nan's life.

Her gaze roamed the small space, made even smaller by the clutter. In the ensuing weeks Nan had been gone a fine layer of dust had settled over every surface... It would take hours to clean all this...

It would take more time to declutter this place, and Doreen would feel terribly guilty if she disposed of anything without Nan's permission.

Nan might love all these mementos, but Doreen felt claustrophobic with all the large dark furniture crammed into the front two rooms. She walked through to the kitchen and stopped. It was cute, quaint and old. Still, if it functioned, it was more than she had otherwise. She opened the back door and stepped out onto the porch that ran along the back of the house. Outside she found the rear garden, rioting in color and completely overwhelmed with knee-high weeds and out-of-control bushes.

As her gaze wandered the length of the gardens she gasped in delight. "Oh, boy, Mugs," she said. "We have our work cut out for us here."

Yet the gardens thrilled her. Gardening was her thing. During her former life she directed gardeners to do the work. Anytime she'd managed to get her hands dirty, she'd been reprimanded because the cuts from the thorns would mar her skin and digging in the soil would break her nails.

She glanced down at her self-manicure. In no way did they resemble the perfect nails she used to show off. "Well, they've already taken a beating, so what's another one."

Mugs stood in the rear doorway and sniffed the air. When a growl came from deep inside his chest, Doreen hurriedly stepped back and peered around the doorframe. While the house fronted a cul-de-sac and sat in the middle of the circle with neighbors on both sides, the backyard went on seemingly forever. Even at the half-collapsed fencing at the back of Nan's property, more land flowed beyond, unmarred by buildings.

"What's the matter, Mugs?" Doreen glanced around nervously. He obviously took well to his new role as protector.

Before this, she'd never paid attention to his heavily wrinkled eyebrows that shifted and moved when he was upset. He really was a watchdog. And something out there bothered him. Feeling a little spooked, she caught him by the collar and dragged him inside and closed the door.

"First thing we need to do is unload the car. Then I want a cup of tea. Afterward we can explore."

She returned to her car. Emptying the contents from the back seat and the trunk of her Honda to the concrete driveway, she stood amid her measly pile of belongings and shook her head. After fourteen years of marriage, she was reduced to five suitcases and two carry-on bags. What a change. Resolutely she grabbed several of her suitcases and took them up the front porch steps and into the house.

She dropped them at the bottom of the staircase. She didn't even remember how many rooms were upstairs from her last visit, years ago, to see Nan. Wouldn't matter now. Nan could have knocked down walls and made two bedrooms into one for all Doreen knew. She wondered if a usable bed was to be found in any of them.

She collected the rest of her luggage from the driveway and added them to the growing pile inside. Afterward she retrieved Mugs's food and water dishes from the front passenger side of the car. On her last trip, she collected his bag of assorted dog food and treats, then made a clean sweep of the Honda's interior to make sure she hadn't left anything behind. She locked the car, walked inside, and shut the front door.

She leaned against it and studied her new home.

Nan had said something about looking after her Maine coon cat that generally lived outside. So far there had been no sign of it.

"Oh." Doreen brightened. "Mugs, is that what you smelled out back? Was it the cat?" She walked to the back door again and opened it. "Hey, kitty, kitty. This is your home, kitty, but Mugs lives here now too."

Mugs growled. Then came a howl and a hiss, before a screaming cat ripped inside the house between Doreen and Mugs. Instantly the dog barked and gave chase. Standing with her back to the rear doorway, in her three-thousand-dollar Chanel suit she had traveled in, Doreen watched as her professionally pedicured dog happily chased the crap out of the ragtag cat that looked to be almost bobcat size.

What the heck had Doreen gotten herself into?

Chapter 2

P ROMISING HERSELF A cup of hot tea in the near future, Doreen took her glass of water and left the back door open—so Mugs could join her if he wanted, especially to avoid that cat. "*Goliath*," she murmured, finally remembering Nan's cat's name. Doreen wandered outside to the veranda, which drifted down the full width of the house, noting a matching set of steps that led to the deck, one from each end of the veranda.

She wasn't hungry, even though it had to be noon or later. After all, she had spent all morning driving here.

With peace established inside—Nan's cat taking refuge under one of the many pieces of furniture cluttering the living room and Mugs no longer barking but feeling proud of himself—Doreen collapsed into the nearest of the two wooden chairs on the veranda and stared at the backyard. A nice deck connected the back of the house to the grassy area of the yard.

It was such a gorgeous afternoon. The sun cast beautiful beams of light across the property, and the waist-high overgrown garden added some shadows too.

Nan's property.

Now Doreen's property.

Legally. Or soon to be. Nan had already started the transfer documents.

Odd to consider this was the first home Doreen had owned herself. Never in a million years would she have expected to end up here in this stage of her life. It was both daunting and exhilarating. Her marriage had been on the rocks for years, and she'd been desperate for a change... but wow. Watch what you ask for.

Looking back, she felt a little guilty and wondered what Nan's life had been like during Doreen's marriage, when Doreen had been led around the world on her husband's arm for years. When Doreen had been a child, she had been best friends with Nan, until Doreen's mother had married up in life, and Doreen had been shipped off to boarding school.

Her mother's death years later had brought Doreen and Nan closer together again, until Doreen had married her own wealthy nightmare. Then Doreen's relationship with Nan had been shunted back to phone calls and the odd solo visit. Mostly when she could get her husband to allow her the time away. Now Doreen and Nan only had each other. And that made it lovely to move closer so they could spend the most of what time they had left together.

Doreen's previous life seemed so far removed from where she'd landed now. Although this house was paid for, she still needed to find a way to make a living to pay her monthly bills and to put food on her table as well as to pay for the dog's food. According to Nan, the water bill here was horrific, and the power companies were thieves. Doreen had not worked the whole time she had been married. Her controlling husband had deemed it "demeaning." So Doreen had job searches and job applications and job interviews to look forward to as well.

But what did she *really* want to do with the rest of her life?

She sighed, shook her head. Those were tomorrow's messes to deal with. Today was about getting moved in and settled for the night.

Mugs walked over and sat down beside her.

He had something in his mouth, but she had no idea what. When he crunched it with a bone-breaking noise, she bounded to her feet and stared at him, aghast. "Where did you get that?"

A bit of grass stuck out one corner of his mouth.

Whatever it was had come from outside the house. But, since Mugs hadn't been in the garden in the front yard or in the backyard yet, chances were that the cat had brought it inside. And that could mean all kinds of horrible things. Doreen had no experience with cats, but she'd heard the horror stories… "Mugs, that's disgusting. Drop it."

When he didn't, Doreen's face twisting in distaste, she leaned over for a closer look. Was it a bone? But what kind of a bone? "Mugs, give it to me. Let me look at that."

He gave her a grunt and backed away.

Crap.

She got on her hands and knees to peer closer. A bone wouldn't be so bad, but something appeared to be sticking out the end of it. She tried to grab it from him, only Mugs backed up again.

Slowly she followed him on all fours. "Come on, boy. You don't want that nasty bone. Give it to me, and I'll get you some proper dinner." Inspired by the idea, she hopped to her feet and ran inside to his stash of goodies, found his treats, shaking the bag as she ran out the back door.

Immediately Mugs dropped the bone and raised his nose to sniff the air. When Doreen held out a chicken twist for him, he smelled it, then decided he preferred the bone at his feet.

"No! Wait, Mugs. No." She shoved the treat into his face a second time.

He gave her an offended look but slowly took the treat, dropping the bone once more.

Instantly she snatched it out of his reach. She turned it over and screamed, tossing the small fleshy thing to the wooden floor of the veranda. Mugs raced for it, but she shooed him away. Using a piece of old cardboard found on the side of the veranda, she scooped up the bone and placed it on the little outside table. Gasping, her heart pounding, she peered closer.

The bone had skin on it—and a fingernail at the end. A nicely manicured man's nail.

Mugs had been chomping on a human finger.

Chapter 3

A N HOUR LATER Doreen faced yet another *first*.
Police. They were as foreign to her as the world they worked in. She'd never met anyone who worked for the police. And hadn't ever needed their assistance. Was there a specific etiquette she should follow? Typical of her husband's overall mind-set in ruling her world and her actions, Doreen shouldn't be so surprised that she would even consider such an issue.

She really couldn't expect to undo all her bad habits formed in her fourteen-year marriage in only six months' time. Yet, she was working on that.

While waiting for the police to arrive, Doreen had transferred the finger from the small table on the rear veranda to the little matching table on the front porch. And she had made sure Mugs remained inside the house, separated from the finger, although she had lost track of Goliath.

As the RCMP car pulled into her driveway behind her Honda, she headed outside and stood on her front porch, wondering at the strange turn her "new" life had taken. The driver got out, and she plastered a bright smile on her face and then immediately wiped it off. This was hardly a social occasion. She could shake their hands. That was businesslike, right?

When the first officer arrived at her front porch steps, she was lost as to what expression was appropriate for the occasion. So she just blurted out, "I think there is a body on the property."

The older man remained silent, surprise lighting his taciturn face.

She stared, fascinated, as his bushy eyebrows rose into his forehead. How did that work? They were like Groucho Marx's in size, only longer. She gave an inward shudder. She wanted to run inside and grab scissors and clip them into shape. If she did that, he'd lock her up as being a lunatic. Half hysterical, she wondered if she could make a business of eyebrow trimming. There was obviously a need for her services in this town, but would they pay her or would she have to pay them to give her the opportunity?

"I'm sorry, ma'am. What did you say?"

She took a deep breath, clenched her fists against her belly, stiffened her spine and said, "Maybe you should come on the front porch, and I could show you instead."

He seemed to be waiting for his partner, who was bent over the cop car, talking on a handset pulled through the open window, standing just outside the car door. The first man was as old and grizzled as the second man was young and dynamite—a tall blond Adonis.

Her breath escaped slowly as she tried to calculate his age.

Early thirties she figured.

Immediately her mind calculated their age difference. There were all kinds of rules to such a relationship. She wanted to race back inside and check. She had them written down somewhere. She should know them by heart. But after Sally Browning had had a relationship with somebody thirteen years her junior and had been ostracized from all the tea parties, Doreen wasn't sure she had the appropriate rules to go by in this instance. After all, Doreen was only a couple years older than Adonis, right?

Right?

Regardless, she thought Sally should've been totally fine dating a younger guy. It wasn't that she and her much-younger boyfriend were doing anything other than having an affair. Everyone knew that, when having an affair, age didn't count. It was only when that affair turned to something long-term that age differences caused eyebrows to raise.

Unless of course money was involved—then all rules were off. Because everyone knew that money made age go away.

And made wives—future and former—come and go too.

"Ma'am, what is it you wanted to show me?" the older officer asked.

She dragged her gaze from the younger officer until he tossed the handset on the passenger seat and stood fully upright. Crap. He was as cute standing as he had been slumped over. Only taller than she expected. Much taller.

Finally pulling her attention back to the officer in front of her, she pointed at the small table off to the side of her front porch where she'd carefully placed the offending bone. "It's that."

He glanced at the table, back at her and asked, "What is?"

She half turned and pointed at the table again. "I put it on the table."

The second officer joined them. She beamed at Adonis.

Both policemen stared at her. "What about the table?" the older man asked.

She exhaled heavily. "Not the table but what's on the table."

Both men stared at the table from where they stood on the ground next to the porch steps. "Just a piece of old cardboard is on the table." The second man's voice was lighthearted and cheerful.

Too cheerful. As if he were humoring her. Instantly his cuteness rating dropped several notches. She glared at the table and froze. *No. No, it can't be.* "Oh, my God, it's gone."

"What's gone?"

She spun around and stared at the younger officer. "I told the dispatcher that I think a body is here."

"And what... made you think... that?" the older officer asked in a slow and patient voice.

She glared at him. "Because of the finger."

At the word *finger*, both men straightened to attention.

She nodded with satisfaction. "I should think so. That dratted cat brought it inside. I swear it was him. Mugs would never have touched it first. But then Mugs took it away from him," she admitted. "I brought it out here and put it on the front porch table, waiting for you guys to show up." She glared the table. "I bet it was Goliath's doing. He never forgave Mugs for stealing it away from him."

"Mugs? Goliath?" the older officer repeated.

She raised both hands, palms up. "Aren't you listening? The cat brought it in."

The younger man smiled. "Is the cat *Goliath* by any chance?"

"I just said so, didn't I?" She turned her back to the men, now so flustered that she didn't know what to do. If she couldn't produce the finger, no one would believe her. Therefore, no one would check out the backyard because she certainly wasn't going to until she got an all clear from someone. Neither would she let that cat back into the house to bring home more body parts. Turning, she announced firmly, "We have to find the finger. The cat probably stole the darn thing back again."

"When did you last see him?"

She stared at the young man she had thought was cute. His brand of *cute* was only on the outside. He had to have a fully functioning brain going on inside to rightly earn the term. "I saw him just a while ago, of course. He couldn't have gone far." She shook her head. "Never mind. The finger must be around here somewhere." She searched the furniture on the front porch. "Check the floorboards. Maybe the cat dropped it. Or maybe he took it inside." She opened the front door and then stopped. "No, it can't be inside. It was here when I heard you drive up." She shut the door and frowned, facing the officers again.

"I haven't seen the cat since we arrived, ma'am," said the younger officer.

The older man walked up and down the length of the porch, supposedly looking for a finger, but he didn't appear to be putting too much effort into it.

She sighed. Loudly. She so didn't need this.

"But Nan did have a big Maine coon cat. She used to take it with her everywhere," the younger man added. "It was a character. Then Nan is too."

"She's my grandmother. So is she yours too?" She studied the man closer. "Are we related?"

The younger officer laughed. "No, the community knows her as Nan also."

"*Great.* That'll make for a confusing few weeks." But it pleased her that Nan was so well-known and apparently well-loved.

Not to mention that she and Adonis were not related.

"She had a cat *and* a parrot," the older man murmured, his gaze still on the flooring of the porch.

"Well, if a parrot is here, I haven't met it yet," Doreen said. "I just arrived. I'm still finding my way through the house. It's a maze of clutter." She frowned. "But I believe Nan did tell me a bird was here. I assumed it was outside."

"Thaddeus tends to wander where he wants. He flies but not terribly well. When you see him, you'll never forget him." The officers looked at each other and grinned.

From the far side of the front porch, she heard a wild squawk. She pivoted and saw a beautiful blue-gray bird standing on the railing, facing her. He was at least a foot tall with long red tail feathers. "Oh, my goodness! Is that him?"

The cops laughed. The younger man said, "Yes, that's Thaddeus."

"Thaddeus is here," the bird said with great stage presence, strutting along the top of the railing. "Thaddeus is here."

"Oh, great. He talks," Doreen muttered, staring at the bird. That was the last thing she needed when Goliath had been dragging human body parts inside the house.

As if understanding her thoughts, the huge orange feline erupted from under the front porch. It raced up a few of the porch steps, then stopped and looked at the humans disdainfully. He took two more steps, dropped his butt, shot his hind leg into the air and proceeded to lick his behind.

In front of one and all.

The only thing that Doreen could think of was how horrified her husband would be with this scene right now. She had to chuckle at that image.

On cue, Thaddeus squawked before speaking. "Thaddeus is here. Thaddeus is here."

Doreen groaned with a shake of her head. "That'll get old very quickly."

"He doesn't say very much, but he is a character." The younger officer walked over and brushed the feathers along Thaddeus's cheek and neck. "He's very personable. Most of the townsfolk know him. Nan, of course, took him with her everywhere too."

"Wonderful," Doreen said half under her breath. "I sure hope no more pets are around here. Mugs is having enough trouble adapting to the cat. I can't imagine him with a parrot, particularly one that talks."

"Mugs?" asked the older man. "Who's that?"

"My dog."

He gave a half snort. "Fun times ahead."

She shrugged. "Not so fun if I can't find the dratted finger again. You two will never believe me without proof." She glanced at the floorboards and found a small hole. She dove to the porch floor and studied the shadows below. "Something's down there. It's just out of reach, and even two of my fingers can't fit at the same time inside this hole. Plus it's hard to see for sure." She thought it was the finger. She darn well hoped it was. She'd already made a fool of herself. She sure didn't want them to think she was a liar too. "I accidentally bumped the table when I came outside. It must have rolled off then."

"Let me see." The older officer got down on his hands and knees. "Well, something's there all right." He twisted his head sideways. "I can't rightly say it's a bone though."

"I've got a pair of tweezers in my purse. Let me go grab them." She dashed inside the house, leaving the door open for just a moment. She found the tweezers and returned to the front porch to find that Mugs was now outside, his tail wagging, as he slobbered his joy all over the officers.

"Darn it… I walked inside for two seconds. What kind of watchdog are you anyway, Mugs?"

"So he only barks when he feels like it?" the older officer joked.

"So far, just when the darn cat ran through the house with the finger. Probably jealous because I think he wanted a fresh bone too."

The two men looked at one another in fascination.

"Sorry." She winced. "I guess you both think I'm a little odd."

The two officers shook their heads very slowly. "No, ma'am. We know Nan well. You are very similar." The older man grinned and stuck out his hand. "The name's Arnold, Constable Arnold Depruis. Welcome to town."

She flushed and shook his hand, still flustered. She brushed her hair back and smiled at the younger man. "And you are?"

"Constable Chester Pearson. But you can call us Arnold and Chester. Nice to meet you."

Tossing a bright smile his way, she dropped back to her knees on the floorboards, positioned over the hole again. The finger had fallen into the hole and rested on a crossbeam underneath. If it had dropped any farther, she'd likely have lost it forever.

She focused and very carefully pulled the offending item out between the boards. "Well, Arnold and Chester, do you think I'm telling the truth now?" She held it up triumphantly and said, "See? I wasn't lying."

Both men leaned in to take a closer look and immediately turned more businesslike. Arnold shifted his hat back and said, "Well, look at that. It's a finger all right."

Mugs barked at her feet and tried to jump for her hand, and somewhere close by a cat howled. Likely Goliath was pissed that he had lost his treat.

Doreen smirked as she laid the nasty thing back onto the cardboard triumphantly. "See? The rest of him has to be around here somewhere too."

But Thaddeus put the icing on the cake. He squawked loud and long, then cried out, "Body in the garden. Body in the garden."

Chapter 4

WHILE THE POLICE searched the property, Doreen searched the kitchen in vain for a teakettle. The police had been here for what seemed like hours, and she needed the comfort of a hot cup of tea. After hunting through the cupboards, she had only found a well-stocked pantry, confirming Nan had lived off canned goods. There were canned beans, canned soup and canned fish. Doreen saw what appeared to be canned potatoes. She stared at it, shuddered and closed the cupboard quickly. Did Nan have any teeth left? Maybe that was the problem.

Doreen knew Nan was a big tea drinker, but Doreen couldn't find any kettle to plug into an outlet. When she opened another cupboard, she found an old-fashioned stovetop kettle. The trouble was, Doreen and stoves didn't get along. Then, of course, she hadn't had much of a relationship with one either. She never had to cook during her entire marriage, and she'd never cooked growing up either. Now that she was single and on her own, she had yet to fathom the depths of how that whole producing-wonderful-food thing worked.

But, if there was ever a time to force herself to try, it was now. Because, above all else, she desperately wanted a cup of tea. That was, if a double-shot no-fat latte or a latte with sprinkled cinnamon on top wasn't available. And, considering her current lack of finances, those fancy coffees would likely never be available to her again.

She pulled out the funky-looking kettle, clicked the button at the top to open the lid and filled it with water from the sink. She walked over to the ancient stove and put the kettle atop one of the rings. She studied the stove for a long moment, but, for the life of her, she didn't know which knob would turn on the right-hand burner in the front. Age had taken its toll on the stove, wearing off all helpful markings—the same as the rest of the house had aged.

She would just have to experiment. She turned on both knobs on the right side where she'd put the kettle. Surely this was intuitive. Unfortunately the smell of gas immediately hit her nose. She shut off both knobs and turned on the other two on the far left side. When she smelled gas again, she quickly turned off those.

Back to one of the cupboards again, she pulled out a couple teacups to peer farther inside, then grinned. She reached far back into the cupboard and pulled out a bright and shiny electric kettle. Nan might not have liked it or used it, but Doreen was thrilled. She filled it with water and plugged it in. "Now we're in business."

For Nan and Doreen, teatime was a beloved hobby. Yet no teapots were visible. At least none that she'd found. But there were teacups. She took out a large one, then found a drawerful of different tea bags and tins full of loose tea leaves.

Studying the varieties, she was astonished at their names, like chamomile tea and dandelion leaf tea. Why would anybody want to put hot water on top of dandelion leaves? Dandelions were considered weeds, the bane of her husband's gardeners. She just didn't get it. But she spied a box of black tea bags, and she figured that was her best option. She dropped one into the teacup and waited for the water to boil.

Leaning against the sink, her back to the window, she deliberately didn't want to look out the window because police officers crawled all over the property. That lovely bone came from somewhere.

As she'd found out on her drive into town earlier this morning, Kelowna was smallish, and the Mission area was tiny. Thus the Kelowna RCMP detachment had only ten full-time staff, as Chester had shared. She swore they were all here in her backyard. Surely they'd be done soon. The property wasn't that large. But she was afraid that, if she went outside, with her luck, she'd be the one to find the body.

Raising even more suspicions from Arnold and Chester.

Beside her, the teakettle whistled. She frowned as the little silver lid snapped up and down. She took that to mean the water was boiling. She poured hot water into the teacup. She sniffed the air experimentally above it, and it did smell like tea, regular old-fashioned black tea. Embolden with that simple success, she opened the back door and stepped onto the veranda.

None of the officers were close to her now. She figured it was safe to sit down and watch their shenanigans. Who knew she had such a gruesome curiosity? Plus her feet ached, and she needed to get off them. She was used to wearing high heels all day long but couldn't for some reason here in Nan's house. Maybe it was the uneven floor. She didn't know.

Her entire wardrobe was completely unsuited for her new lifestyle. Along with that fact came another—she had no money to change it. And she wouldn't have a clue where to buy everyday jeans. The only jeans she owned had designer labels on them, were skintight and didn't wear worth a darn. Whereas everybody she'd seen so far in this town wore blue jeans or leggings that looked durable.

That was what she needed. Something she could afford and which would last. She might have to follow Nan's advice and go to the church bazaar and find something secondhand. Just the thought made her shudder.

She wasn't snooty or too proud. She just wasn't at that point yet of trying to navigate the process. Wearing other people's hand-me-down clothes made her wonder about the original owner. Who they were? Why they'd discarded the clothes? Had they gained weight? Lost weight? Changed jobs? Speaking of jobs, how much could she expect to earn from a job here in the Mission? Heck, she had no idea what kind of a job she would be suited for. Would anyone want to hire her? Her, a discarded rich man's trophy wife?

As she looked down at her Chanel suit, she figured it would probably take a year's wages at whatever new career she found in this small town just to pay for another one of these. On the other hand, she didn't need any more Chanel suits. She had those already, should they ever be needed on occasion in Lower Mission. Still, it would probably take a year's worth of time for her to no longer worry about whether she was perfectly coiffed, all to avoid getting snarky, nasty remarks from her husband.

Only after she fully got away from her marriage did she realize the stress and pain involved in maintaining appearances for his sake. And how his constant criticisms—when she didn't achieve the required level of perfection—were more about him and not so much about her.

How her nails had always been the wrong color, her lipstick had always been too bright. Her eye shadow had never been stylish enough. He said her hair, the last time she had it done, made her look like an old woman.

Of course it hadn't made her look old, but, in his eyes, he was ready for a younger trophy wife. Well, he had found her in Doreen's divorce lawyer.

How was that for irony?

One thing Doreen had learned from that mess was to laugh at herself. She knew she was an anomaly. Nobody would feel sorry for her after her years of the rich and lavish lifestyle. But rarely did people see the other side of that lifestyle. How Doreen needed to be perfectly fit, a perfect decoration always. To smile, even though she hated the people her husband brought through the house. And, when his hand cupped her butt blatantly in front of others, how hard it was to not turn around and smack him for his lack of respect.

She took it because, most of the time, he was fine. He was worse in front of his peers. When she had first met him, she'd been totally in love with him. That had faded quickly. But, by then, she had already been groomed for her role as his wife. Another pretty bauble for him to show off. Never mind that she had a brain.

But what about her growth as a person? Nobody ever really cared about that. A decade into her marriage, well, that was a whole different story. She finally woke up to seeing how much she was missing in life. Things she'd never have a chance to experience. She didn't know who she was, what she was, or who she wanted to be. All she knew was what *her husband* had expected her to be while married to him. But what did *she* expect to be, to do, to become?

"Find time to figure that out, idiot," she said out loud but with affection. "And you promised to never put yourself down again."

She had taken enough of that from her husband. Almost worst was his sister. That woman had hated Doreen. The feeling had been mutual. Doreen had never been allowed to say anything catty or mean to her back then. Of course not. Her dratted husband wouldn't have allowed that. And he'd ruled the roost.

"Ma'am?"

Startled, she stood, her tea sloshing, almost spilling on her suit. She walked to the railing to see the younger officer, Chester, standing at the foot of the nearest veranda steps, which led to the uncovered deck in the backyard. "Yes?"

"Have you been in the backyard at all?"

She shook her head. "I told you that I just arrived today, around noon, moving into the house."

She really wondered why the people in this town didn't understand what she was saying. She was a British Canadian living in a British Canadian town. It wasn't like she was French Canadian with an accent. Before she'd lived only a five-hour drive away in the British Properties area of West Vancouver. Yet it seemed she had to keep repeating everything she said three or four times since arriving here. "I can prove that I drove all the way from Vancouver this morning," she said, "if you don't believe me."

He gave her a surprised look and shook his head. "It's not that I don't believe you. But we found a lot of footprints back here."

"What?" She leaned forward but couldn't see anything

where he pointed. She set her teacup on the little table and walked down the veranda steps using the wobbly railing for support. The old place was falling apart. As soon as she stepped on one of the wooden planks of the deck, it squeaked and groaned under her weight. And she knew for sure that, at five feet seven and 125 pounds, she was not overweight. No matter what her husband said.

Shrugging off her husband's insults, she walked toward the officer, now at the far edge of the deck, and noted as he pointed out several footprints in the yard. The area had been roped off to avoid any further contamination of the scene.

"But those could've been here a long time. Maybe they are Nan's."

He looked down at her, his head cocked. "You don't have anything to compare them to right now. But they're large, like a man's size eleven."

Her eyebrows rose. "No, not Nan's. Those are big feet."

He pointed at his. "Mine are a ten. Those footprints are bigger than mine."

"Maybe they belonged to the dead man?" she asked, her voice rising in horror.

He stopped and stared at her. "Do you know who the dead man is?"

She frowned. "No." *Be patient, Doreen.* "Remember? I just got here." Man, she wanted to put that sentence into audio format and just hit the Rewind and Play buttons. It would save her a lot of time and effort.

But Chester still stared at her as if he couldn't figure out what made her tick.

Good luck with that. How could he know when she didn't?

Finally he shook his head and said, "No sign of a body

yet."

"Well, unless somebody is walking around town with an amputated finger and just accidentally left the appendage here on my property, I suggest you keep looking." She glanced at her heels and said, "I could change my shoes and come out to look too."

"No, just stay where you are. The less people out here, the better."

She chuckled and looked at the dozen people already on her property. "What possible difference could one more person make?"

"We're all professionals, ma'am. We know what we're doing."

"It doesn't look like you do, when you haven't found the body yet," she said in exasperation. She held up her hand to stop him from speaking. "Okay, fine. I'll go sit on the veranda." She delicately made her way to the steps. Before she reached them, she turned to Chester and asked, "Did you check under the deck?"

He instantly spun to address her. "Why would I check *under* the deck?"

She stared at him wordlessly for a full moment, getting a grip on her frustration. "Because it's a possible hiding place to put a body?" From the doubtful look on his face, she didn't think she would get any kind of a meeting of the minds here.

"Of course it's a great hiding place. I just thought maybe you knew that's where the body was."

"Let me tell you *one more time*. I haven't been in this house in years until I arrived about noon today from Vancouver. I don't know who the man is who belongs to that finger. In the three hours or so that I've spent here today—the last two hours of which I have had policemen crawling all over my property—I never saw anybody else in this place, and I did not put a dead body under the deck." On that note she turned away, gingerly went up the steps, retrieved her tea and stalked into the house. Her last act of revenge was to slam the door. Hard.

Chapter 5

B ACK INSIDE SHE decided to take Mugs for a walk. She
changed her heels for Nan's bright pink garden shoes
on the back veranda, put Mugs on a leash, grabbed her purse
and walked out the front door. If the police wanted to talk to
her, they could call her. Because she'd had enough of them.
She sauntered down the street, waving at a couple neighbors
who called out to her. She pretended not to hear them when
they asked questions, and she just kept on strolling by.

What was she supposed to say? *Oh, the police? No problem. I just have a body in the garden.* Or how about, *Oh, it's
nothing. I'm sure that finger I found wasn't connected to
anything to be concerned about.*

She refused to contemplate what happened to the poor
man normally attached to that finger. Best scenario was a
neighbor lost the finger in an accident using power tools.
Her husband always said they were dangerous things.

As a vehicle slowed while passing her, the driver's gaze
curious, she stared resolutely ahead. Not the preferred first
day to her new beginning that she'd hoped for. These people
barely knew her, and Nan was already eccentric enough.
Apparently everyone was checking out Doreen sideways to

see if she would be a chip off the old block. According to Chester and Arnold, she probably was.

Just as she got to the end of the block, she heard a single *flap* sound behind her. She turned to see Thaddeus flying— no, make that coasting—toward her. He landed on top of Mugs, who immediately twisted in a circle, trying to get at the bird riding him like a horse.

Goliath streaked past too, the huge cat brushing up against Doreen's calf in the process.

"Oh, for God's sake." She brushed the bird off Mugs's back. The bird immediately hopped to her arm and did a weird slide step up to Doreen's shoulder.

"Thaddeus is here. Thaddeus is here," he squawked in her ear.

"Really? Like I didn't know that already?" she cried out, trying to stare at him. He cocked his head at her. "You can't just sit there." She'd come to a complete stop on the sidewalk. How was she supposed to walk with him on her shoulder? But Thaddeus had no problem with it. His claws dug into her shoulder but never hard enough to really hurt. Nan had obviously trained him well. Besides, he was beautiful.

He looked down at her… as if waiting for her to sort herself out.

"Okay, fine. But you behave yourself."

"Thaddeus is here. Thaddeus is here." Instead of shouting it, he crooned it softly, rubbing his head along hers.

She nuzzled back, grinning in spite of herself, and then proceeded to walk toward town.

Instead of being upset by the crap going on in her back-yard, she had a spring in her step. Maybe this would work out after all. She didn't have any chosen direction to walk or any definitive purpose for going to town. She just needed to take Mugs for a walk and, well, to get away from the madness at her house.

She turned right, taking a path along the creek.

She crossed one of the small footbridges and stopped, looking at the water below. It really was beautiful here. She could see how Nan would've enjoyed her years spent in this town. Doreen brightened. Maybe that's what she should do—visit Nan. The retirement home wasn't very far away. Nan had one of the outer studio apartments on a corner with lots of light where she had French doors leading to a patio and a small garden. She could have her meals at the main center, or she could do her own cooking. But Doreen knew Nan. She didn't do much in the way of cooking. And only cooked what came from a can, apparently.

Doreen grabbed her phone and called Nan. "Are you up for a little bit of company?"

"Oh, my goodness. I would be delighted," Nan said. "When?"

Doreen laughed. "I'm walking toward you right now. Thaddeus is on my shoulder, and I've got Mugs beside me. And the cat is sauntering close by too."

"Oh, my dear, that would be absolutely wonderful. I'll put on the kettle."

When her grandmother hung up the phone, Doreen had to laugh. Nan wasn't one to hold the phone to her ear while preparing tea. But then Nan had been late getting into the Technology Era. She still felt the phone—a plugged-in landline no less—belonged in the hallway near the front door and nowhere else.

Doreen changed direction and kept walking until she could see Rosemoor, the retirement home, up ahead. It had both full-care and partial-care facilities. She really didn't know anything else about it. She had never known anybody who lived in one, until Nan. And this one appeared to be unique in a town that didn't have a large population, so they had gathered together a lot of people with various needs into a single building. One end was a full nursing home for people mostly bedridden. On the opposite side were small independent living apartments. That was where Nan currently lived. Doreen assumed, when people's conditions worsened, they were moved to the north end of the complex.

That kind of sucked. But, on the other hand, Nan was still in her right mind, so maybe it was all good.

As Doreen walked up to Nan's apartment, Nan stepped onto her patio and waved. Thaddeus immediately left Doreen's shoulder and flew across the beautiful lawn toward Nan and landed on her shoulder. Even from this distance, Doreen could see the affection between the two. Her heart warmed. Maybe having Thaddeus around wouldn't be so bad after all.

Doreen was supposed to go inside the main lobby entrance and around to the front door of Nan's apartment, but, with Mugs and the bird and the cat, she knew she wouldn't be allowed inside. So, ignoring the Do Not Walk on the Grass sign, she cut across the lawn and quickly stepped onto the stonework patio.

Hearing the horrified gasp at the edge of Nan's patio, Doreen turned her head and stared at an older man. She hadn't seen him working in the gardens from the sidewalk. He glared at her and pointed at the sign.

She winced, gave him an apologetic smile and quickly turned away. *Shoot.* She didn't want to make a bad impression in her new life, but, so far, she'd done nothing but.

"Don't worry. That's Grumpy George," Nan said with a chuckle. "He's a stickler for rules and keeps track of the blades of grass here, like a farmer does his sheep."

Chuckling at the nickname, Doreen bent to give Nan a hug, amazed at how strong her grandmother's hug was. Nan, while aging gracefully even with her somewhat gnarled fingers, was petite with her tiny wrists. And the smile on her face was, as always, full of pure love. It brought tears to Doreen's eyes. She'd missed this woman a lot.

"Take a seat, dear."

Doreen pulled out the other little wrought-iron chair and sat down at the small bistro table. The patio wasn't much bigger than a ten-by-ten-foot square, so there wasn't a whole lot of room for furniture. It was cozy and suited this downsized version of Nan. As Doreen looked at the teapot, she frowned. It appeared to be a flower upside down with its stalk as the spout. "That's quite a teapot, Nan."

She laughed, her voice rippling around the garden, seemingly making even the sunshine brighter. "Isn't it? I picked it up at a secondhand store. You have to go over there, my dear. They have treasures unlikely to be found anywhere else in this world." She shook her head and smiled, patting the little teapot. "I know it's an oddity, but, at my age, I should be allowed a few of those."

"We should be allowed those at whatever our age," Doreen said with a big smile.

"And yet, you don't." Some of Nan's bright laughter fell away, and Nan's voice sharpened. "You were barely even living before, my dear. But look at you now. You're not coated in makeup, and your nails look like you have lived a normal person's life instead of a model's. That smile of yours—it's the best part—because that's the first real emotion I've seen on your face in a long time."

"That's not true," Doreen protested. Inside, she hoped it wasn't true.

"No, maybe not," Nan admitted. "Your only other emotions lately have been the pain and loss of your husband to your divorce attorney and the loss of your marriage—or more the loss of a way of life and your complete lack of comprehension of what that meant for you." Nan shook her head. "I never said anything all those years you were married. But you never looked happy. It's like you were shaped into a Barbie doll, and that was the role you played. And you played it well. Until your husband was no longer happy with Barbie and changed it for a china doll." She waved her hand up and down at Doreen. "Look at you. Your super expensive suit, and yet, those must be my gardening shoes." Nan bent forward under the table to stare at them. "Oh, my goodness, where did you find them?"

Doreen kicked out her legs. "They were on the back veranda."

Nan laughed. "See? That's what I mean. A year ago you never would've been caught dead in them."

"But they're comfortable," Doreen said. "Besides, I had to run out of the house and get away from the cops."

Silence fell at those words. Nan stared at Doreen, and her jaw slowly dropped open. She leaned forward. "What have you done that the cops are in the house?"

Nan didn't know anything about it. "Oh, my goodness, I didn't do anything. I blame your cat for this." She quickly explained what the cat had brought home and how Mugs had stolen the finger from the feline.

When Doreen got to the part about the dratted thing dropping the bone onto the front porch and then disappearing in the cracks of the floorboards, Nan shook her head and giggled. "You are a disaster." Then her giggles turned into full-blown laughter. "I love it."

"You love that a body's on your property?" Doreen stared at Nan for a long moment, wondering where her grandmother's humorous reaction came from. As far as Doreen knew, her grandmother was one of the sweetest old ladies ever. On the other hand, sweet old everyday ladies could have a dark side. Doreen leaned forward and asked, "Nan, did you kill somebody and bury him in the backyard?"

That sent Nan into absolute hilarity. By the time she finally calmed down, Doreen wondered if she should call somebody. Tears poured down the old woman's face, and she held her sides to the point that she looked to be having a heart attack.

Just as Doreen rose to race inside to get medical attention, Nan said, "Oh, my goodness, I needed that. You have no idea how boring my life has gotten lately. I'm so glad you decided to move to town, my dear."

Doreen settled back in her chair and stared at her grandmother. "So does that mean you did or did not murder somebody and bury him in the backyard?" She narrowed her eyes suspiciously at her grandmother.

Several more chuckles slipped out as Nan regained control. She wiped her eyes with a napkin from the table. "No worries. I never murdered anybody." She pointed a finger at Doreen. "Now I might have wanted plenty to be murdered. But it's just so messy."

Doreen stiffened at those last words. She knew her grandmother would never have been involved in a murder. But, when she said how it was *too messy*, Doreen fixed her gaze on her last living relative and asked, "How would you know it's messy?"

That sent Nan off again.

Grumbling about being the center of so much laughter, Doreen reached for the teapot and poured the two of them some tea. Maybe that would help Nan calm down. Or maybe not. She appeared to be enjoying herself way too much.

Chapter 6

THE WALK HOME was bright and sunny. After an enjoyable hour with Nan, where it appeared she hadn't had anything to laugh about in months, the two women had settled down to a nice chat. Nan tried to explain how the stove worked, but it was a bit too confusing for Doreen. Especially in the abstract, what with the ancient stove not on hand for an actual demonstration. The discussion on how the washing machine worked also went over her head. But she promised Nan that—somehow—she would figure it out.

It seemed like Thaddeus had the best visit, as he'd spent much of his time on Nan's shoulder, crooning and rubbing his beak along the older woman's cheek.

With tears in her eyes, Nan lightly stroked the beautiful bird. "The worst part was leaving the animals behind. I do so thank you for bringing them for a visit." She stroked the sprawled-out cat, acting sedated around Nan—not like the hellion at the house earlier.

"And I'll bring them again. Besides, you can visit anytime you want," Doreen said as she gave the woman a goodbye hug, dropping a kiss on her cheek. "Do take care."

"*You* take care, my dear. You're the one who has a dead

body in your garden." And she snickered.

"Murder is not exactly a joke, Nan," Doreen admonished. "Let's hope there's no body at all." She walked across the lawn, and Thaddeus flew to join her, perching on her shoulder. With Mugs happy to be once again on the march, and the cat lollygagging behind, the four of them slowly walked toward her house.

She stopped on the little footbridge and stared at the happy creek bubbling under her. It really was a beautiful place here. She still hadn't spent the night at the house or bought any food, so her dinner would be whatever traveling snacks she had left from her car trip.

Doreen had lived in a world where food arrived on platters, beautifully presented. And now she lived in Nan's world, where food was prepped overnight, and then something magical was done to it the next day. *Or cans were opened up*, she thought with a shudder.

Since her separation, take-out and sandwiches were more the norm until even takeout cost too much.

And all that kitchen magic from her mansion-living days was black magic to her now because Doreen had yet to make anything work in her grandmother's kitchen, other than an electric teakettle. She sighed. Her new life was a challenge. But she had often thought she was bored before, so maybe this was a *good* challenge for her.

As her little house came into sight, her good mood fell away. Some people were hanging about the yards nearby, watching her place. And the police were still there. Really? How long would it take them? How was she supposed to adapt and spend her first night in the house in this her latest version of "alone" when she wasn't even alone?

With a heavy sigh, she walked up the front porch steps

and into the house. She unclipped the leash from Mugs, who ran to the back door and barked. Thaddeus jumped off her shoulder and flew to a tall perch in the living room. *So that's what that was for.* She likely would've tossed it out otherwise. But Thaddeus stood tall and proud, surveying the world below him. Goliath slunk into the kitchen, probably to scare the bejesus out of Mugs. They were darn near the same size. She closed the front door, crossed into the kitchen to put her purse in a cabinet and stared out at the rear garden.

She pushed the back door open and stepped onto the veranda, leading out to the adjoining deck in the yard. A half-dozen men were working underneath the wooden slats.

"Did you find anything?" she asked.

Chester, the younger police officer, popped his head out from under the deck and smiled at her. "There you are. Yes, it looks like we found something."

"Under the deck?"

He nodded. "Appears somebody was buried underneath. It was a garden at one time. And this deck was built over the top."

She stepped back and looked at the deck, only six feet wide maybe. New planking was on the far side, above the spot where they searched. And, of course, a body was darn near the same size as this newer deck addition.

Also a large cutout on the deck accommodated a huge azalea bush. *How odd.*

She hadn't really noticed the azalea growing *through* the decking or the new extension before now. But both made sense under the circumstances. And the police would surely destroy the newer deck area to get to whatever lay underneath.

As she watched, one of the officers tested the supports

and found several beams perpendicular to the ground with the newest deck section atop them. With four big strong men strategically positioned, they literally picked up this extension and moved it off to the side. Everyone stared down at the space below. Several flowering bulbs had sprouted through the ground but were suffering without sunlight.

"Oh, my goodness. Those are begonias."

An officer pulled out the green-brownish shoots and stared at her in surprise. Then at the handful of gnarly bulbs he held. "What are they?"

"Begonias," she said in delight. "I didn't realize they grew here. I figured the winters would be too hard."

"Lady, I don't have a clue what you're talking about." And he proceeded to dump his handful of bulbs onto the ground, off to the side.

"Oh, be careful," she cried out. "Those are beautiful plants. We need to give them a chance to grow."

All the men stopped to peer up at her, then looked at the backyard's massive garden, completely overwhelmed with weeds and unruly overgrown bushes, and finally at each other.

She frowned. "I just got here. Like five, six hours ago. You have to give me an opportunity to fix the garden before you judge me for it."

A similar piece of cardboard to the one the finger had been resting on had been discarded halfway under the railing. She snagged it up and then headed down the deck steps until she was at ground level. She picked up all the discarded begonias and placed them on the cardboard. "When you pull out more," she instructed the policeman, "put them all here."

"Lady, this is a murder investigation," the officer said.

"We are not concerned about where we put the garbage."

"They are not garbage," she snapped in outrage. "And, if you are pulling out any true garbage from this spot and are planning to throw it all over my property, then you're wrong to do so in the first place. You can darn well get a garbage can or a garbage bag and put the trash in it." She glared at him. "Do you understand me?"

The cop who'd spoken turned to look at the others. Then he shrugged. He pulled up a few more of the bulbs and said, "Whatever." But he did add those to the indicated cardboard.

"That's much better. Thank you."

The other officers rolled their eyes at her.

"It's not that hard to save a life." Nobody had any appreciation for plants. She'd found that out a long time ago. It had been one of the hardest things to accept with her gardening staff. So often they were there for the job and didn't give a darn about the plants. She'd had enough of that attitude.

That wasn't her. And, if she could get along with these policemen, then they would have to get along with her too.

Suddenly one of the men gave a startled exclamation.

The others rushed to his side. She looked where he pointed. All the men gathered around, squatting around something. She walked closer and peered over their shoulders.

And, sure enough, a hand missing a finger poked through the dirt. "Oh, finally you found it. That's excellent." She beamed. "Now kindly remove it please."

Arnold, the older grizzled cop who she'd met first, stood and said, "All in good time. It won't happen that fast. You need to be prepared for that. The coroner will be here shortly. Properly digging out a body takes a lot of time, and we need to gather forensic evidence as we do." He spoke in such a ponderous tone, as if this was super important.

She sniffed. "It wouldn't take ten minutes to dig up that body, if you really cared to."

"It's because we care that we aren't doing it that fast." He glared at her. "If any forensic evidence is in this dirt, we need to find it. We need to know who put this body here and what killed him."

She stared at Arnold for a long moment, her jaw opening as realization dawned. "You're talking *days*, aren't you?"

He shrugged. "Potentially. But likely tonight and tomorrow. So why don't you go on back inside and let us do our job."

She fisted her hands on her hips and stared at the group of men, all shaking their heads at her. She tapped her foot and said, "Okay, but if you find any more begonias, you put them all in one pile. I'll collect them later and give them some water. Don't kill them. I've got to have one place where I can put them and keep them alive without the police destroying them."

She turned and headed inside. What she really needed was food and a cup coffee. Her blood sugar was dropping. That was the only explanation for her being more concerned about the begonias than the dead body. But really, begonias were so much easier to think about than a body in her backyard, you know?

Not exactly a warm welcome to her new home. And a rather ominous start to her new life.

Still, she was here, and she had to make the best of it. And while the men worked outside, she searched the tea drawer for coffee beans. Thankfully she also located a simple-enough coffeemaker. Now if only she could find the blasted coffee, figure out the portions, and find something to grind the beans in. Meanwhile, the hostess in her wondered if she was expected to share her coffee with the uniformed officers outside. Because that would put a major drain on her resources and her patience. *Was she supposed to feed them too?* She wasn't sure there was food enough for her own dinner.

She forgot about making coffee as she heard several more vehicles pull up her driveway. A look outside from her living room window confirmed more people had gathered out front. And two more police cars parked behind her Honda, confirming in no way would she get a meal prepared if she couldn't drive her car to buy some groceries. Damn. She did have some nuts, cheese and crackers, leftovers from her travel snacks. That would be a pitiful dinner, but it looked like that was all she had. At least until the men were done. Or maybe she could order some dinner in. A walk back to town would not happen. She was already tired, and her feet still hurt.

Nan was her best source of information for takeout.

With that bright idea, she picked up the phone and called her. "Nan, I can't get out because of all the police cars here. Is there any place I can get food delivered?"

"There's a lovely little Chinese restaurant around the corner," Nan said. "I used to always get their wonton soup. Win and Len Yee run it. Lovely couple."

Nan rattled off the phone number while Doreen quickly wrote it down. "Thanks, Nan." She hung up, wondered if it would be too expensive for her present situation. But she had to eat. And, so far, today was a complete wash. She had a sinking feeling that tonight would be just as bad. She had to wonder if she would get any sleep as she watched the new arrivals bring out what appeared to be large floodlights and tarps.

By now a bigger bunch of onlookers stood on the street, watching all the activity too. This *so* wasn't the impression she'd wanted to give on her first day in town. She sighed and muttered out loud, "The Mission will never recover from my arrival."

Chapter 7

AFTER TOO MUCH of her lifetime spent worrying about appearances, this didn't exactly bode well. She peeked out the living room window to see dozens of strangers standing outside watching the goings-on at her house. She wanted to creep out the back, run around, and join them, blending in so they wouldn't know who she was.

She walked back into the kitchen, Mugs very close to her heels. *The poor guy is hungry after walking into town and back again.* She should have fed him before they left, but she had been too angry to think straight. Yet, his food was easy to take care of. She had both wet and dry food for Mugs.

She lifted the appropriate bag onto the table, and gathered his food and water dishes. With his bowls now filled, she looked around the kitchen for an out-of-the-way spot where he could eat in peace. There really wasn't any area that worked with the natural traffic patterns in this room.

She could put Mugs's food and water bowls on the deck, but not right now as dozens of people were working around the house. And probably not a good idea anyway given she didn't know what other animals were out there. She went into the entrance hallway where a bench had been situated so people could sit to put on their shoes, and that vacant space underneath the bench would work, but it would only be a temporary fix—not exactly where she wanted to keep the dog's food and water bowls when company arrived. She returned to the kitchen and studied the lower cabinets.

One of the lower cupboard doors hung at a slight angle. She opened it up to find the shelf on the inside was askew too. This house was falling apart. How had Nan stayed here for so long without repairing stuff? Doreen tried to straighten the shelf so it would be usable again, only it broke into two pieces while in her hands. "Great."

She tugged the pieces of wood free. It came loose suddenly, sending her flying to her butt. Doreen sat there, glaring at the now-empty space. It was a rather large cupboard, accessible. "Mugs," she called out.

Mugs sniffed around, already at her side, his big jowls waggling back and forth in joy. She glanced at her messy suit, Nan's old gardening shoes on her feet, while considering the fact she sat on the dirty kitchen floor, holding a busted shelf. Tears came to her eyes as she dropped the shelf pieces beside her. She threw her arms around her beloved dog and held him close. But he could only stand that for a few minutes before he wiggled free. She moved her legs out of the way, and instantly Mugs walked into the cupboard.

The cupboard was at least three feet across. It didn't make any sense to have it here. The door didn't fit properly. She assumed a different door had been here at one point in time. Neither did the flooring go all the way to the end of the cupboard. How wrong was that? On the other hand, it was a potential place to put Mugs's food and water bowls.

At least with them in there, the bird wasn't likely to eat it all either. She hoped. She kicked off Nan's old shoes, got to her feet to retrieve the dog's food and water bowls, and put them inside the cupboard. Mugs didn't seem to mind his accommodations at all. He dug right in.

"Dinnertime. Dinnertime."

She spun to see Thaddeus strutting back and forth on the kitchen table. He stopped beside the open can of wet dog food and pecked away at the little bits of food still stuck to the bottom of the can. As if getting the scent of the dry dog food, his head flew up. He cocked it sideways to look at her first and then at the bag where the dry dog food came from and carefully walked forward, his neck fully extended. When he got to the bag, he stuck his head inside, pulled back, and stuck it in again. This time he came out with a dry kernel. He put it on the table and pecked at it, then said, "Dinnertime. Dinnertime for Thaddeus."

She wasn't sure she would survive all this domesticity, taking care of not only herself and Mugs but now a bird and a cat. *Probably like taking care of children.* Something else she had no firsthand experience with. Not even secondhand experience. Too bad she and Nan couldn't share this old house now that Doreen had arrived and also share the pet-related responsibilities. But hopefully she would be working a day job, away from home, so she knew it was better that Nan have twenty-four-hour assistance available at Rosemoor.

Groaning, her legs not working quite the same as they had before her walk, Doreen trudged over, while Thaddeus pulled out one more kernel from the dog food bag and put it on the table. She said in a firm voice, "That's Mugs's dinner."

She closed the bag, cleaned up the kitchen, and then studied the room. Surprisingly Thaddeus had been quiet all this time. She needed to get Thaddeus some food, or they would have an all-out war over the dog food soon. But where was the bird food, and what did a parrot like this eat? She'd forgotten to ask Nan about that. Darn. Mugs had already adjusted to a much cheaper dog food than he was accustomed to, but she didn't need Thaddeus eating it any faster.

Who had Nan left in charge of him and Goliath for these three weeks before Doreen arrived? Or had Nan walked back and forth each day to feed her animals? Or was that the Marge Nan had mentioned when Doreen first arrived? Nan cared for her animals meticulously and obviously wouldn't have let them suffer. Thaddeus was an African Grey, Nan had said. It would outlive both Nan and Doreen.

That didn't bear thinking about.

She searched the kitchen cupboards, looking for bird food but finding none. She turned in frustration, the bird staring at her, his head cocked to one side.

He spoke again. "Thaddeus is hungry. Thaddeus is hungry."

She glared at him. "Do you have to say everything twice?"

"Yes. Yes."

She groaned. "Enough."

"Thaddeus is hungry. Thaddeus is hungry."

In defeat she pulled out her phone and called Nan. "Have you got food here for Thaddeus?"

"It's in the front closet on the top shelf," Nan said with a giggle. "Is he eating the dog food yet?"

"Well, he is trying to. I presume he also eats Goliath's food too?"

"Who's Goliath?"

Silence overtook her. Doreen frowned into the phone. "Your cat?"

"Oh, well, Goliath is a better name than I gave him."
Nan giggled. "Cat food and bird food are all in the closet.
Don't leave the door open, or Thaddeus will get in all the
food."

With Nan still on the phone, Doreen headed to the closet and tried to open it. "Why would you lock this closet?
The bird can't turn a doorknob."

"It isn't locked. It's just got a strong spring, so it shuts
firmly. Turn the handle and tug real hard."

"Really?" She squeezed the phone between her ear and
shoulder, and, with both hands, she turned the doorknob
and gave it a sharp tug. It opened easily enough, considering,
sending her backward. "Well, you're right about it sticking."
She looked up at the corners, realizing the door had swelled,
and that was why it had been stuck. "This door should be
taken off its hinges and sanded down," she said to Nan.
"There are some things I know need to be done as I oversaw
the work at the estate, I've just never done it myself."

Nan laughed. "That's a minor thing. Wait 'til you see
the rest of the things falling apart in the house."

"Oh, great." But bags of pet food were up on the shelf.
She pulled out the cat food and some of the bird food. She
found another set of food and water bowls that she could use
to feed the cat, since Doreen hadn't seen any others out in
the house already. Did Thaddeus eat and drink from a bowl?
So far she'd seen him eat off the floor and the table. The rest
of her conversation with Nan was about how much Doreen
was supposed to feed Thaddeus and Goliath and where to
feed them.

"He has two bowls. One for water, but he prefers my
tea," she chuckled. "And loves the blue bowl with chips out
of the side. He's partial to that one but will eat out of

anything. It's important that you put Thaddeus on his roost after eating. He's very good at keeping the house area clean in general, but you have to change the newspapers around the base of his stand."

While Thaddeus ate on the kitchen table—a habit she really didn't want him to continue—Doreen walked to the bird's perch and stood, staring at the soiled newspapers positioned around the base of the stand, and saw what Nan had been talking about. Doreen's long-sounding sigh had Nan giggling on the other end.

"Did you really think he didn't have to go to the bathroom when inside the house?"

"How many times a day does he go?" Doreen asked suspiciously.

In a way-too-innocent-sounding voice, Nan said, "Not too often. Just change the newspapers whenever you can. Every day would be good." And then she hung up.

"Darn." After the day Doreen had had, what was a little poop? She rolled up her sleeves, gathered the dirty newspapers together and laid out fresh newspaper from a nearby stack—now understanding why they were in this corner. Along with a collection of plastic grocery bags. She grabbed one of those too and filled it with the newspapers to discard.

She certainly didn't want this mess inside the kitchen. She looked outside at the people standing around where her garbage can was. What a long walk it would be to get the bird-poop papers down there with everybody's gaze on her. And how hard it would be to get past those people watching her without them noticing her.

Then she got mad. So what if they were watching? She'd been through a heck of a lot worse since the holidays last year. So many people had looked on, snickered and outright laughed at her circumstances.

She'd be darned if she'd let these gawkers make her sleep in the same house as the rather overwhelming collection of bird poop. She walked back into the kitchen, slipped her feet into Nan's shoes, picked up the bag of poop-coated newspapers and opened the front door. Instantly a murmur arose from the crowd at the base of the driveway. She closed the door behind her and strode, staring straight ahead, to the garbage can. There she lifted the lid, put the garbage inside and slammed the lid down a little harder than necessary.

Instantly silence surrounded her.

And still the *clang* of the metal-on-metal rang clear. She winced, turned and walked back toward the house. Not a soul said a word. As she entered her front door, neither had she.

She stopped in the threshold, wondering how to turn this around. Normally she'd say she was a wonderful hostess, knowing how to smooth over any awkward moment. She'd prided herself on that to make her husband's social evenings work. Yet, here she was, in the middle of two worlds, a bridge that she had crossed. But she had yet to figure out a way to bring her previous experiences with her.

She pivoted for one last look at the crowd. And tried to smile.

All eyes stared back at her. Nobody moved.

She took a deep breath, twisted fully to face them and said, "Hello. My name is Doreen. Nan is *my* grandmother."

Not a word was spoken in response. She shrugged. Well, she had tried. She turned again.

And just as she was about to shut the door, somebody from the middle of the crowd called out, "Did you kill him? Did you kill the man in the garden?"

"Of course not," she yelled. "I just arrived today."

"And yet, there is a dead man in your garden."

"No," she hollered at the top of her voice. "There is a dead man in Nan's garden."

And with that the crowd gasped in shock.

"Nan wouldn't kill anyone," someone yelled.

"And neither would I," Doreen yelled back. She glared at them, spun on her heels, then slammed the door shut. If only she could shut out the world that simply. She leaned against the door, tamping down the scream in the back of her throat.

Just then Mugs raced through the hallway, Thaddeus riding his back and screaming at the top of his lungs, "Thaddeus is here. Thaddeus is here."

Doreen grabbed her hair, pulled and joined in, screaming at the top of her lungs.

Chapter 8

F ROM THE DIN inside, it was almost impossible to hear the knock on the door. Wiping the frustrated tears from her eyes, Doreen scrambled to peer around the corner of the living room window. A massive crowd remained outside. If anything, it appeared to be larger.

She glared at them from her hidden position. But someone at the door pounded again. The whole darn frame seemed to shake at that movement. She peered around the corner, but all she could see was someone big, and she chewed on her bottom lip, wondering if she should answer. By this point Mugs thought he should add to the noise again. He barked and barked and barked.

What now? I'll never get to eat at this rate.

If for no other reason than to shut him up, she walked to the front door. With her chin held high, she flung it open. And her jaw dropped. A man—huge, broad, sexy as hell, and a bit older than she was—filled the doorway.

He looked at her and smiled and asked, "Doreen Montgomery, I presume?"

She stared at him suspiciously. "How do you know my name?"

"I work with law enforcement. So I already know who you are. Besides you're in Nan Montgomery's house."

"But my married name was Merriweather."

"Have you reverted back to your maiden name?"

"Paperwork is in progress," she admitted. "But Montgomery's the only name I'll answer to now."

He motioned to the living room behind her. "May I come in?"

She crossed her arms over her chest and glared at him. "Why?"

He laughed.

That made her even more suspicious. "Are you just one of the many who wants to come here and gawk?"

"Hell, no, I don't. I'm the investigating officer for the Serious Crime Unit here in town."

She bolted backward. "Does that mean I'm a suspect?" She outstretched her arms as if to ward off an attack. "I didn't do anything, honest." Then she stopped and stared at him suspiciously. "Do I need a lawyer to talk to you?"

"Whoa, take it easy. No. You are not a suspect but more of a witness after-the-fact. My brother is a lawyer, if you *want* to talk to one. I almost went to law school with him." He smiled reassuringly at her. "We both work on the side of the good guys."

"There is no such thing when it comes to a lawyer," she snapped. She narrowed her gaze at him and asked, "ID?"

He raised an eyebrow, pulled out his wallet from his back pocket and extracted a card from inside. With two fingers, he held it out to her.

She read it. *Mack Moreau.* He looked like a man called *Mack* should look, as he was the size of a freaking Mack truck.

And the card presented him as Corporal Moreau of the Kelowna RCMP Serious Crime Unit. So at least he was who he said he was. If that made any difference. "Why are you here, and do I need to get a lawyer of my own choosing?" Yet, she had absolutely zero trust in them at this point in her life.

He shook his head. "No, you don't. Things are done very casually here. I came to welcome you to our town and to see what the hell was going on in your backyard. More cops will be here anytime now."

"*More* cops?" She waved at her backyard. "How can there possibly be more cops working for this small town? They're all in my backyard already."

"A lot of times we deputize civilians if we need them."

She stared at him as the information computed in her brain. "So you can deputize me to work in my own garden?"

At that he gave a boisterous laugh. "Well, if it wasn't your garden, and there wasn't a body found on your property, without that conflict of interest, if you are in fit physical form to assist us as needed for the case, then it's possible."

She stared at him, disgruntled. "I'm fit."

His gaze went from the top of her no-longer-coiffed hair all the way down her very bedraggled suit to Nan's pink garden shoes on her feet. In a very gentle voice he said, "It looks like you've had a very difficult day." He motioned to the kitchen. "Why don't we put on a cup of tea?"

She couldn't decide if he was being patronizing or compassionate. She decided she'd had enough of the bad guys, and she'd take his compassion if it were there. "Fine. But watch out for Mugs and Goliath." She turned to find the giant of a man busy rubbing Mugs's belly as he lay on his back, his stubby legs in the air, a serious groan coming from his mouth. "I don't think I've ever heard him make that sound before." She stared at the man and shook her head. "I suppose you think you can charm anyone?"

"Nope. But dogs are easy."

"How do you feel about cats?"

Goliath snuck around the corner of the hallway toward Mack. He gave the cat a great big scratch on its back and under its chin. And, just like that, he'd won over Goliath too as the traitor dropped to the floor and purred like a lion. Doreen stared at Mack. He had an affinity for animals she'd never really had a chance to explore. Before today.

"How's Thaddeus?" Mack straightened and walked toward Doreen, glancing over at Thaddeus on the tree post. "I'm used to seeing him on that roost all the time."

"He seems to like that place." She put on the teakettle, grateful she knew how to do that much. Too bad she hadn't made any coffee. She'd have it to offer him now. But what would she serve him with the tea? "I haven't had a chance to go shopping yet," she said. "I wasn't sure the crowd outside would let me."

"If they're bothering you, I can have them dispersed."

She faced him. "Can you?"

"Sure. They're just curious. Those are all your neighbors, plus a few from surrounding neighborhoods it seems. They want to know what's going on. They're harmless enough."

"How can you tell? One of them might be the murderer. Isn't it true that murderers often stick around when the police arrive at the scenes of their crimes?"

"Usually with a fresh one. Not so much when it's been buried for a while. Although this one is a relatively recent murder, as I understand flesh is still on the bones." He tilted his head toward her. "But you are correct in that criminals do return to their crime scenes. And they do seem to enjoy watching everybody scurry around to solve the mystery."

"I thought so." She opened the tea drawer. "I don't know what tea to serve you."

"How about coffee instead?"

She eyed him suspiciously. She had heard the hopeful tone in his voice. "The coffeemaker is right there. Feel free."

He walked over, swung out a basket from the top of the coffeemaker she hadn't known existed and dumped out its contents in the trash can under the sink. He opened the drawer below the coffeemaker, pulled out a coffee filter, stuck one in and then reached for a bag of coffee.

And she didn't even know it had been coffee. She walked over and studied the bag. "Nothing on it says *coffee*." She felt his stare of surprise.

He quietly said in a calm voice, "It says *espresso*."

She nodded. "I read that. I didn't realize that was the same kind of coffee one could use to make coffee in a coffeemaker."

"Absolutely. Espresso makes some of the best coffee."

"Good, because I really could use a cup." She walked over to the table and sagged into a chair. At that moment, Thaddeus decided to walk across the kitchen floor, strutting his stuff but coming from the other side of the kitchen. "Where the heck were you?" she asked in an accusing tone.

"Thaddeus is here. Thaddeus is here." He ruffled his feathers and jumped onto the table.

And then she got it. She leaned forward and studied the dog food. "You were in the cupboard, eating all the dog food, weren't you?"

"Thaddeus is here. Thaddeus is here."

"You might not be for long though," she threatened.

"Thaddeus is a long-term character around this place." Mack walked over and brushed the side of the African Grey's cheek. "Hello, Thaddeus. How are you doing?"

Thaddeus lifted a foot to the man's finger, bobbed his head, proceeded to hop on, and then walked all the way up to Mack's shoulder, where he sat quite comfortably. "Thaddeus is fine. Thaddeus is fine."

"Glad to hear that, big guy. I'm sure it's been a pretty tough adjustment for you not having Nan around."

"Nan is gone. Nan is gone."

But Thaddeus's tone of voice had changed to a soulful mourn, so much so that Doreen could feel his grief.

"Nan is not gone," she reassured Thaddeus. "Remember? I took you to see Nan today."

"Did you? How is she?"

Doreen looked over at Mack and said, "Honestly, she seems quite happy there. I was expecting her to be in worse shape."

Mack pulled out a chair beside Doreen. As he sat down, Thaddeus maintained his position perfectly on his shoulder.

The smell of coffee filled the air. She turned and looked at Mack. "I should've asked earlier. How much coffee did you put in?"

"Two scoops," he said without missing a beat. "And the scoop's inside the bag."

She stored that information away for later. She so wanted to learn to make a decent cup of coffee. Even if it took her ten pots to get there. She was a little desperate for her caffeine.

"And your relationship with Nan?"

Her gaze focused on him, her mood mellower now that she knew coffee was coming. "My grandmother. She's the only family I have left. I didn't get to see her very much when I was married. We did phone a lot though." She smiled. "Nan used to tell me how her life was busy and not to worry if I didn't have more time for her."

"Did you believe her?"

"No, I think she often said that to make me feel better." Doreen looked at him. "My marriage wasn't exactly the easiest. Nan seemed to call at my low points. She always cheered me up. Just hearing her voice made me happy. She was also the one who constantly told me how I had choices in life."

"Did you agree with her?"

There was no probing. His questions just seemed like simple curiosity. So she answered him the same way. "At the time, no. When you're in the middle of a situation, it's very hard to see options. But now I can laugh and realize— looking back over the years—how upsetting the situation was, and yet, how many options I did have at the time. I wish I'd listened to her earlier."

At the last gurgle of the coffeepot, Mack nudged his shoulder, and Thaddeus walked to the table. Mack rose and filled two mugs with coffee, bringing them back to the kitchen table. "I think everyone feels that way at some time or another about their lives."

"And, if they're smart, they'll listen to the advice given to them by those who are older and wiser." Her gaze fell on Thaddeus, busy preening himself. After all, he had just finished eating the dog food. Time to clean himself afterward, right? "I'm surprised Nan didn't find a home for her pets though."

"Except for one thing," Mack said quietly. "She *did* find a home for them."

She raised her gaze, startled at his words. "Me?" When he nodded, she laughed. "I meant a *good* home."

He tilted his head to the side and studied her carefully. "And why is it you can't provide them a good home?"

"I have no idea how. I haven't had to provide for myself until now, and, at this point in time, with three animals..."

"But you're resourceful. You're a survivor. You can do this."

She openly stared at him. And she had to wonder. Was he right?

One thing she did know. He was too handsome, too suave to believe most of the time. But maybe those most recent words from him were just what she needed to hear.

Chapter 9

"WHAT QUESTIONS DID you want to ask me, Corporal Moreau?" Doreen studied Mack, wondering at his earlier insight. Mugs walked over and sniffed his shoes.

"Just call me Mack. I'd like you to tell me what you saw outside and what you found." He gave her a gentle smile. "Just start from when you first arrived."

She rolled her eyes. "That'll take a while. I've been here a whole six or so hours, and unlikely events have taken over my life." But she launched into her story. Doing the best she could to leave nothing out, she brought Mack up to date on everything that had happened so far.

"Do you have any idea why there would be a body in the garden?"

She looked at him and said, "No."

"Any idea why Nan would have somebody buried in the garden?"

She narrowed her gaze at him. "No."

He nodded. "Do you have problems with anybody from this area?"

"Maybe the entire neighborhood for all I know," she

snapped. "Remember that part about how I just got here? Today? At noon?"

"What about Nan? Did she have any enemies?"

Instantly her ire subsided. "Hell no. Nan is one of the nicest people I've ever known." She waved her hand around at the small house. "Maybe you should talk to the neighbors about that. Because I really don't know. If they do have something to say, maybe you'll fill me in. As far as I know, Nan didn't have any arguments with anybody. However, Nan is alive and well in the retirement home, so maybe you should talk directly to her."

"And I will," he said, tucking away his notepad.

He'd been writing something on those pages. She watched him pocket his pen. "Can you tell all those policemen to get out of my backyard now?"

"Not until they are done."

"And the mess they're making?"

He glanced out the window at the completely overgrown garden and said, "How can you even tell?"

She stared at the garden area. "Nan couldn't do very much gardening for the last few years."

He waved at the grass. It was well over knee-high, so were the weeds all throughout the yard. "At least that long."

A few trees in the back badly needed pruning. When she had the time and energy and money, she would get those done. Nan must've needed help with everything. All of it piling on top of her and just not enough energy to even care anymore. Between the garden, the house and the animals, it had all gotten to be too much for her aging grandmother.

Guilt shot through Doreen. Poor Nan. She'd really hoped to stay here in her own home until she died. Maybe Doreen should ask Nan once more if she wanted to come live here with her.

"Any idea what brought about her decision to move?"

Doreen slowly faced him, her eyebrows raised. "You know? I never asked her. Maybe I should."

His voice dropping yet again, he said, "Maybe you should."

As he walked away, she studied his back suspiciously. "What do you mean by that, Mack?"

He turned and smiled. "It might just have something to do with your circumstances."

She stared at him blankly for a moment, and then it hit her. She gasped in horror. "You're not saying Nan moved into a retirement home so I could have her house? That would be horrible."

"Why would it be horrible?" He leaned against the doorjamb, crossing his arms as he studied her. "Sometimes it takes other people's circumstances to make us realize it's time for a change."

She huffed.

He grinned. "Then, because of your circumstances, it might've been the final straw that led Nan to making that decision."

Somehow that sounded better, but, at the same time, it wasn't what she wanted to hear. She planned to ask Nan… she just needed the right time… She didn't want to make it sound like she was ungrateful for all Nan had done. Neither did she want Nan to feel obligated to help her out. Doreen could stand on her own two feet. She had no experience doing so, but she was gutsy and getting more so every day.

There was something incredibly freeing about her new life.

Just then a knock came at the back door, and she opened

it, amid Mugs's crazy barking, to let in the same grizzled cop she had met at the very beginning of this strange day—Arnold. She couldn't begin to remember his last name. Carmichael maybe? No, that wasn't it. No matter. Chester said to just call them by their first names.

He nodded, took note of Mack and said, "Good evening, sir. I didn't realize you were here."

Mack nodded back at him. "Any forensic finds?"

"Not that we noticed yet. The coroner is ready to take away the body. Did you want to see the backyard?"

Mack said, "Yes, actually I would like to."

"I would too," Doreen growled. She headed out to the back veranda behind them. When she saw how much of the garden they had dug up getting to the body, she winced. "You know? The least you guys could do is dig up the entire thing." Several blank faces raised in her direction. She sighed. "Never mind."

Mack laughed. "They will get the joke later."

She followed Mack from the kitchen back door to the far set of veranda steps down to the decking nearest the grave. She stayed on the veranda steps while Mack walked around one six-foot-long pit, a couple feet wide, barely big enough for a body, and only a couple feet deep. "I thought you're supposed to bury bodies at least six feet deep so that animals can't smell them?"

One of the officers turned to look at her. "That would be in ideal circumstances."

She nodded. "So somebody didn't intend for this body to be here for very long?"

Arnold faced her. "Maybe *somebody* buried it just recently."

A sour note had entered his voice. As if Doreen were

somehow responsible. She glared at him. "It wasn't me. Remember that part about me not being here until six hours ago?"

"But you could have been here a couple days ago, coming in secretly, burying a man in the backyard and then coming back again when you moved in. All looking innocent like that." He brushed most of the dirt off his hands and clothes.

She glared at him. "Why would I bury a body in my own place?"

"I haven't figured that out yet. But I will." Arnold gave her a surly look and walked around the house.

Several of the other men were busy walking the rest of her property.

She waved a hand toward them. "What are they looking for?"

"Anything and everything," said the younger cop, Chester. "We must search to find any forensic evidence that would explain how and why this happened. And, most important, by whom."

"I understand that, but do you have to check in the garden like fifty yards away?"

"If you were to stand on that deck," Mack began, "and were to toss a murder weapon into that mess, how far do you think you could throw it?"

She turned to Mack and answered his question. "I don't know. Maybe thirty to forty feet?"

"If you were a fit teenaged male, how far do you think you could throw it?"

She studied the back of the garden and said, "Fine. I guess somebody good at pitching a softball could throw all the way to the back of the property. But it's getting too dark to see anything."

The young cop said, "That's why we will be back first thing in the morning."

She stared at him in surprise. "You guys will be here again tomorrow?"

Mack cleared his throat beside her. "We'll be here every day until we have searched the whole place."

She stared at him. "Why?"

"Because a dead body was found on your property."

She closed her eyes, hating the idea of starting a brand-new life immediately ravaged by something as nasty as a murder. Then she nodded. "That's fine, but I want to know exactly what you take out of here."

"We can do that. We'll give you a list of items before we leave with them."

She asked Mack, "If you guys are leaving now and coming back in the morning, how the devil will you know if the killer comes back and takes whatever it is he might've thrown out there?"

He looked at her and just smiled.

She shook her head at his failure to answer her and was about to go back inside, but Mugs sniffed around the bottom step. "Did you happen to check under these veranda steps?"

Everyone still in the vicinity stopped and looked at Mugs. He sniffed from one side of the step to the other. Then he jumped down into the grave. "No, Mugs, no."

But Mugs ignored her command. With his short stubby legs, he dug deeper in the spot where the policemen had dug. Instantly several of the cops came back over with flashlights to look closer underneath that final step nearby the grave. And she had the sinking feeling they'd found something.

Mack, disregarding his suit, jumped into the grave, picked up Mugs and put him at the top of the veranda steps beside her. "Can you keep him here until we find out what it is he smelled?"

She nodded and grabbed Mugs by the collar. Goliath wandered out, completely oblivious to the fact that a dozen men surrounded the veranda. "What is it, Goliath?" She didn't expect the cat to answer, but he walked back and forth over the top of the same step Mugs had sniffed and swished his tale. She wasn't sure what that meant in cat language, but she presumed it was significant. Between the findings of the two of them, something had to be under there.

When somebody tore off the bottom veranda step from its supports, set it to one side, and dug underneath, she winced and said, "Please tell me a second body isn't down there."

"I don't think so." The cop pulled out what look like a briefcase. "A man's laptop bag or something similar." In the dark, it was hard to see, but the item was black and about the right size for a briefcase.

The men kept digging a little more and came up with a dead squirrel.

"Oh, that must be what the dog was after."

The cops shrugged. The squirrel was tossed into the nearest garbage bag beside them. One of the men asked the cop holding the briefcase, "Now this briefcase, that's a different story. The animals weren't necessarily interested in it. But is it the dead man's briefcase?"

"It's a reasonable assumption," said the cop holding the new evidence.

With a flashlight turned on the briefcase, the cops opened it up to find papers. Lots and lots of papers.

Doreen leaned in to make sure nothing pertained to Nan. A couple of the cops looked at her funny, but none told her to go away. They'd better not. Without her and Mugs, they wouldn't have known the briefcase was even here.

Mack pulled out several documents. "These look like investments, stock portfolios."

"And is Nan's name on there or not?" Doreen asked.

Mack looked at her and understood. He walked up the steps and turned on the outside light for more light on the veranda and the deck then he went through several of the papers. "I'm not seeing Nan's name on any of these forms."

Doreen's shoulders sagged with relief. "Thank you. I just want to make sure this guy hadn't ripped her off or something. Nan must have had a really bad time financially these last few years, and I'd hate to think somebody took advantage of her."

"Forensics will get these original documents first. I'll get copies and go over them in detail," Mack said. "If there's any mention of Nan on these, I'll let you know."

He collected the pages, put them back in the case, gave it a good bang to ensure some of the dirt came off and then joined the other policemen on the yard.

Chapter 10

DOREEN LOCKED THE front door once Mack and some of the other officers had gone, then, needing a better outlet for her growing frustration, ended up kicking it too.

"Ouch." *Okay, that was stupid.* Hobbling gently, she walked to the kitchen window where she watched from behind the curtains as the policemen slowly collected their tools and belongings and then left her garden. When the backyard was clear, she walked into the living room, just in time to see several cop cars pull away.

A few stragglers remained from the crowd that had been outside, standing around, staring and talking. Several even had what appeared to be mugs of tea or coffee. She supposed this was their local entertainment. With a sad shake of her head, she turned toward the coffeepot.

At least she'd learned how to make coffee. If she were lucky, there'd be a cup left.

She perked up at the idea and walked to the pot. No such luck. It was a small pot, and between her and Mack, the coffee had been finished off. She pulled out the coffee from the drawer where she'd seen Mack grab it, and, true enough, the scoop was inside. So now she could make coffee herself.

But, just in case, she jotted down his instructions on a notepad so she wouldn't forget.

She was hungry too and still had her lack-of-food issue to deal with. The Chinese food delivery would have to wait for another day. She was just so tired, but she forced herself to sit down and eat the rest of her traveling snacks. After the first few bites she felt better. By the time she'd polished off her meager meal, she was more than ready to go to bed.

She grabbed several of her suitcases and marched upstairs. She hadn't unpacked her bags yet, not with so much happening on her first day here.

With all the animals following behind her, she opened the first room to see a small bedroom with ancient wallpaper and dingy curtains on the windows. In spite of the looks she smiled. This had been the room she'd stayed in as a child. There had been a bathroom across the hallway. Crossing the hallway she found the bathroom as she remembered, which at least looked serviceable. The master bedroom was at the end of the hallway. This was Nan's room. She gasped in delight as she walked in. It was huge. This would work.

Of course it was also jam-packed with all kinds of shelves and old furniture. She had no idea what Nan needed with all this stuff. But amid all this clutter was a very large bed in the center. She walked over and sat down experimentally. Loud squeaks and groans of metal springs erupted from underneath. She closed her eyes in defeat. "Really, Nan?" Was this the same old bed she'd always had? Hadn't she upgraded anything? Doreen stared at it in disbelief. "This thing will break my back. I just know it."

Immediately she chastised herself for the uncharitable thought. It was probably all Nan could afford.

Doreen pulled back the bedding to see that, indeed,

clean sheets were underneath. Nan had probably left it ready for Doreen's arrival. Which Doreen appreciated, but, at the same time, she wondered at the sense of just taking the mattress off the noisy steel springs and putting it on the floor. She wasn't sure she'd be able to sleep on the bed as is. She was starting to feel like the princess with the pea—only right now she was more pauper than princess.

Two very large double closet doors were on the opposite wall, and that was a plus. But as she opened the doors, the closet overflowed with everything else stored away in this house. It would take days, if not weeks or months, to sort through and toss all this clutter. Why hadn't Nan done this first? She'd known she was leaving this house.

When Doreen had a chance, she'd ask Nan. Doreen's little Honda was too small to haul everything out of here, and she had no money to pay for somebody else to get rid of it all. The living room and dining room downstairs were full as well. But she hadn't really expected this bedroom to be also. She turned to see Thaddeus, sitting on the foot railing to the bed. "Oh, I don't think so. This is where I sleep, not you."

But as she studied him and the newspaper on the floor under him, she wondered if that really was his sleeping spot. "Oh, my God! Please don't tell me that you poop in here too?"

As if knowing exactly what she said, Thaddeus gave a tiny squirt, and a white splotch appeared on the floor.

It was just too much. It was *all* just too much. She could feel hot tears burning in the corner of her eyes. She brushed them away impatiently. By the time she cleared her eyes, she could hear a weird groan. She glanced over at the bed again to see Goliath dead center, curled up in a ball. Nan probably had lived with her pets as if they were family.

The trouble was, they were *Nan's* family. Doreen wasn't at all sure they could become hers. Did she have any choice?

Mugs stood up on his back legs, his front paws on the bed, took one look at the cat asleep there and barked.

Doreen rushed over. "Oh, no you don't. You're not jumping on that bed." But before she reached him, he lunged and ended up on the bed too. The bed squeaked and bounced with his movements. The cat didn't even open an eyeball. Mugs sniffed at him hard and then circled around and dropped at the foot of the bed, stretched out, taking up over half of it.

If she'd ever wondered how much her life would change now, here was her answer. The proof was right here in front of her. She would never be the same again.

She turned her back on them and surveyed the rest of the room. She couldn't deal with the animals right now. *Later.* Spotting a door on the far side, she walked over and pushed it open. And cried out in joy. Of all the things she hadn't expected, it was this huge en suite bathroom with a large soaking tub, a separate shower and double sinks. When had Nan redone this room? Whenever it was Doreen would be forever grateful. And right now a hot shower would do a lot to ease her mood.

She walked to the window to check if anybody could see her. The master bathroom looked over the backyard. Outside of the neighboring yards, only trees and grass stared back at her. She stood here, slowly unbuttoning her suit jacket as she stared out at the massive garden. Tracks and shovel marks and trampled grass reached all the way back to the dilapidated fence. Such an invasion of privacy. She knew she shouldn't feel violated, as it didn't feel like home yet, but she was more outraged for Nan's sake.

Yet, she knew Nan didn't give a crap. In Nan's mind, this was done and gone, and she wasn't coming home again. And that was just that.

As Doreen glanced back out into the evening light, something twinkled. It winked and flashed as if something metallic or mirrored had moved. She frowned and stepped behind the curtains. Was somebody out there?

Of course people were out there. She had had curiosity seekers watching the events here all evening. Just because the cops had left, did that mean the gawkers had too?

No other houses were behind hers. She should have complete privacy here. Except for whatever was twinkling in the night.

As she glanced up, she could see the moon rising off to the left, sending a sharp ray of moonlight down on the back garden. Well, that explained the twinkling and flashing going on, but what was the moonlight hitting? She contemplated heading out there to look but knew that she couldn't see anything in the dark. Did Nan have a flashlight among all the stuff stored in this house?

Sleep would elude Doreen while that shining thing was out there. She didn't know if it was important or just a piece of garbage. But what if it had something to do with the murder?

This was Nan's house—regardless of what Nan thought or said or did—and Doreen had to do what she could to protect it. With a groan, she buttoned up her suit jacket once more and headed back downstairs, shoving her feet into Nan's shoes. Doreen searched the kitchen drawers until she found a flashlight and then headed outside.

With both Goliath and Mugs moving excitedly at her

side, she propped the back door open so the animals could come and go as they pleased and then headed outside. She went down the veranda steps, carefully making her way around the huge hole that the police had left, striding toward the area where she'd seen the twinkling light. Thaddeus flew up, joining the trio, and landed on her shoulder. She stroked him, her heart more affected than she thought.

He crooned against her cheek, "Thaddeus is here. Thaddeus is here."

And she was so grateful that she would not be totally alone in Nan's house.

With the animals at her side, the flashlight giving her limited visibility, she slowly made her way through the backyard. Going by the landmarks she'd memorized while looking out her upstairs window, she focused on the big window in the master bathroom, gauging where she'd find the shiny thing. She shone the flashlight around but saw nothing. She walked the area for a good ten minutes but couldn't locate it.

"Well, Goliath, you're the one who brought the finger bone inside. Can you find this other thing? How about you, Thaddeus? Can you find the reflective thing?"

Maybe his species was attracted to shiny stuff. Or was it magpies that stole the shiny things? Crows? She shook her head, not having any answers to her own questions. "What about you, Mugs? How about you root around and dig up stuff? Isn't this what you wanted a garden of your own for?" She knew she was talking out loud just to keep herself focused on why she was here. In the dark. By an empty grave.

Mugs had been denied access to the garden in the big house where they used to live. He had his own little dog run where people came and cleaned up behind him every day.

But now he had a real garden, where he was allowed to roll around in the dirt. She knew he'd be much happier here. Just like she would be.

She stopped, took another assessment from the angle upstairs where she'd been and walked about eight feet forward. As she moved ahead, Mugs dove into the grass in front of her. It was tall enough and deep enough that it darn near split and flattened in half with his weight. She shone the light to see what he'd found. And, sure enough, something was in his mouth. She grabbed his collar so he wouldn't run away with it. She'd had more than enough of that earlier with the finger bone. She shone the flashlight at what was in his mouth, and it was indeed metal. It was a small flat piece. But Mugs wouldn't drop it easily.

She found a stick and made a trade.

Grudgingly he accepted the stick. She stared at the metal and wondered what the heck it was. Probably nothing but garbage. She checked out the spot where it had been. With the dog now happily chewing on the stick beside her, the cat roaming the garden and Thaddeus staring over her shoulder, she found the rest of it.

It was a small metal box half buried in the garden. She didn't know if it had been uprooted by the police or whether one of the volunteers had found it or if it had lain here for decades. She dug around it and lifted it from its surprisingly deep home, realizing it had been in the same position for a long time. Nothing was inside the metal box, but, as she removed it, she found something below it. Gradually she moved away more dirt and grass and then reached inside the hole. And what she brought back up made her blood run cold.

Thaddeus squawked in her ear. "Murder in the garden. Murder in the garden."

Chapter 11

"MACK? CORPORAL MACK Moreau?" she said into the phone. She rubbed her hand across her forehead and stared at the item she'd brought into the house.

"Yes, this is Mack. Who's this?"

She rolled her eyes. "It's Doreen."

"Doreen?" he asked cautiously.

"Remember the crazy lady with the bird, the dog, the cat and the dead body in the garden?"

There was an abrupt silence before he said, in a much warmer tone, "Yes. What can I do for you?"

"I found something in the garden. Honestly I wasn't looking. I wasn't trying to interfere. But I was getting ready for bed, and I could see something shining in the back corner of the garden. I guess the moonlight hit the metal. Anyway the four of us went outside, and I found a metal box. It looked like it'd been disturbed while everybody was searching, but nobody probably really did see it because it was covered in dirt."

"And what was in the box?"

She said, "Nothing. But a bottle of arsenic was buried below it."

"What?" His voice turned businesslike. "Please tell me you left it in the garden."

"Oops," she said into the ever-widening gap of silence.

"Of course you didn't. Did you bring it all inside?"

"No, just the bottle of arsenic. It appears to be empty though," she hurriedly added. "Honestly I didn't want to leave it out there. What if some animal got a hold of it?"

She could almost see him ready to pull his hair from his head. It was very nice hair. She really didn't want him to pull it out. But she understood how his lack of control over her could be a little on the frustrating side. "You have to understand. This is my property, and it reflects on Nan's reputation, and I am feeling a little responsible for what's going on here."

"Where is the arsenic now, Doreen?"

"In front of me," she said. "On the kitchen counter."

"I'll be right there."

"No, you don't have to—" But it was too late. The phone was dead in her hand. "Wonderful." She glanced down at her clothing. "And my shower will have to wait. Again."

No getting away from this visit. She'd called him, and she would have to see this through to the end. She walked to the front door, opened it to let in the evening air and stepped on the front porch, waiting for Mack to show up.

She was grateful that, at this time of night, her house had long lost interest for all the neighbors. For the first time, she could see the beauty of the small cul-de-sac with its collection of little houses. Everyone took care of their yards. They were large properties. Nobody could see into the other houses' windows. There was a lot to be said for this place. She would enjoy seeing more of this area as she walked into town to visit Nan every day or so. She just wasn't so sure about that whole gossipy thing going on right now.

Or the dead body.

Of course, if she hadn't been at the murder scene, maybe it would've been just fine. She sat with Goliath in her arms, Thaddeus walking back and forth on the porch railing and Mugs sleeping at her feet until she saw headlights coming. A car drove up her driveway and stopped.

Mack got out and walked over to her. "You okay?"

She shrugged. "I'm exhausted. I'd really like to get this over with." She stood slowly, handing him Goliath. "The arsenic is in here." She proceeded to lead the way.

Goliath didn't seem to care that he'd been passed over to the big man. And neither did the man. She watched Mack as he shifted the large cat in his arms and followed her.

Now that was a decent guy. Her husband would've stepped back before the cat made contact with his suit. He'd have shot Doreen a horrified look, as if she'd tried to kill him. But then he hated cats. Apparently Mack didn't. And she trusted Goliath to know a good man when he saw one. Although she had no idea where she'd heard that old wives' tale about cats being able to discern that. So far Goliath hadn't been around many people. But what did Doreen know? She'd been a cat owner for less than half a day. And so much had happened in that time to distract her from watching Goliath's reaction to various people.

In the kitchen, she pointed out the bottle. Mack glanced at her. "I don't suppose you wore gloves when you picked it up."

She winced and shook her head. "No, I never thought of it."

He directed her to the sink. "Wash thoroughly."

Immediately she turned on the water, soaping up, chastising herself for not thinking of that first. She could have poisoned her pets. She glanced at Goliath. "I was petting him too."

"When you're done, grab the brush and give him a good brushing. Chances are, he'll be fine, but you don't want to take a chance. Then I want you to show me where in the garden you found it."

She grabbed the towel, quickly dried her hands, walked over to the pet closet where she'd seen a brush along with the cat food and pulled it out. Between the two of them taking turns, Mack and Doreen made Goliath think he was royalty. They managed to get a solid layer of fur off him.

When that was done, she picked him up in her arms, and tossed him over her shoulder to carry him like a baby. Armed with her flashlight again, she led the way to the far back corner of the yard. It took a moment for her to find the exact spot. She had to look back at the master bathroom window several times. But finally she pointed. "There."

She shone the light on the metal lid she and Mugs had discovered. Of course Goliath sat right beside the place she'd been looking for. Was it on purpose? Or a coincidence. She shot him a suspicious look but he just stared back at her.

Mack walked over, pulled some gloves from his back pocket, put them on and squatted beside the lid. Mugs snuffled the ground at his side. Mack gently scratched his neck as he studied the box. "Did you move anything?"

"Just the box and the bottle. The metal box was on top of the bottle," she said. "I think the lid caught the moonlight and was twinkling, which drew my attention. When I realized it was a box, I lifted off the lid. But the box was empty. So I unburied it, and then I found the arsenic." She shone the light around the area and cried out softly, "Oh, my goodness! These are azaleas."

He turned to face her. "I gather you're a gardener."

"I'd love to be a gardener. Up until now I've only directed gardeners."

He shot her a look of wonder.

She shrugged. "What can I say? My soon-to-be-ex was extremely wealthy. I wasn't allowed to touch anything, including cutting flowers from the garden for vases inside the house."

He shook his head. "A different world."

"A very different world."

He lifted the lid, checked it, found nothing. He lifted the metal box. Examined it and again didn't see anything. He shined his flashlight all around and took a closer look at where the box was. "I'll take the box and the lid with me. I doubt any fingerprints are left on it—other than yours." He shot her a look.

She gave him a half smile of apology. "I'm really not up to all this stuff. Not exactly sure what I'm supposed to do when I find things like poison in my garden."

He nodded. He collected the box and the lid and straightened. "In the morning I'll come back and take another look." He motioned to her. "Lead the way back to your house."

Scooping up Goliath again, who seemed to be completely content to be carried, she led Mugs and Mack back to the house. Thaddeus half-flew, half-walked beside them.

When they got to where the big empty grave was, Thaddeus perked up. "Murder in the garden. Murder in the garden."

Mack laughed. "Did you teach him that?"

She shot Mack a look. "You really think I want him to repeat that?" She shook her head. "He said that when we first found the arsenic."

Mack studied Thaddeus. "Interesting. I wish I knew where he learned that from."

"I don't know much about him," she admitted, then considered Mack's words. "You don't really think someone taught him that, do you?"

"I doubt it. Why would anybody? It's hardly something you want your bird to tell people. They would start to wonder if it was telling the truth. *Body's in the garden. Body's in the garden.*" He mocked the bird with his last words.

She stopped, looked at Mack. "Actually that's what he said when we found the finger. *Body in the garden.* Now he says, *Murder in the garden.*"

"Smart bird."

"Why?"

"Because the progression of events is exactly as he said. First, it was a body in the garden. But now it's proof of a murder in the garden."

"You're saying that man was murdered...? Of course he was!" She felt a little ill at the thought. She hadn't really considered it an actual murder. A real murder. "I know I've called it a murder and even asked about murderers watching in the crowds, but the reality of that event just now sunk in." She had assumed from her nice, easy, safe existence that he had died of natural causes and that someone may have buried him. No, that really didn't make any sense. She was such a fool. Why hadn't she jumped to this conclusion immediately?

Frowning, she walked back into the kitchen. "Sorry," she muttered. "It never occurred to me. I guess maybe I am still in shock over this whole mess."

"Don't worry about it. We don't have any details on it yet. But I highly doubt he met his death in any natural way."

"Well, he might have. What if he just keeled over and had a heart attack?"

"Then why bury him? Why not call an ambulance to haul away the body?"

She stared and shook her head. "I don't know. I can't come up with any scenario that makes sense."

"Exactly, which usually means murder."

"But neither can I come up with a reason why anyone would bury the body so shallow and so close to the house with the animals all around."

"Usually it's a case of expediency. Accidents happen, or an argument gets out of control. Somebody kills somebody and must get rid of the body real fast. Or maybe they couldn't move the body very far. If you think about it, the grave was right near the bottom of the steps."

"Which is a stupid place to put a body."

"Let's say a garden was already there."

She frowned at him. "Well, the cops did pull out begonia bulbs. Normally they come up in spring. It's an unseasonably warm April, but it's still too soon for begonias to show much more than shoots. And, depending on the climate, they could be left in the garden. Although they have to be insulated in cold climates or better yet they get pulled and replanted after the ground warms."

"So, the garden is likely freshly turned, with bulbs breaking up the dirt underneath, so that makes it easy digging." He cleared his throat. "And of course there's the new deck over top..."

She stared at him suspiciously. If anybody said anything

against Nan, Doreen wasn't having any of that. "I don't like what you're implying, that this could be Nan's work."

His eyebrows shot up. "Why is it I would be implying it's Nan?"

"It's her house. It's her garden. She's a small and aging woman who couldn't pull the body very far."

He nodded soberly. "And, in that case, you'd be quite right. However, it also fits other people."

"Like who?"

He gave her a grim smile and said, "There is somebody else. She's standing right in front of me. She could've come several days ago and done this. She's not very strong, but she's certainly determined."

Chapter 12

Day 2, Thursday

DOREEN WOKE UP the next morning to a sore back and the not-so-musical sound of the bed springs. Mugs had taken up residence at the base of the bed near her feet. Goliath had taken up the other half of the bed. And, yes, Thaddeus appeared to be snoozing on that old metal railing at her feet. And every time she rolled, the bed springs squeaked and groaned.

"Not sure how long I can live with this noisy tortuous bed. It's not conducive for actual sleeping. But getting a new bed is out of the question for a while."

She stared up at the old ceiling and thought—although it would take a lot of time, effort and money to fix the house—it was a gift in her time of need. It was a far cry from where she'd been, but it was hers alone. There was a certain sense of peace and security with that.

With a hard realization, she looked back over the years where she'd spent money indiscriminately because it was always available. It was… there. She'd bought jewelry, clothes and knickknacks for the house, and she'd never thought to put away any cash. When she'd married, she had believed in forever. And, sure, she'd wanted out of her marriage a lot of times. But it had never occurred to her she would be replaced. How was that even fair? Or legal?

She'd been married for fourteen years. He had built up his business during that time, with her help as his hostess for all his social events. She had no intention of ripping off her husband, but she'd wanted some compensation for all those years she had invested her time and effort into his businesses. But, according to her lawyer, Doreen wasn't entitled to anything of his, including the house, his cars and their bank accounts. The only reason she had the Honda was that it had been her personal car before they married, and she had convinced her husband to keep it, if only for having on standby so the maid could run to the grocery store.

So Doreen was lying here, not even able to afford a new bed, and he had the contents of the whole house to himself. Well, he and his new arm candy, Doreen's divorce lawyer.

Doreen did have one thing from her marriage. Her survivor's spirit.

Of course, she'd been the fool for signing the divorce agreement—only she hadn't realized it until afterward, when it was too late. Or was it? She'd revisit that thought later.

One crisis at a time, please.

She threw back the covers, hopped out of bed and walked over to the bathroom. Once again she stopped in the doorway and smiled. Not only did she have her spirit, she had this bathroom. And this was one room in the house that mattered. She danced inside and turned on the shower, delighted to feel lovely hot water almost instantly with copious pressure.

After a vigorous scrub and several shampoos of her hair, she almost felt clean again. Between the dead body and rummaging through the weeds, she was dang sure she'd brought in more than her fair share of the dirt. She'd like to blame the animals. But she'd been in and out constantly herself.

Back in her room she opened her biggest suitcase, looking for a pair of pants she could wear around the house. She had no idea what she was supposed to do with all her expensive clothes. Her designer shoes. The thought of ever wearing them here was highly unlikely. Could she sell them? She knew it was probably a foolish idea. But she'd do almost anything to get a new bed.

Once again the animals waited for her as she made her way, now dressed, to the kitchen for her next attempt at making a pot of coffee. While it dripped, she fed the animals. At least their food would last them for a while. Then she turned her attention to herself, because, after all, dinner had been almost nothing, and this morning's offerings weren't looking much better.

With a fresh cup of coffee, she opened the fridge, another archaic-looking thing she couldn't believe still worked. She'd seen them in old movies but never imagined they'd be in household use today. It was empty except for a box of baking soda on the shelf. She didn't understand why that was there. The half-freezer above was also empty.

So Nan had used up or given away or tossed all the perishable food before she left, and that was probably a darn good thing. But it also meant Doreen couldn't put off grocery shopping for much longer. She gathered all that was left of her traveling food on the table—some dried fruit and nuts. Obviously that was her breakfast.

As soon as she ate, she grabbed her purse, poured the last of the coffee in her travel mug and headed for her car.

As she opened the front door, she gasped to see an older woman, her hand in the air, ready to knock.

The two women stared at each other in surprise before Doreen pulled herself together. "Hi. How can I help you?"

The older woman smiled. "I'm Ella, your neighbor." She turned to point at the house on the far right of the cul-de-sac. "I just wanted to say hello and to welcome you to the neighborhood. It's been a bit rough for you, so I wanted to let you know we're not all nosy busybodies."

How lovely. Doreen beamed at the first true welcome she'd had. "Thank you so much. You're right. Yesterday was a bit rough, but today is a new day."

Ella laughed. "I see you're heading out." She motioned at the travel mug in Doreen's hands while backing down the front porch steps. "So feel free to stop by and say hi sometime. We'll have a cup of tea together."

She skipped down the last few steps, waved and strode home, leaving Doreen to stare after her neighbor, wondering if she should have changed her plans and visited with the woman. Still, the moment had passed. Shrugging, Doreen got into the car. Nan had said a grocery store was just down the road. If nothing else, Doreen could live on bread and peanut butter for a while. The peanut butter was a memory from her childhood. She'd never been allowed to have it while married. Like so many other things.

She hated to leave all the animals inside the house. Plus, she expected the cops back again, but she had to leave before they blocked her in once more.

She drove down Lakeshore Road, ignoring the many people out walking their animals and staring at her. Several blocks later she came to a grocery store. She pulled into a parking spot, got out, grabbed a cart and went in. Now she had to enter that food nightmare. If she could cook, it would be a different story, but chances were she'd burn everything. Although the coffee this morning had tasted like coffee, which was a huge improvement.

She still didn't understand the mystery of grocery stores. She understood fresh food was supposed to be on the outside perimeter, and the food she was to avoid was on the inside of the store. Why would they sell food that you're supposed to avoid? And why put it in the middle of the store, exactly where everyone was going? Her husband had been a fresh-food freak, and that was great as she'd obviously remembered some of his rantings. She wandered down the store aisles, figuring out just what she could buy in this small town with an even smaller budget.

She quickly collected fresh greens, spinach and kale. Maybe she could get her smoothies back into her routine again. She didn't know if Nan had a blender. Checking the secondhand store for one was a place to start. Maybe she could find a teapot too. She kept on going through the fresh veggies, picked up some fruit and wandered into the meat section. This was where that whole cooking mystery began. Nothing made sense to her. But she needed to eat protein too.

By the time she finished her shopping, she was confused, tired and frustrated. But she pushed her small cart to the cashier. The clerk, Cherry, according to her name tag, gave her a wide-eyed look, then pinched her mouth shut and rang up the groceries. Doreen assumed Cherry must have heard about the body.

Figures. Doreen pushed her prepaid card into the card reader and punched in her security code so she could access her remaining funds, heaving a breath of relief when the transaction was approved. She had saved most of her "allowance," then had bought a prepaid card before she made the five-hour drive here. She didn't want to carry any cash on her while traveling alone, and she felt the prepaid card was safer, plus it was insured for theft.

But she did need to check its balance. She was afraid to look and confirm how little was left, but, at the same time, she needed to know the exact figure. She sighed, deciding to check the balance once she got home.

Just as silently, she grabbed her bags, put them in the cart. She thanked the clerk with a polite smile before wheeling the cart to her car. It was such a relief to be back out in the fresh air and sunshine again and to not have to worry about anybody saying anything. As she thought about it though, nobody spoke to her at all—as if a town conspiracy of silence was the best way forward.

When she drove into her driveway and parked, two unmarked vehicles were already parked at the curb. She figured they were cops, working in the back garden. She opened her trunk, pulled out her bags and walked up to the front of the house. Instantly Mugs barked.

"Mugs, it's okay. It's just me."

Mugs barked again, not having any of it. Since strangers were in the street and the backyard, she couldn't blame him. She unlocked the front door, let the dog race outside to confirm nothing was there and carried the bags to the kitchen. Setting everything on the table, she walked back to close the front door. She shrugged out of her sweater, laid it over the back of the couch, dropped her purse on the kitchen table beside the groceries and opened the rear kitchen door so she could step out and see what was going on. Mugs barreled ahead of her.

Sure enough, four men were in the garden where she had found the arsenic last night. She recognized Mack, who raised a hand in greeting. Beside him, she acknowledged Chester and Arnold with a wave and returned to the house. She stood just inside the door and wondered aloud, "Should I put on coffee? Or tea? I'd offer cookies if I was at home." She frowned, walking over and staring out the kitchen window.

She'd been forced to learn a lot of etiquette rules when she'd been married, as they were different from the ones for unmarried women, according to both her uppity mother and her controlling husband. It had taken forever before any of it came naturally to Doreen, but eventually it had. With her separation, that had been one of the first things she'd stopped worrying about.

Until moving here for some reason.

She decided it was probably prudent to be ready with coffee if Mack did come in. At least she'd have a cup for him. So she put on a second pot. It was a small pot after all, and she'd drink it all herself if she had to. She quickly set the coffee to dripping, put her perishable foods in the fridge and then figured out where to put a few canned goods of her choosing when the cupboards were already full.

A knock came at the back door. Mack filled the open doorway.

She smiled brightly at him. "Good morning."

"Good morning. You weren't here when we arrived, so we went straight into the backyard."

She nodded. "I needed to get a few groceries." Her tone was formal. Even though she was trying to be friendly, it was still odd to see somebody like him doing what he was doing.

He nodded formally as well. "How was your night?"

"Outside of the fact that you were here late last night, and the bed I slept in must be from the early 1900s, and every time I rolled over, the bed squeaked and bounced and pinched my spine…" She gave him a wan smile. "I'll probably be heading for a nap at noon because it was so bad."

"Sorry about that." He winced. "It's really important to have a good bed."

"Well, I won't be getting one anytime soon, since I have no money for anything like that."

He shrugged. "At least you have a home."

She gave him a flat stare. "There is that."

"You know…" Mack began.

Her eyebrows raised, she waited for him to continue.

"I don't mean to meddle," he said.

"Go on. I can at least listen to what you have to say, then I'll decide. Right?"

"You could have an estate sale."

"But, but… isn't that when someone has died?"

"Call it a garage-and-house sale if it makes you feel better. Get rid of what Nan doesn't want and buy a new bed."

"*Hmm.*" She wasn't sure what that type of sale entailed but it was an idea. She just wasn't sure it was a good one. And would it actually bring in enough money to buy a bed?

"You could make it one day, or a weekend or even a one-week-long neighborhood event, where you could get the neighbors to join in. It would give the community a new way to view you after all this murder business."

Her eyebrows shot up at that. "I don't know," she said slowly. "I will consider it, but it's going to take time to sort through this stuff. I have to ask Nan about most pieces."

"There's no rush though, is there?" He smiled at her.

"Except you could use a new bed sooner than later."

With a nod of her head, she said, "Thank you, Mack."

Thaddeus walked in and straight up to Mack. "Thaddeus is here. Thaddeus is here."

She smiled down at the bird. "Good morning, Thaddeus."

He tilted his head sideways and rolled one eye up at her. He hopped onto the kitchen counter and walked back and forth. "Coffee. Coffee. Thaddeus smells coffee. Thaddeus smells coffee."

"I've never heard that word out of him before," she exclaimed. She brushed a finger down the bird's neck. "I really have no idea what I'm doing with him."

"Looks like you're doing just fine."

"Just goes to show you that appearances can be deceiving." She straightened and gave Mack a pleasant smile. "Did you need something?"

He nodded. "That's why I came in before we left."

"Left?" She glanced out at the garden and saw it was, indeed, empty. "Oh, good."

"You don't have to sound quite so happy."

"Given what I've been through these last twenty-four hours, I so do. I want this over with." She motioned at the coffee. "Would you like a cup? It's fresh."

His face lit up. "I'd love a cup, thank you." He pulled out a kitchen chair and sat down at the table. "Besides I have some questions for you."

Crap. She knew she shouldn't have been so friendly. "Questions about what?" she asked as she poured two cups full of coffee.

"Questions about the murdered man."

Chapter 13

DOREEN STARED AT Mack in shock. She sat down hard at the table and said, "I don't know who the murdered man is."

"His name is James Farley. He was an insurance salesman."

"Well, Mack, I'm not at all surprised an insurance salesman was murdered," she murmured. "According to my almost ex, they are all scammers."

"Well, you're *almost* not married anymore," he said shortly. "Make your own decisions."

She narrowed her gaze at him. "Somebody murdered him. Why do you think I would know anything about him?"

"That's why I'm here." He proceeded to ask her questions, like; did she recognize the man's name? Did she know the family? Had she any insurance? Could she have bought some from this Farley person? What about Nan? Did she have any insurance?

The answers were easy, as she didn't know anything about the dead man or insurance. Neither did she know anything about Nan's knowledge of the dead man's family or if Nan had purchased insurance from him. "You'll have to ask Nan." When he was done, she crossed her arms and slumped in the chair. "You've told me who he is. I still don't *know* him."

"Have you seen any correspondence from Nan around the house with that man's name on it?"

She shook her head. "I've been a little busy over the last twenty hours or so since I arrived here, so you need to direct those questions to Nan."

He nodded and stood. "That's where I'm heading next."

He walked to the front door, she trailed behind. "Don't upset Nan when you go there," she said. "The last thing I want is for her to have a heart attack over this."

"I won't do anything to upset her if I don't have to. However, we do have to find out who killed this man."

And then he was gone.

There was no friendly belly rub for Mugs or a stroke behind the ears for Goliath. Not even an acknowledgment of Thaddeus. Businesslike and simple. A few questions and he was gone. But it left a chill.

She locked the front door behind him. She knew how this looked. Yet, that didn't change the fact that neither she nor Nan had killed this man. Perhaps somebody had known the house was empty and thought nobody would notice, so they had deliberately placed the body here to implicate Nan or Doreen. Or as a temporary measure until they could move it again but... *ewww*. Not to mention that decking over the body looked pretty permanent.

Either way it sucked. Nan was a wonderful person, and she didn't need this. And that meant somebody had to find the right answers. Not just the answers that would fit and make a case for the police. Because, if that case closed around Nan, then the conclusion was wrong. Somebody would have to set them straight. That somebody would have to be Doreen.

Nan had done a lot for Doreen over these last few rough months, and that was without taking into account all the times she'd been there for Doreen over the years. The least she could do was return the favor. She'd find out who killed that man. She rolled up her imaginary sleeves and stormed into the kitchen.

She snagged a cup of coffee and stepped onto the back veranda, considering what to do to clear Nan's name. Her gaze studied the proximity of her house and yard to the neighbors' yards, wondering if she should talk to the neighbors. Maybe they had seen something between the time Nan moved to Rosemoor and when Doreen arrived yesterday.

But the state of the backyard distracted the gardener in her. Nan's back garden was fully fenced although those fences were badly in need of TLC, like the gardens themselves. Doreen had lots of TLC to give, but she wasn't so sure about the fence repairs. Still, if a hammer and nail would do the job, she could work with that. Besides the physical work would help rid her of some of the building stress.

But solving the dead man's mystery came before gardening. Her laptop was still packed away upstairs. She went inside, retrieved it, set it up on the kitchen table and searched for James Farley. Thank heavens the house had internet. Thanks Nan.

He'd lived and worked in Kelowna, in British Columbia, Canada. But he wasn't from the Mission area of British Columbia. Not that that made him an outsider. Mission was just one of many communities that had pulled together and suddenly became a town as it grew. No way to keep the growing parts and pieces separate anymore, so they'd been incorporated into the city of Kelowna.

Farley was employed by an insurance company downtown. Maybe it was time to take Mugs for a walk along the boardwalk and check out where this guy had worked.

Had the insurance company called him in as a missing person? Or had he been one of those employees who traveled most the time and only checked in occasionally, and the company didn't know when he was coming back? Didn't they realize he was missing?

Unable to leave it alone, she quickly toasted herself a piece of bread to-go, then loaded Mugs into the car. She locked Thaddeus and Goliath in the house. With both cat and bird staring out the living room window at them, she got in the car and drove downtown.

A lot of the downtown parking you had to pay for, unless it was on a weekend. Today was Thursday. So she parked for free down by the beach, hooked Mugs on his leash and proceeded to walk toward the business district. Several blocks later and around a corner, she found the small insurance company. She glanced up at the second floor to see the company name written on the window. Lifelong Insurance, Inc.

"Yeah, it didn't do him so well, did it?" she asked Mugs. "His lifelong ended up being a pretty darn life*short*."

As the words fell off her lips, the door opened and out stepped a balding redheaded mailman with more freckles than she'd ever seen. A big bag over his shoulder, mail in his hand, he smiled at her and moved out of her way. "Sorry," he said cheerfully and, with a jaunty step, headed down the sidewalk.

She pulled open the door, and with Mugs at her heels, they climbed the stairs to the small office. Lifelong Insurance was on the right at the top of the stairs. No lights appeared to be on inside. She turned the handle and pushed, but the door was locked. No Closed sign was on the door though. She knocked several times, but there was no answer. Did James Farley own Lifelong Insurance? Was he the only employee?

With those thoughts running through her mind, she slowly made her way back downstairs, stopping at the first landing. And came face-to-face with Mack, who was on his way up.

She smiled. "Great minds think alike," she said gaily.

"What are you doing here?" His tone was much less than happy.

She stuck out her chin. "I wanted to see if I could find some answers myself. I don't want you thinking that Nan had anything to do with James's murder. And I know I didn't do it, so, therefore, somebody else did."

"Oh, no you don't. I don't want you nosing around, asking any questions," Mack stated in an unequivocal term. "You leave that to the police."

She'd perfected a flat stare a long time ago. But it seemed to have no effect on him. She gave up and smiled sweetly instead. Nan had always said honey worked better than vinegar. "Obviously I don't want to step on any of your toes. I just wanted to know where Farley worked." She glanced over at the door above and behind her. "It's his own business, is it not?"

Mack nodded. "Yes, he's the owner and operator of Lifelong Insurance."

"Right." She was pleased to find that out on her own.

She tossed him a bright smile. "Have fun."

He probably had the right to go inside the office, even if locked and vacant. She watched as he carried on up the stairs, unlocked the door and entered Farley's office. Unable to help herself, she tiptoed back upstairs and stood in the open doorway. And cried out.

Mack stood in the middle of the destroyed office and glared at her. "Don't come in here."

Immediately she shook her head. "I won't. I promise I won't. But look what they did."

"They?" he asked, suspicion coloring in his tone.

She glared at him. "What? I didn't do it."

"Didn't you? Funny how I just came in as you're leaving."

She pointed at the doorknob. "It was locked, remember?"

This time his smile was less than pleasant. "Easy to lock it if you had already unlocked it to get in."

She glared at him. "I had nothing to do with this."

"Good. Keep it that way." He made a motion with his hand to shoo her out of the doorway. "I've a forensic team coming in here. Don't touch anything, and stay out of the way."

She backed away but went to touch the door.

"What did I just say?"

She pulled her hand against her chest. "I tried to open it earlier. So my prints will be on the doorknob. And I knocked, so my knuckle prints are on the glass," she added in a rush.

He shook his head and glared. "Great. Now you mucked it up with your prints too."

She winced. "I'm sorry. It just never occurred to me that trying to talk to someone at an insurance company would cause trouble."

"That's because you didn't think. Everything regarding James Farley is now a police issue. Please go home. Let the police handle it before your prints are everywhere and cannot be ignored."

She sniffed, turned on her heels and slowly walked back down the stairs. Trouble was, Mugs didn't want to go. He stared at the top of the stairs, and short of dragging him all the way down, he wasn't interested in leaving the office. Groaning, she stepped up a couple risers and said, "Mugs, what's wrong with you?"

"What's going on?" Mack asked from the doorway.

"I don't know. I just asked him that," she said in frustration, glaring at Mack. "He doesn't want to leave."

Mack walked over, and in a mood completely opposite to the cold, irate cop from seconds earlier, he bent and scratched Mugs behind the ear. Mugs wagged his tail, sniffing all over Mack's shoes. While Mack was busy scratching the dog, she hadn't been paying attention, so when Mugs tugged on his leash, it fell from her fingers and he darted right between Mack's legs. Right inside the insurance office.

"Oh, no," she cried out. "We have to get him." She darted around Mack, dashing into the office.

Mack was on her heels.

Inside the office, she stopped and stared. There was no sign of the dog. She spun on her heels and cried out, "Where is he?" Turning back to the trashed floor, she called out, "Mugs! Mugs, come on, boy. Where are you?"

No answer came.

Mack searched the other rooms. She followed. There was a single small office, a bigger office and a private one that looked like another small office in the back. By the time they made their way to the bathroom and the storeroom, she found the office was larger than she'd initially thought, deeming it just one of those tiny seedy-looking single rooms with a bathroom. But it was set up to hold five to six staff offices.

Only there was still no sign of Mugs. "Where could he be?"

Behind her was a muffled bark. She spun around to see Mugs underneath a large boardroom table, but with all the chairs pulled up around it, she couldn't see him there. She pulled out a couple chairs to find Mugs lying on his belly, panting. A mess of papers was on the floor in front of him. She grabbed his leash and tugged, but he wouldn't move. He stretched his neck forward and barked at the papers.

"No, Mugs, you can't have those papers. I know you love to rip apart paper, but you can't have these papers."

Instead of listening to her, he lunged for a big stack, growled and backed up under the table. Mack grabbed the leash and brought Mugs out from underneath. By then Mugs had a mouthful of paperwork.

She gently opened his jaw, telling him, "Who's a good boy, Mugs? I promise I'll find you a newspaper at home. You can rip that up."

He gave her one of those hangdog looks, as if to say, "Sure you will."

"Wait." Mack dropped to his knees beside the dog. Using a pressure point in the back of the dog's jaw, Mack forced Mugs's mouth open. The stack of papers dropped. Mack snatched them up but not before she saw the top page.

"That's got Nan's name on it."

"Yes, it does." He patted Mugs. "Thanks, Mugs. This is a great lead."

Chapter 14

DOREEN MOVED CLOSER to read more, but Mack removed the papers from her sight.

He glared at her. "Official police business, remember?"

She shoved her chin out front and forward. "Official family business, remember?"

He chuckled. "You've got a point." He laid the papers on the table, and together they searched through them for Nan's name.

Doreen tapped three different sheets. "These relate to Nan."

Mack pushed the first one off to the side. "This is her personal history, medical, etc. You always get that done when you make an insurance claim or when buying insurance coverage. This one appears to be his notes about Nan's family history. Your name is on it too." He tapped the center of the page.

She peered closer, and there was her name. She tapped the mention with her fingernail.

He set those two sheets beside each other, then pulled out the third one and studied it. "And this is a copy of a life insurance policy on Nan... until she reaches age 95."

Doreen focused on it and snatched it from his fingers. "Why would she do that?" She studied the document. "This is for half a million dollars!"

"Yes, but this was taken out a long time ago. And it's not from Lifelong Insurance. So he found an insurance company that had a policy for Nan. And it lists you as the sole beneficiary."

She stared at him. "Does this mean it's still in effect?"

He turned his gaze from the paper to her. "It appears to be. You didn't know anything about it?" he asked curiously.

She shook her head. "No. I had no idea." She stared at the paper in wonder. "She had no money. This must be important to her."

"Do you know for sure she had no money?" Mack asked delicately. "Because, many times, older people just can't spend their money or don't feel like they should spend it or aren't interested in spending money. They like the comfort of all the old things they have around them."

She pulled out a chair and sat down hard. "I honestly don't know. And I feel very invasive having that conversation with her. She used to travel a lot when she was younger. Then she stopped. I figured it was because the money ran out. Plus, look at her run-down house and gardens. If she had money, wouldn't she have renovated her house and the yards?" Doreen shook her head. "I've never asked Nan for any money or for anything else for that matter. I thought she was broke. Why buy a life insurance policy?" she muttered under her breath. "I always thought they were just scams."

"Lots of people believe the whole life policies are, and yet, lots of other people believe the term life policies are a good investment. Plus these term policies are the cheapest, so it may not be the hardship on Nan that you think. Then there are equity insurances and too many other combinations to list."

"How can it be a good investment if it only pays off after you die?"

"So true." He laughed. "But it also goes to show you that Nan loves you."

What a lovely thought. She stared at the sheet of paper and thought about how much her husband didn't love her and then thought about how Nan was in the background doing something like this for Doreen. And never telling her. "I'd never have known about this if I hadn't come here."

"Maybe it's not a good thing for you to know." He shuffled the rest of the papers. "If she runs out of money and can't maintain this, then you might have the expectation of money when she dies, but it won't be there."

"If she needs the money, I'd be happy for her to cancel it. She doesn't get any money back, does she?"

"Not on a strictly term policy. Not any way of knowing that without reading the policy. Some of them are structured differently."

"My soon-to-be-ex-husband is paying for one on me. I didn't know about it until he flung that information at me during a fight in our last year. It still makes me cringe, even after the first few months of our separation. Just the thought that maybe he'd knock me off somewhere. But, since I wasn't the one paying the premiums, I didn't have a copy. So I have no idea what the details are."

He shook his head. "You have every right to go to the insurance company and say you fear for your life, and you want the policy canceled. I don't know what they'd say, but, if you are seriously worried, then you should do something about it."

"And that'll likely involve a lawyer or cops. And lawyers are not people I trust." She forgot who she was talking to.

He straightened and focused on her again. "Lawyers get a bum rap. But they are not all bad."

Her gaze went flat, and she stared at him. "My lawyer completely screwed me over on the separation and upcoming divorce and is now my husband's current fiancée. According to her, I wasn't entitled to anything. And I, fool that I am, believed her."

He stared at her. "Oh, shit."

"Oh, shit, indeed." She turned her focus to the papers atop the table. "Are you taking these? What about the stuff on the floor?"

"I need to spend a few hours going over some of these papers. It's hard to know exactly what's been going on here, but with the vandalism, I have to consider somebody was looking for something."

"How can you tell if they found it?"

He shook his head. "With a mess like this? The only person who knew for sure is dead. So likely we'll never know."

For her that wasn't good enough. She needed answers, not more questions. "It doesn't make any sense that he'd have copies of Nan's old insurance papers. If he was trying to sell her insurance, he would know she wouldn't need another policy."

"Perhaps he was hoping to get her to transfer it or to create a new policy or to sell her something else."

"That's possible. I don't know what Nan is like with business. She always kept that to herself. In fact, I can't ever remember her talking about money."

"Is that why you believe she doesn't have any?"

"Yes, plus everything in the house is in disrepair and seriously in need of updating. Lots of canned food but no fresh food or new furniture and the bed..." She closed her eyes, a shudder rippling down her spine at the reminder of the night. "That bed is something else."

"Maybe she has many happy memories of all that furniture. The house is worth a fair bit. It's in a nice little area. The whole of the Mission has skyrocketed in real estate prices. She could've sold her home at any point in time if she needed to. Instead, she gave it to you. That, in itself, means she obviously felt she had enough for her own needs without selling it."

She stared out the window. The Okanagan area—including a lake, a valley and a river—was well known for its resort-like location and balmy weather almost every day of the year. And, true to form, a blue sky and sunshine were out there today.

The talk of her grandmother made her homesick to see her again. She'd stop off on her way home for a visit. Maybe she'd bring up this insurance policy.

"Was it that tough?" Mack asked, pulling her back to the conversation.

"Between my husband and my lawyer, I get nothing." She said it in a brisk tone, hating to let him know just where she was at financially. But there was no point in putting on airs that she was anything but completely destitute. "My lawyer explained how I had signed all my rights away."

"How long were you married?"

She looked at him. "Fourteen years. I helped him build his business, clear off his debts, yet somehow ended up with nothing."

"How long have you been separated? Have you actually

divorced yet?"

She frowned. "Separated for months, almost six now. He told me right before the holidays. And, no, we can't file the divorce papers until one continuous year of separation later, but I've already signed everything. I just didn't realize I had other options when I was signing. *Obviously.* I let my lawyer handle it. But, of course, I didn't know my lawyer was on my husband's payroll and had screwed me over." Her laugh was bitter. "And apparently screwing him at the same time." She shook her head. "I didn't even think things like that could happen." She turned and strode from the room. "Believe me. Some lessons you just can't walk away from."

"But there might be something you can do about it."

She froze, turned and looked at him. "And just what would that be?"

"You could see another lawyer. Yours obviously did not have her client's best interests in mind."

"She only had her own interests in mind. And a lawyer means more money. Remember that part about being cleaned out and not having anything?"

"Another reason to have the garage sale."

Doreen shook her head. "I'm buying a bed first. Everything else will have to wait." She picked up Mugs's leash. "Come on, Mugs. We've had enough of a bad trip down memory lane for today. Let's stop at Nan's and see if we can find a little sunshine in her life today."

"And consider letting me and my brother take a look into that separation agreement before the divorce goes through," he said. "My brother is a practicing lawyer, and he's a good, fair man."

She looked over her shoulder at him. "I don't have any money, so your offer, although generous, still requires some form of payment. I don't have anything to give. Maybe later." She nodded at the forms on the table. "I'll ask Nan about James and the insurance policy. Maybe she can shed some light on this." She headed down the stairs.

When she got to the front door, Mack called out to her. "You didn't even ask how much he'd charge."

She looked up the stairs to where he stood. "Doesn't matter. My last one got every drop of money out of me. So it doesn't matter how much he charges. Even your idea of a garage sale, if I pull that off, is only a one-time thing. I need money coming in monthly. If I don't find a job soon, I'll be heading to the food bank." She turned and walked out.

As the door slammed behind her, she smiled. There was something freeing about stating the truth about her current situation.

Instead of depressing her, the action made her feel better. If there was one sentiment Nan had impressed on Doreen repeatedly throughout the years it was, *When you're down, look up. That's the only place left to go.*

She glanced up at the bright blue sky and the sunshine beaming across the small town. "You know? I'll be totally happy to go up for a change. Being down really sucks."

She walked to her car, loaded Mugs into the back seat and went around to the driver's side. She closed the door and buckled up her seat belt to find Mack standing at the front of the car. She rolled down the window and called out, "Now what? Did you find something?"

"You mean, besides a very frustrating, irritating woman?" he asked. "No."

She glared at him. "Then what do you want?"

"To offer you a part-time job," he said in exasperation. "But why I want the added frustration, I have no idea."

She froze. Then stared up at him in delight. "What kind of a job? And, yes, please."

He shook his head, stared up at the sky for a long moment, then raised both hands in the air and said, "Whatever." He walked around to the driver's side, leaning in the window. "You might not like it."

"It doesn't matter if I like it or not," she admitted quietly. "I need it." She waited for him to say more.

"Do you like gardening?"

She nodded. "I love gardening."

"My mother's house is only a couple blocks away from you, and she can't get out into the garden anymore. I told her that I'd come and look after it, but it's more than I have the time for. I wouldn't be able to pay you a whole lot... but maybe an hourly wage that we could agree on would make us both happy."

She grinned. "Absolutely. Give me the address, and I'll look at it on my way home."

He gave her the address, watching as she wrote it down. "Don't talk to my mom yet though."

She merely shook her head. "Okay, I won't. I just want to see what kind of work I'm looking at."

"Good idea. And, after you do, give me a shout. We'll discuss price." He pulled out another card, this one with his home number on it and handed it to her. "In the meantime, stay the hell out of my case." He glared down at her as if for good measure, then abruptly walked back into the Lifelong Insurance building.

She turned on the engine, and in a much happier mood, she said to Mugs, "See? Like Nan said, there's only one place to go, and that's up."

Chapter 15

DOREEN DECIDED TO visit Nan tomorrow and to check out Mack's mother's garden today. When she finally located the address, it was within walking distance from Nan's house. Just a couple blocks down, like Mack had said. In that sense, it would be perfect. She wouldn't have to use the car to get to work, so the cost of gas wasn't an issue.

She drove past the house slowly, looking at the front yard. It had a lovely front garden with a bed full of perennial bushes with a few annuals dotted around. A nice combination of colors. And it was in decent shape. The grass needed to be mowed, and that could present a problem as she didn't have her own lawn mower.

Neither did she have the money to buy one. As for the weeds, well, some had definitely taken advantage and needed to be pulled. Many of the bushes were overgrown and needed to be trimmed too. She wanted to get out and wander around to the backyard, but she didn't want to disturb his mother. Looking at the yard, she thought she saw an alleyway behind the house.

She drove around to the back of the house, parked and got out, then looked over the short fence at the backyard.

She couldn't remember if he had said both gardens or just the front. But the back garden was in worse shape. His mother probably tried to do what she could out in the front to keep up appearances. But the backyard required more than she had to give. Like so many people who owned homes, the work got ahead of them, and catching up was brutal.

Considering how much work Doreen had to do on Nan's garden, she understood. In Doreen's case, fences needed mending, the patio was overgrown with weeds, and likely the concrete blocks making up the patio weren't worth keeping either. Not to mention the beds had to be redefined. She'd need a full-time paycheck just to get it back into shape.

But some of it had to be done, even without money, applying a lot of physical labor.

It would take a day or two to fix up the front yard of Mack's mom's house, but the back property would need a full week, and she could use some added muscle. Several shrubs needed heavy pruning. And some fallen garden logs needed to be replaced. Still, it was all doable.

A dog barked at her side. She spun in surprise to see an older gentleman staring at her, his nose in the air, a disapproving look on his face.

She glanced from him to the fence she'd been peering over and flushed. "I was just looking at her garden," she rushed to say.

His gaze narrowed.

Flustered, she returned to the driver's side of her car and quickly backed out the alleyway. As she came to the end of it, she realized she could have just driven forward past the older man.

"Crap," she muttered, still flustered. But at least she

hadn't backed into anyone's fences on her way.

Smack.

She froze, then closed her eyes and dropped her forehead on her steering wheel. Finally she raised her head and looked behind her. And grinned. She'd hit a harmless street sign delineating the road and alleyway. She hopped out and walked around the car to see the damage but could only find a scrape on her bumper. And it was hard to see because the bumper had been well decorated in the same manner long before she'd bought it.

Happier, she got back in her car and drove home. She pulled into the driveway, parked and let Mugs out. He barked immediately. She looked around but didn't see anything. "Mugs, what's the matter?"

He kept barking, then ran around to the rear of the house. She followed at a slower pace. In the back, she couldn't see anything wrong, but she could hear Goliath inside the house, howling. Obviously he wanted out too. She made her way up the back steps to the kitchen door and opened it. Instantly Goliath shot out, screaming across the backyard property. Now the two of them were out there. She propped the kitchen door wide open to let some fresh air in, and, sure enough, Thaddeus flew out the door to land on the railing.

"Thaddeus is here. Thaddeus is here."

"Of course you're here. I can see you," she said in exasperation.

The bird cocked his head at her, and the big guy blinked. She tilted her head to the side and patted her shoulder. Instantly he hopped up. She threw her purse and keys down on the outside table and marched to the rear of the property.

For whatever reason, both the dog and cat were howling at something in the back corner. As she made her way to them, she assessed the manpower needed to restore the back garden to its former glory. And groaned. It would take a lot of work. A lawn mower would help a lot, but again she didn't have one.

The fence wasn't as bad as she had thought, if she looked past the multiple types of fencing that dotted the yard. The support posts were solid. A hammer and nails would put the sagging boards back in place. A can of paint would give it a face-lift. Part of the fence was an open-picket style, with just crossrails instead of solid wood. Several of which had fallen off. Still, she could see the neighbor's house on the one side and out the back alley.

Alley? That was the first time she realized an alleyway was behind the house. In that case, it would've been easy for somebody else to access that side of Nan's backyard to bury the body.

Nan's property backed onto Crown land. One of the advantages was owning a home where you could open a gate and walk the dog for miles out on public property. Or a disadvantage if Mugs ran off.

"Mugs! Mugs!" she called out. As she reached the back fence, she found the gate was open. "Oh, dammit, Mugs. Come on, Mugs."

She pushed the gate wider and stepped out. Instead of grassy fields, she found a good-size creek ran along here. She looked back at Nan's house and the fence. "Why would you fence off the river? This is too pretty to hide."

What she'd thought had been an alleyway was a bit of a walking path alongside the back of all the fences, which buffered the creek edge to the fence line. Plus a little footbridge was built over the water. "Oh my, this is beautiful."

"Beautiful. Beautiful," Thaddeus crooned in her ear.

It would be even nicer to get rid of the broken-down fence to open up the view of the creek to Nan's house. It would also allow her to see the wildlife, as plenty of small critters of all kinds would gather at the water. That would be something she'd love to watch.

Feeling so much happier at the sight of the creek, she studied Nan's house from here. A lot of bushes and trees blocked the view. But, with a good heavy pruning, she could turn this backyard into something spectacular.

She hopped up onto the little bridge and called out, "Mugs! Mugs?"

On her shoulder, Thaddeus opened his mouth and cried, "Thaddeus is here. Thaddeus is here."

"I know you're here, silly," she said. "But where's Mugs?"

Suddenly Thaddeus made a great big screech and flew off her shoulder, down to the far side of the bank.

She ran after him. "Wait, Thaddeus. What did you find? Mugs? Where are you?" She ran over the little bridge. As she put her foot on the last board, it gave way beneath her. And down she went.

She cried out as one of her feet hit the water, her other knee buckled and her butt hit the little bridge. Taking a deep breath, she tried to assess what just happened. One foot was caught in the framework of the little bridge. She was forced to twist around, using her hands to clamber back up, afraid to put any weight on her ankle or the bridge.

She glanced down at her designer jeans and sandals and cried out, "And these are ruined now too?" She shook her head but was much less concerned over her outfit than her missing dog. "Mugs, where are you?" She whistled for him.

Still there was no answer from Mugs. Clumsily she stood on her feet and tried to shake the water off her sandal. But it and her jeans were drenched to her knee and covered with mud. Hesitantly she placed her weight on her sore ankle, grateful it could at least sustain her weight. Her leg was scraped by the broken slats, but her ankle didn't appear to be sprained.

Now that she was on the other side of the creek, she could see a small pathway, overgrown by brush. She managed to get up onto the path and followed it after Thaddeus. "Come on, you guys. Where are you? Don't make me search for you."

Bedraggled and limping as she was, she hoped to heck she didn't meet anybody. It was bad enough being Nan's crazy granddaughter in the eyes of a few. But, if anybody saw her now, they'd have no doubt she was nuts.

In the distance, she heard a bark. "Mugs?" She ran, although lopsided. But at least she was moving. She got a few steps down the path when she heard Mugs's barking go up a notch. She picked up her speed, broke through a pile of brush and came to a sudden stop, staring at her crazy trio. Mugs was still barking like crazy. Goliath sat on a tree stump staring up a tree, his tail making short hard twitches. Thaddeus wandered back and forth like a bloody little soldier. Marching ten steps, turning, and marching back again saying, "Thaddeus is here. Thaddeus is here."

She shook her head. "What is wrong with you guys? Why did you take off?"

Only Mugs wasn't listening. He insisted on barking as he looked up a tree. She groaned and walked closer. She grabbed for his leash. As she looked up, eyes looked down at her.

She shrieked and stepped back. That set Mugs off again. She hesitantly took another step forward and peered up into the foliage. "Hello?"

"Hello" came the boy's small voice.

"Are you okay?" she asked. "Mugs won't hurt you."

"He's barking."

"Yes, he does that a lot all of a sudden." She sighed. "I can't seem to find a way to stop him." She peered through the foliage to see a young child sitting on a branch way too high up for her to even reach. "How did you get up there?"

"I climbed."

"You climbed?" She shook her head. "Do you need help getting down?"

The child looked down at her and said, "You're the crazy lady, aren't you?"

"I'm not the crazy lady," she protested with a winning smile. At least she hoped it was. "I'm Doreen. I'm just a normal person."

The child giggled. And pointed at her leg. "But you're wet and covered in mud."

"Yes, but that doesn't make me a crazy lady," she protested. "I fell through the slats on the little bridge back there when I was chasing after my animals. Now that I've got my dog and Goliath, not to mention Thaddeus…"

At that moment Thaddeus flew up and landed on her shoulder again. He stared up into the tree. "Thaddeus is here. Thaddeus is here."

"I know you're here. Stop talking, for crying out loud." She groaned. "Okay, maybe I look a little crazy. But I'm not, honest." Then she shrugged. Why was she explaining herself to a child?

"Why do you call him that?"

"It's his name. What's yours?" she asked, wondering if he could get down on his own.

The child swept to the bottom branch and scampered down the trunk like a monkey. He stopped and looked up at her. "I'm Travis. And you look crazy to me." And then, without another word, he ran full steam in the opposite direction.

Leaving her standing with her mouth open.

Chapter 16

S HE HEADED FOR the kitchen, determined to face this room of such mystery. She had deliberately picked up simple foods at the grocery store this morning. Everybody can make a jam and peanut butter sandwich. Trouble was, she wasn't interested in having one now. She'd bought sliced ham for sandwiches, and also she could fix cucumber sandwiches with mayonnaise too. Or a ham-and-cucumber combo sandwich. Each, she knew, she could manage.

Just to find some success in her day had her keeping her lunch to a simple sandwich. She pulled out two slices of bread and started building. It was fun. She could see that maybe this cooking thing wouldn't be too bad after all.

With a sense of pride, she cut her sandwich into four triangles, placed it on a plate, put on the teakettle to make a cup of tea and sat down at the table to enjoy what she had made. She took the first bite when Thaddeus landed on the table beside her.

He cocked his head and said, "Thaddeus is here."

"Thaddeus is here," she joined him. "I wish you would stop saying that all the time. Please."

He opened his beak and to shut him up she reached for

a piece of cucumber still on the cutting board and held it up to him. He looked at it, snagged it in his beak and laid it down on the table where he broke it off into little pieces and pecked away at the center, then lifted the food with his foot, and ate it.

But at least he ate it. So that was good. Or maybe it was not good. Were birds supposed to eat cucumbers? She had no idea. She grabbed her laptop and pulled it toward her and quickly checked. *Yes, cucumbers are allowed. Good.*

She glanced around to see Goliath, sitting on the chair beside her, studying the ham left on the cutting board.

"Oh, no you don't. That is for me, for another sandwich. And I might just need a second one." She was starving.

She hadn't had very much to eat since she'd arrived in town. And she really wanted a full meal. The thought of making it herself was daunting. Most of her earlier attempts while at the apartment had ended up in the garbage. And she couldn't afford to waste food then or now. When she counted that cost of ruined food against what the restaurants charged, she'd chosen the restaurant more times than not over the last six months.

But she didn't know very many restaurants here in Mission. And, if she could just learn to cook for herself, it'd be that much cheaper. She picked up the second quarter of her sandwich and studied it with a smile. "This was easy. So surely I can find something else just as easy to fix too."

She set up a search on her tablet for easy meals for new cooks. And she munched away on her sandwich and studied the recipes.

"They don't look that hard." She chose one with a chicken breast and vegetables. When she finished her sandwich, she rose, walked to the fridge and studied the package of chicken. It was too much for one meal, so she opened it, put one piece on a plate, added the spices the recipe called for, putting it in a quart-size zip-bag, placed it back in the fridge, and froze the rest. She'd done her first step to getting dinner ready. Good. Next step was to clean up her lunchtime mess. Something else she never had to do while married.

She turned to see Goliath running off, a big piece of ham hanging out his mouth. And Mugs in chase.

"Mugs! Come back."

But the dog not only had a chance to chase the cat but ham was his prize. No way would she be able to call him back from that. She took advantage of both of them being gone to quickly pack up the rest of the ham and put it back in the fridge. As she turned around, she caught Thaddeus working away on a large bit of cheese. She lifted the package, dumped the little bits and pieces on the table for him and wrapped up the rest.

"I can see that keeping food away from you guys will be as much of a challenge as not burning it," she scolded. "You might be cute and fluffy, but you can sure destroy a block of cheese fast."

As she turned around after closing the fridge, Goliath sat there, staring at her with a grin lighting his eyes.

"Oh, no you don't. You had your share, and that's all you're getting."

But the cat didn't move.

And she wondered out loud, "Unless Mugs got the ham away from you. Did he?"

Feeling stupid but unable to help herself, she opened the ham and handed down a little piece. The cat grabbed it delicately and swallowed it.

She stared at him. "Did you even chew that?"

Silence. Not even a purr.

She gave him another tiny piece and wrapped up the ham, put it in the fridge and slammed the door shut. She glared at him. "That's it. I have to eat too."

Resolutely she walked to the table and finished packing up the rest of the food. Thaddeus had started working on the lettuce. She ripped off a couple pieces, laid it on the table, packed it up in its bag and collected the bread too. She didn't think he'd gotten to the mayonnaise, but who knew?

She returned with a wet cloth to the table, wiped it down, brushing the crumbs onto her plate. She surveyed the clean area with a smile. "There. That wasn't so hard."

She dumped the contents of the plate into the garbage, then went back to the sink, where she washed her plate. She could almost get used to this. It was kind of boring and tedious work, but it was doable.

And speaking of *doable* and *work*, she needed to phone Mack.

She pulled out his card, dialed his home number and waited until he answered. "I drove past your mom's house today. Are you interested in having the front yard and backyard done? Or just one of them?"

"How bad are they?"

"The front isn't too bad. It'll take a day at the most, I'd think. And it'll take a couple hours a week to maintain it," she said. "The backyard, however, that's a much bigger job. Doesn't look like it's been mowed in quite a while. The front needs to be mowed too. But the back is much worse. The gardens are overgrown and need pruning, etc."

"I honestly haven't been in the backyard in quite a while," he said. "I'll do the mowing. It's my mower anyway.

I usually bring it over. I'll take a look this weekend."

"So I'd estimate the front would take six hours initially. And that would mean trimming the bushes, pulling out the deadwood, pruning back the perennials that are more like weeds and giving it a general clean-over. The weeds should be pulled on a regular basis. You already know that. If you want, we could arrange for me to spend a couple hours every week just to keep on top of it. The backyard, well, I'd have to go in and take a closer look before I can give you a better idea on the time needed."

"When can you start work on the front?"

"This weekend?" It's not like she had anything else to do. Except find out who murdered a man in Nan's garden.

"Okay, we can do that. I'll come over with the mower at the same time."

They decided to meet on Saturday morning at nine. Just before she rang off, she said, "Did you know that the backyard of this property ends at a creek?"

"I took a quick glance over there when I was walking the property," he said. "But it's sealed off."

"No, there is a gate in the fence," she said. "It was a little hard to open, as it's broken, yet I slipped out earlier and found a footbridge that crossed the creek."

"So your backyard is fairly accessible. Is that what you're saying? I'm tied up at the moment, but I'll come by this afternoon to take a quick look. I thought the fence was sealed, so somebody would have to climb over it, in which case the whole thing would likely fall down and leave an obvious trail."

With the call done, she went back upstairs to Nan's—now her—room. She wanted to unpack, but had no idea where to put away Nan's things, currently taking up the closet.

She walked into the spare bedroom and opened its closet. It was stuffed. No surprise there. She grabbed what looked like old winter coats. None of these were her style, and surely Nan didn't need all these. Honestly the coats looked like clothing from the 1940s. She studied the labels, and a couple of them were real fur.

She frowned. Why did Nan have fur coats? Especially at this stage of her life? They looked like they were well cared for. Or had critters gotten into them? Fur was notoriously difficult to look after.

She continued studying the labels, realizing the coats were of seriously good quality. She pulled out her phone to call Nan.

"Nan, you have fur coats in your spare bedroom closet. What do you want me to do with them?" She turned to look at the dozen hanging coats. "Do you have someone I could give them too?"

"Oh, those old things? Why don't you take them to the consignment store and see if you get anything for them."

"Consignment store?" She wasn't sure people did that with clothing. She'd heard of it being done with art and furniture, not so much for clothing.

"Yes. If they accept them to sell, they'll give you a percentage of the money."

"You mean, give *you* a percentage of the money," Doreen corrected. "This is all your stuff here. If you didn't want any of it, why didn't you sell it or give away some of the clothes?"

"Because I knew you needed the money, dear. You go ahead and get what you can for the stuff. In fact," Nan said, "When you're ready to move out some of the clutter, feel free. I was going to, then thought you might enjoy the process. Besides you might be able to get a few dollars from selling some of it. I have everything I want with me right here."

Doreen straightened. She looked around at the roomful of stuff—exactly the same as what the rest of the house looked like—and her eyebrows shot up. "Nan, are you sure?"

Even if Nan said she was sure now that didn't mean she wouldn't change her mind down the road. Better to take it slow and make sure Nan really was ready to let go of her memories. As she opened her mouth to say so, Nan laughed. "I'm serious. Except for you, Mugs, Goliath, and Thaddeus, everything I cherish is in my apartment with me every day."

At that, Doreen's eyes clouded with tears. "I don't know what your finances are like, and I don't want to pry, but neither do I want to take any money that you need for yourself." Then she remembered. "And speaking of money, you never mentioned you were paying on a life insurance policy that has me as the beneficiary. Are you sure you should be doing that?"

"Oh, dear, you're so sweet. I'm fine for money. That policy has been around for decades. I bought it when you were still in school from a nice insurance man here in town. He sold the business years ago, but I did confirm with the new owner that everything was still in place. When I'm gone, you'll be fine. In the meantime, you go ahead and sell anything you want in that house. And check the pockets first. I was really bad about leaving money in pockets." Nan hung up without so much as a goodbye.

Instantly Doreen shoved her hands into the nearest pockets and retrieved several crumpled-up twenty-dollar bills. And, for her right now, that was a gold mine. Excited beyond belief, she systematically went through the pockets of the fur coats, checking both the inside and outside pockets. In each coat she found money. Then she put them on the hangers, giving them a good shake out before rehanging them in the closet in the spare room.

Deciding to be systematic, she took a picture of the fur coat against the closet door. It gave a good idea what condition it was in, then she proceeded to document all the others. She shook her head. "Dear Nan, how the heck did you manage to get away with this all these years?"

But Doreen didn't mind. It was like treasure hunting. And, if there was one thing she could use right now, it was a bit of treasure.

Chapter 17

THAT AFTERNOON DOREEN loaded up her car with Nan's fur coats, several of Doreen's suits and designer shoes she would never likely wear again and other bits and pieces from Nan's spare bedroom closet and drove to the consignment store. She'd already called them and had a conversation about the items she was bringing. The owner was interested but hesitant to say that she'd accept them until she'd seen them. Fair enough.

Doreen parked out front and carried in the items. She didn't quite understand how this worked, but, as the store was empty, she didn't feel quite so bad if she made a blunder in the process.

The shopkeeper's name was Wendy Markham. A robust buxom lady with a brilliant smile. She took one look at the fur coats and exclaimed, "Oh my, those are real."

"Exactly."

Doreen appreciated the woman's reaction. She was afraid Nan's things would be discarded as junk. And that wasn't what Doreen wanted. At the same time, there was no point in keeping these things, cluttering up closet space she could use herself. And, if Nan didn't want them, it was better to put them to good use. Maybe somebody could still appreciate them. Besides, money was money.

"I'll get a few more things from the car." It took her three trips to bring it all in.

By the time she was done, Wendy had sorted through the clothes, placing them into Accepted and Not Accepted piles. Thankfully eighty percent of it went into the Accepted pile. Yet, she worked fast and efficiently as she made her decisions almost instantly.

Wendy said, "It'll take a little bit to figure out prices for the fur coats, but I can tell you right now what kind of prices the suits will bring."

She named off a price that had Doreen's eyebrows rising. That was way less than half of what the suits had cost but still was a tremendous amount of money for her right now. Just to be sure she asked, "And how much of that is commission?"

"I take 30 percent, and you'll get 70."

"That's more than fair. Now, is this too much stuff for you? I have more closets of clothing to go through still."

"I've had a couple really big sales which cleared out my stock," she said. "So why don't you bring me another load, and we'll see how quickly the items move. I have a decent number of return clientele here. With any luck, some of these pieces could go right away. After a piece has been here in the store for sixty days, I discount it. You have the option to take it back if you don't like the discount option."

Doreen smiled. "Discount if you need to. Hopefully not too much will be left by the end of sixty days."

In a much happier frame of mind, she got back in her car and headed home. As an afterthought, she took a left turn toward Mack's mother's house. Doreen considered the amount of money she could earn in return for her hours estimated to do the job at the agreed-upon hourly rate, and it was probably a fair deal. But gardening always entailed more than first envisioned. Tomorrow was only Friday. Her fingers itched to get at Mack's mom's gardens now but would have to wait until Saturday. For now, she must keep working on Nan's closets. She had promised another load for the consignment store today, which was more money in her pocket potentially.

Doreen drove home, headed back upstairs and went through another huge stack of Nan's well-kept clothing, creating a Goodwill pile, a consignment store pile and a Keep pile of a few items she thought maybe she would wear, as they were quite funky and cute and fit her.

By the time the lunch hour had arrived, she was tired. But the car was full with yet another load for Wendy at the consignment store. Doreen decided to drop that off first, then maybe pick up something to eat. She'd take Mugs with her this time.

After the consignment store and dropping off the Goodwill stuff, Doreen headed to a park. With Mugs on a leash, Doreen spied the huge food truck. Such an odd icon, but they served hot coffee during the summer here. She bought a coffee and took Mugs for a long walk. On the way back, she picked up fish and chips to-go, returned to her car, and drove home. As soon as she entered the house, Goliath was all over her.

"Did I forget to feed you this morning?"

But, as she walked into the kitchen, she glanced to the left corner where the broom closet was and could still see food in his bowl. The fish smell in her to-go bag had attracted him. She grabbed a plate, opened the back door, and sat down on the rear veranda with her fish and chips. Thaddeus immediately flew to the nearby railing. She probably shouldn't give him anything fried or too salty. Luckily her fish and chips had been served up on a bed of lettuce. She gave him a wilted leaf. He put it on the railing and pecked at it. Goliath, on the other hand, wasn't interested in the french fry she offered him. He hopped up on the table and batted at her fish.

"I didn't buy enough to share with you guys," she complained but good-naturedly broke off a piece of the white flesh his paw had touched and gave it to the cat. Mugs didn't appear to be bothered that she had fed the other two animals first. He just stared at her. She gave him a french fry, which he sniffed, then grabbed and walked over to the far end of the veranda and lay down. But he ate the fry.

She shook her head. "Who knew all the animals would eat vegetables like that?"

After cleaning up after her meal, she headed back upstairs. She was determined to at least get the spare bedroom sorted out. She had an assortment of money and collectibles from Nan's pockets, which had made this a fun treasure hunt, amassing over $260 so far. And a bundle of change she hadn't even counted. She had brought a kitchen bowl to the bedroom to hold the various little bits—the paper money and the coins, a ring, and a chain. She continued checking the pockets of the rest of the coats, finding another $38.42. A small fortune in itself.

But she had another load to sort through. She sorted the clothes into various boxes, marked Consignment, Goodwill, and Dry Cleaning for the things Doreen would keep. After boxing everything up and making several trips to move the boxes downstairs near the front door, she finally had the spare room closet completely empty. But only the spare room. And only the closet. Still, it was later than she'd planned. So she'd deliver the goods tomorrow.

She focused her attention on the dresser next. The bottom three drawers were full of sweaters. She bagged up several for the consignment store and kept one that appealed to her. In the top drawer she found a novel. Stuck inside, like a bookmark, was a Lifelong Insurance business card. Slowly she set the open book on top of the dresser.

"Is this important?" It showed that the dead man and Nan had connected at some point in time. Then she'd mentioned having checked with the new owner of the insurance company and confirming all was well with her original policy. Doreen flipped through the rest of the book but didn't find anything else inside it. On the back of the card was a time, as if Nan had set up a meeting with the dead man. Doreen set it off to the side.

Letting herself be distracted for a few moments, she finished going through the top drawer, finding scarves, several belts and another $12.00. At this point, she wouldn't be happy until she completely gutted Nan's house, finding all the hidden money. Leaving the book where it was, she sorted and boxed up the rest of the clothes from the dresser, whether to sell at the consignment shop or to donate to Goodwill. She added these boxes to those already near the front door.

She didn't want to load up her car this late in the evening.

Not to mention she had no idea what the crime rate was here but where she used to live, leaving a vehicle full of boxes was asking for someone to break in and steal them.

She'd load up her car tomorrow, right before leaving to

make her deliveries.

As she returned to the spare bedroom, only the night table and the bed were left to inspect. She quickly stripped the linens off the bed, checking out the pillowcases and under the mattress, ensuring Nan had no money stashed underneath. The mattress and box spring were in good shape, intact and didn't have any holes where something could be stuffed inside.

She stared at the box spring on the frame, knowing it would be heavy and awkward to move. But then she decided, if she was going to do this job, she would do it right and proper. She took the top mattress off, leaning it against one wall. With both hands, she grabbed the box spring, lifting it a bit. Finding nothing underneath, she dropped it. But she noticed something was caught underneath. She flipped the box spring on its side this time and found an envelope taped underneath. What on earth had Nan been up to that she'd felt compelled to hide so much stuff?

Doreen rearranged the angle of the box spring so she could reach the envelope, pulling it free to place it atop the dresser before quickly putting the bed back together again. Although she was curious about the envelope, she wanted to finish this room before she went to bed tonight. So she went through the night table and found another $42.00. Glancing at the night table lamp, she picked it up, making sure nothing was underneath the base.

Now with the room back to normal, she picked up her bowl of money and trinkets she had found in the room, the open book with the business card and the envelope. She headed back downstairs.

She picked up her phone and called Mack. "I've been cleaning up Nan's spare room," she told him. "In the top dresser drawer was a book." She looked down at it. "It's a copy of *Moby Dick*. Inside is a Lifelong Insurance business card."

"Interesting," he said. "That means Nan did meet him."

"I don't know that she met him." She then explained what Nan had said to her, adding, "But somehow the business card is in her house, and ten o'clock is written on the back. So it could be from her meeting with him way back when."

"I'll be over there in a few minutes," he said. "And we have to postpone our Saturday clean-up session at Mom's. I've got too much else going on to squeeze that in. I'll reschedule something with you later."

She ended the call, reached for the brown legal envelope taped shut on the back flap. She ripped off the tape and flipped up the flap. She went to pull out all the contents but slowly placed it on the table, suddenly unnerved.

What could possibly be in this envelope that Nan would've taped it underneath a spare bed?

Then Doreen frowned and thought, *What if Nan hadn't taped it there? What if somebody else had?* Doreen stood and paced the kitchen. She had no reason not to see what was in the envelope, but for some reason, she couldn't bring herself to. Realizing Mack would be here any minute, she washed her hands and set up a pot of coffee. It was the least she could do.

"I hope it's a decent cup," she muttered to Mugs, now sitting at her feet. She bent down and gave him a hug. "Tell me what's wrong with the envelope."

He barked.

She nodded. "Yeah, that's about how I feel too." She lifted the envelope and held it for him to sniff. He backed away instantly.

She frowned at his reaction, then held it out for Goliath.

Goliath hissed, and his tail poofed.

"Wow. Okay. So that's a really serious reaction. What about you, Thaddeus?"

Curious to see what the bird would do, she held up the brown envelope to Thaddeus, who immediately took flight, screeching, "Murder in the house. Murder in the house."

Chapter 18

A LITTLE UNNERVED at the animals' reactions, she dropped the envelope on the table and refused to inspect it further. Mack was on his way. He could dang well deal with it. She wasn't superstitious by nature, but something about the reaction from all her animals had her nerves on edge. Of course Thaddeus storming around the house, saying, "Murder in the house. Murder in the house," wasn't making her feel any better.

She again washed her hands and walked over to the coffeemaker and pulled two cups from the cupboard above it. She waited until it finished brewing, then poured one. Mack could pour his when he got here.

She sat down heavily at the table and stared at the envelope. It wasn't like it would reach out and bite her. But Thaddeus was correct—or almost correct about it being murder in the garden—but was it also murder in the house? And how could that be? That envelope had upset everyone. She stared at it. It was just an envelope. What could it possibly contain? And why did it bother her so much?

Still, she never had been a coward in her life. She reached for it and quickly dumped the contents onto the table.

Photographs. Taken in the upstairs bedroom from the looks of the wallpaper. Photographs of a dead man. She shook her head. No. There was no way to prove he was dead. He looked dead, but... he could have been sleeping. If he were dead, there should have been blood, lots of it. Right?

She slowly picked up a picture and stared at the tiny details. Was it really Nan's upstairs spare bedroom? Could she prove that? She turned it over to see a date from thirty years ago. "What the heck? Has this photo been under the bed all this time? Why would Nan do that?" Then it hit her. What if Nan had nothing to do with it? How long had Nan lived here?

Doreen frowned, thinking back. Nan had lived in this house for all of Doreen's life, she thought, but it was hard to remember. She picked up the next picture, a similar shot— same man, same bed, slightly different angle. It showed a wider view of the dresser and the closet. Enough to confirm it was Nan's upstairs spare bedroom.

She picked up the envelope, and something was in the bottom. She gave it a bit of a shake upside down. A crumpled piece of newspaper fell out. She opened it up to find a 1988 article on a missing man, Jeremy Feldspar. The headline stated, "Man Accused of Murdering His Mother with Arsenic Now Missing Himself."

Doreen sat back and stared. "Arsenic and a dead man. Like both the arsenic and the dead man found in the garden." She shook her head. "*This* can't be a coincidence."

Mugs barked then he stood on his back legs and put his front paws on her legs. Given his earlier reaction, she placed the newspaper clipping on the table and gave him a hug and a cuddle.

"It's okay, Mugs. It's okay. I'm not sure what this is all about, but we'll get to the bottom of it."

Thaddeus hopped up on the table and walked across it toward the items there. The bird stared at them with one eye. Then the feathers along the back of his neck ruffled upward.

Not sure what the bird was up to, Doreen quickly re-packaged everything into the envelope. As she put the crumpled newspaper page inside, she noticed an odd residue on her fingers. She inspected it closer and froze at the fine white dusting. Her mind immediately jumped to the worst-case scenario.

The trouble was, she had no reason to think that way except for the headline on the newspaper clipping and the arsenic bottle she'd found in the back garden.

Just what the heck was going on? And why hadn't Nan spoken about any of this? Granted Doreen would've been five years old at the time and living with her parents. Still, a murder in your grandmother's guest room would make for an interesting topic to tell many years afterward.

Yet Doreen had never heard anything about a dead man being found in Nan's spare bedroom.

Two dead bodies on Nan's property? Granted, they were thirty years apart, but it did beg the question—were these two cases related? Doreen shook her head, confused and unnerved by her recent findings. She rose, walked to the kitchen sink and carefully washed her hands right up to her elbows several times.

As she finished, the doorbell rang. Thank heavens. That should be Mack. She rushed to the front door and opened it. Her hand went to her chest. "Oh, thank God, you're here!"

Midway over the threshold, he froze and asked, "What's

wrong?"

She took several deep breaths. "You better come in while I explain." She led him to the kitchen where she quickly poured him a coffee. "Sit."

He sat down heavily, his brows creased in the middle. "What's this all about?"

She sat down opposite him and pointed at the envelope. "I found this cleaning out Nan's things in the spare bedroom upstairs."

She launched into an explanation of her day, about the fur coats and the clothing, of Nan's habit of leaving money everywhere. She pointed at the bowl on the table, full of money and things. But as she spoke faster and faster, she could see the confusion on his face.

Finally he held up a hand. "Stop."

She gasped for air, realizing she was barely coherent. She shook her head. "I'm so sorry. I'm so sorry. I'm just really unnerved."

"I can see that," he said. "What does any of that have to do with this envelope?"

She took a deep breath. "Because I found so much odd stuff as I went through everything, and, when I flipped the mattress and the box spring, I saw this." And she held up the envelope for him to see.

His eyebrows shot up.

"I know. But I wanted to make sure I checked *every-thing*," she emphasized. "And taped to the bottom of the box spring was that envelope." She watched as enlightenment whispered into his eyes.

He gazed at the envelope, put down his coffee cup, and said, "What's in it?"

"I think you better check," she said quietly. "I'm really

hoping it's not what I think it is."

He shot her a look as he donned a pair of plastic gloves, reached for the envelope and pulled out the pictures.

That was a much smarter way to retrieve the contents, unlike how she'd just upended it, making a mess. And she noticed a fine dusting of white everywhere. She stood, dampened a paper towel and came back, wiping the table, then used a dry paper towel afterward. "I don't know what this powder is, but it's from the envelope." She sat and stared at him. "Say something." Why wasn't he saying anything?

He stared at her, then focused on the pictures again. "You know what room this is?"

She nodded, her breath shaky as she answered in a low voice, "Yes, the one I was cleaning upstairs."

He nodded slowly. He reached for the brown envelope again and found the crumpled newspaper article inside. He studied that, looked at the man in the photograph and said, "You know something? I think I remember this case." He tapped the newspaper article with his gloved finger. "I certainly remember that headline as the case is one we went over in my training."

"The thing is, as soon as I saw the word *arsenic* in the newspaper article and the pictures of the dead body, I thought of the dead body in the backyard and the empty bottle of arsenic I found in the garden."

He nodded. "Obviously the mind makes a kind of a connection, but we have to be careful not to assume anything."

"How can I not assume?" she cried out. "It's obvious this guy's dead in the picture. If it's the same guy as in the picture, he supposedly killed his own mother with arsenic. And I've got a dead man and a bottle of arsenic in my own garden." And she pointed her hand to the table. "And here is more white powder. I'm terrified that's arsenic."

He froze, staring at the white powder in the envelope. "And you could be right." He got up slowly. "Do you have a vacuum?" He pulled out his cell phone and carefully took pictures of the table, envelope and the floor surrounding where they stood.

She shook her head. "No. I can wipe it up though." Very carefully they moved everything off the table, and she came back with more wet paper towels that she could then throw away. They cleaned up all the powder on the table. She glanced over at Thaddeus. "Thaddeus, go away. You need to get away from this white powder."

He looked at her and said, "Murder in the house. Murder in the house."

"He really has a flair for the dramatic, doesn't he?" Mack asked.

When they finally had it all cleaned up, she turned to him in distress and asked, "Do you think the animals got any?"

"They look clean to me. They're all doing fine. Arsenic is a fast-acting poison, although it can be used for long-term slow killing, as small amounts of it accumulates over time. It's one of the favorite methods of wives getting rid of their husbands."

She stared at him. "You're kidding, right?"

He shook his head. "Poison is very much a woman's tool. I know several cases where the wives slowly poisoned their husbands with arsenic in their lunches. It's supposedly tasteless and slowly builds up in the body to a point that eventually kills them."

"That's horrible." For good measure, she grabbed yet

more paper towels, slightly dampened them, and wiped the table again, taking careful note of the cracks and indentations in the table. Then she dropped to her hands and knees on the floor and scrubbed away.

"I'm pretty sure it's fine now," Mack said.

"*Pretty sure* isn't good enough." But finally even she had to admit there couldn't be more on any of the surfaces here. "Can you get that powder analyzed?"

He nodded. "I'll do that as soon as I leave here." He held up the envelope. "Have you shown this to anybody else?"

She shook her head. "No, I haven't. I don't know anybody else to show it to. And I knew you were coming, so it just made sense to give it to you anyway. I presume the man in the pictures is dead?"

"He *appears* dead." He studied the picture still in his hand. "But, with no visible injury, it's hard to say." He sighed. "You know Nan owned the house thirty years ago, right?"

She stared at her hands and nodded. "I know that." She raised her gaze to his. "But I also know there's no way Nan killed anybody."

"What if he deserved killing?" he asked, his voice quiet, soft. "We're all capable of killing if put in the right position to do so."

She shook her head vehemently. "No," she said softly. "Nan is the gentlest of women. She'd never kill anyone." She studied Thaddeus, now relaxed at the far end of the table. "And would it make any sense at all to keep an envelope with incriminating photos and evidence like that in her own house?"

"I've seen all kinds of strange things people do that don't make any sense," Mack said.

Just then, in a weird, slow humming voice, Thaddeus said, "Murder is everywhere. Murder is everywhere."

Mack departed, business card in hand, soon afterward, leaving Doreen pale but composed by the kitchen table. She wasn't exactly sure where on his suspect list Nan would fall, but Doreen knew her grandmother was the priority for her. No way would she talk to Nan on the phone about this. Doreen wanted to see her reaction, to watch her facial expression. Doreen needed to find out the truth.

And hated the necessity of doing even that.

But it was too late tonight for a visit. This would have to wait until the morning.

Chapter 19

Day 3, Friday

THE FOLLOWING MORNING she quickly made herself some toast and jam to go with her coffee. She walked out the door twenty minutes later.

She wanted to get to Nan first thing. Leaving Goliath sitting on the front railing, completely disinterested in where they were walking, Doreen led the way to Nan's retirement home apartment, Thaddeus riding on her shoulder and Mugs strolling at her side.

With still a block to go, she grabbed her phone and called her grandmother. "Nan, you there?"

"Of course I am, dear," she said in a gentle tone full of exasperation. "Where else would I be?"

"We're walking toward you. We're a couple minutes away," Doreen said with a big smile. It was so hard to believe Nan would be mixed up in anything like murder. She just couldn't be. It wasn't possible.

"Oh, that's delightful. I just made a full pot of tea. I must've known company was coming."

Doreen laughed. "You're a psychic now?"

"Wouldn't that be lovely if I were?"

Doreen shook her head and ended the call, pocketing her phone. She wasn't sure how to broach the subject of the photos. Nan's life was so very different than Doreen's had been. But anybody who had lived as many years as Nan had must see life from a whole different perspective.

Just look at me. In the last six months, everything had changed for her. Imagine if she had survived what Nan had gone through. She'd been married a long time ago, had a son, only to have her husband die soon after. When Nan had married again, her second husband died as well. Then she had decided marriage wasn't for her and had traveled the world. Sure, her son had been Doreen's father. But her parents split up when Doreen was little, her father dying soon after. Yet Doreen's mom had been friends with Nan before she had married Nan's son, and their friendship had continued afterward for Doreen's sake.

Doreen, as a child, had spent a lot of time with Nan. Doreen's mother wasn't the maternal type but enjoyed living a single's tennis-club life. She'd remarried twice since then and had distanced herself a little more each time from her motherhood role, but that was okay because Nan took over, being a true mother to Doreen. When Doreen had gone off on her own, she'd missed Nan.

But, as Doreen had built a life with her husband, it became easier and easier for her to acclimate to her mother's lifestyle. Her new life quickly filled with new people, new experiences—as her husband's ever-increasing control of Doreen's world worked to separate her from everything and everyone from her past, except for those things and people he knew and wanted in her life.

She didn't blame him entirely. She'd been young and naive and so wanting to please. But, over time, her previous life and the people in it had drifted farther away.

Now there was no need to let go. Doreen needed somebody. Nan needed somebody. And they were gravitating toward each other again.

Reaching the corner of Rosemoor's property, she could see Nan sitting in the little garden she had all to herself.

Nan raised her gaze, caught sight of Doreen and waved.

Mugs started to bark.

"Yes, that's Nan." Doreen loved how Mugs had taken to Nan so well.

Of course maybe it was a case that Nan's animals had taken to Doreen, and so her animal had taken to Nan, understanding the loving bond between the two women. Somehow Doreen was already thinking of Thaddeus and Goliath as hers. And this was only the beginning of her third day here, and since her arrival, there had been nothing but chaos. Maybe the animals clung to the familiar face of the person who was in residence. Maybe they didn't give a crap who was there as long as somebody was feeding them.

How fickle animals were. She glanced at Mugs and wondered. "Mugs, if I were gone, would you just take to the next person?"

He barked.

She took that as a yes.

She rolled her eyes, let him off the leash and watched as he ran toward Nan. She stood away from the table and bent to give him a big greeting.

Once again Doreen crossed the grassy lawn, breaking one rule, and also knowing she wasn't allowed to bring the animals here either. Yet she felt less criminal because she was doing something, for once, that was against the rules, yet was doing a lot of good for an eighty-something-year-old lady.

Laughing at her granddaughter's antics and with her arms out, Nan gave Doreen a hug.

Doreen gently hugged her back, with Thaddeus taking the opportunity to shift from one shoulder to the other. Sitting down, Doreen watched as Mugs and Thaddeus claimed Nan's loving attention.

"Where's Goliath?" Nan asked.

"He was lazing on the porch railing when we left."

Nan nodded. "I'll see him next time."

"What's this? A new type of tea?" Doreen sniffed the air experimentally.

"It's brand-new. A friend of mine just came back from China and brought me some authentic Ceylon tea to try."

Doreen didn't have the heart to tell her grandmother that the island named Ceylon was later named Sri Lanka. And the black tea of Ceylon was now grown in India and China as well. But Doreen would appreciate the drink anyway.

Nan poured two teacups full as Thaddeus looked on from her shoulder. "It's lovely to see you again, dear. Has everything calmed down at the house now?"

It was all she could do to hold back an unending stream of questions. "Oh, it's calmed down somewhat," she admitted. "But then something else came up."

"Oh, dear." Nan stared at her in fascination. "I lived in that house for forty years, my dear, and I never had the kind of excitement you're having."

Doreen studied her grandmother and smiled. She could use that opening. "I sorted through the spare bedroom yesterday. I already took a couple loads to the consignment store. Have another ready in the car now."

Nan clapped her hands in joy. "*Aah*, wonderful. It'd be

nice to see some of the clothing go to good use."

"I also took a couple big bags to Goodwill," she confessed. "Wendy wasn't interested in those items."

Nan nodded. "That makes sense. I hope you checked the pockets before you sent everything out." She shook her finger at Doreen. "Remember? I never could keep my pockets empty."

"That's the truth. You could not keep your pockets empty. I found well over $300.00 in all those clothes. Not even counting the change yet."

Nan's face froze for a moment, and then she burst out into joyful laughter. "Well, how lovely." She chuckled again. "You needed money, so there it was. And who knew I had left so much behind."

Doreen instantly felt bad. She leaned forward. "I never thought to bring it to you. It is your money."

Nan lifted a hand and waved it at her. "I told you everything in the house is yours, my dear. I already have enough for my needs."

"And what about your wants?" Doreen asked softly. "Is there anything you *want*? You can't spend your entire life only looking after your needs. Is there anything you want just because it's pretty or makes you smile? What about a book from your favorite author? Or a new bedding set? How about a holiday?"

A quiet silence followed as Nan contemplated… something. Doreen had trouble deciphering the look on her grandmother's face. But she waited.

Nan said in a gentle voice, "My dear, I've already lived well over twice as long as you have. I've had lots of wants taken care of, but now the only thing that matters is making sure your needs are met. I have very few needs in this world."

There was such a sad element attached to that statement.

Doreen tried to understand, but it was hard. She settled back and picked up her tea and took a sip. The tea was wonderful, full-bodied, and it was just the perfect drinking temperature. She cupped her hands around the teacup to absorb some of the warmth. "This tea is lovely."

Nan agreed. "It is. I've been enjoying it."

After that they shared little conversation as Doreen contemplated her grandmother's words. She took a deep breath. "Nan, because I found so much stuff hidden all around in your clothing and drawers, I made sure I did a thorough search of the room—cleaning it out, you know?"

Nan nodded and waited.

"I even flipped the mattresses."

Nan stared at her in amazement. "Oh, my goodness. I wouldn't even be strong enough to do that."

And Doreen sat there with that truth staring at her. Of course Nan wouldn't. Even thirty years ago she wouldn't have been able to. Nan was tiny. Doreen doubted Nan could pick up twenty pounds. A man could have handled the mattress, most likely, but that would not be an easy feat for Nan.

Doreen shook her head. "I didn't think of that before."

Nan leaned forward. "Think of what, my dear?"

Doreen settled back and smiled. "I found a brown 9x12 envelope taped to the bottom of the box spring."

"Oh my, this is getting interesting. What was in it?"

Doreen explained about the contents, including the white powder and the newspaper article and the pictures of the dead man from thirty years ago. She studied her grandmother's face intently, looking for any sign of foreknowledge of the package. But Doreen saw nothing but sheer astonishment in Nan's expression.

"What a delightful mystery." She shook her head. "And

in my spare bedroom." She sat back with her tea, staring at it for a long moment. Almost as if looking down the tunnel of time and seeing if it would give her the answers she needed. Then she looked up and said, "I wish I had seen the pictures of the man."

"Oh," Doreen said. She quickly pulled her phone from her pocket. "I didn't even tell Mack I did this." She lowered her voice to a hushed tone. "It just seemed important that I remembered the dead man's face." She found the photograph of the man and held it up for Nan to see. "I took a picture of the picture."

"Oh, dear, that sounds very complicated." Nan reached for Doreen's phone and brought it closer, pulling the glasses off her head and putting them on her nose to peer at the picture intently. "He *almost* looks familiar." She lifted her gaze apologetically. "I know my memory isn't quite the way it used to be, but I can't remember ever seeing this man in my house."

Doreen nodded. What could she say? "The thing is, Nan, it was definitely taken at your house. These pictures were of the spare room, with the same curtains, the same wallpaper and the same dresser."

Nan stared at her in surprise, her mouth forming an O. She turned her attention back to the picture. "I just don't understand how that could be."

"Did you go away on a holiday thirty years ago? Were you visiting a friend? Did you let somebody stay in your house for a little while?"

Nonplussed, Nan continued to stare at Doreen. "All of that is possible. But it was thirty years ago, so I really can't be sure of when."

Doreen patted Nan's hand. She didn't want to upset her grandmother. "If you do remember, let me know. Just be aware that Mack is likely to come by with questions."

"Mack?"

"Corporal Mack Moreau. He's the officer investigating the case." Under Nan's prying gaze, Doreen could feel the heat rising up her neck. She shook her head. "No." She made sure to use a strong, firm voice. "There's nothing between us."

Nan nodded slowly, but her gaze twinkled. "Of course not." She settled back and took another sip of her tea. But a smile played around the corner of her lips. "He's a good man. I know his mother. Interesting history there." Then she sealed her lips and went quiet.

Doreen eyed her suspiciously but knew there was no point in pushing her grandmother. She could be stubborn when she wanted to be.

Thaddeus took that moment to jump on the table. He studied the almond cookies that neither of the women had touched, looked over at Nan and said, "Cookie please. Cookie please."

Doreen gave a startled gasp. "How is it this bird has so many phrases in his vocabulary? He continues to amaze me." She glanced at Nan. "Where did you get him from?"

"An old friend brought him over one day years ago, hoping I'd take him in as he'd been abandoned. He had no details on his history, but Thaddeus chose to stay behind, and we've been friends ever since."

"Amazing," Doreen said, eyeing Thaddeus in a different light. "He's very smart."

Thaddeus gave a weird chirp and pecked at the closest cookie.

"It's not just that he has all these words," Nan said gently, "but the way he puts them together so they make sense. Well, sometimes it's downright freaky."

Chapter 20

"LADIES?" MACK'S HARD voice cut through their peaceful teatime only to be drowned out by Mugs's sudden barking as he woke up from his nap. Goliath had accompanied Mack on this walk and ignored the dog and jumped into Nan's lap.

Doreen looked at Mack in surprise, but he ignored her to study Nan's face.

Doreen hurriedly stood and pulled up a spare chair. In a bright voice she said, "Join us."

He sat down in the very small chair, making her wince. He glanced at her, even as he scratched Mugs's ear. In a droll voice, he said, "I'm sure it will hold my weight."

She flushed immediately. "Sorry," she muttered.

"Oh, what are you sorry for? Coming here to see Nan before I have a chance to question her?"

"Why shouldn't I be allowed to talk to her? It's not like this has anything to do with the current murder at my place, and it's not like Nan is a murder suspect," Doreen said dismissively. She picked up her tea and took a sip. "Or is she?"

He glared at her. "Every time I turn around in this case,

I am tripping over you. If it isn't at Lifelong Insurance, then it's here at Nan's."

Doreen straightened in outrage. "Well, I'm sure your investigative work entailed more than those two places. And obviously I have to check into anything that might involve Nan. And I did show you the things I found in Nan's house."

"Dear, it's okay." Nan reached over and patted her wrist. "Don't worry about it. Mack's just a little upset that you got here before him."

"A little upset?" She glared at Nan. Mugs, sitting underneath the table, stood up on his back legs, his paws on her knee and growled at her tone. She patted his forehead. "It's all right, Mugs. I'm fine."

"Is he a good guard dog?" Mack asked, a frown on his face as he studied the basset. "They were originally bred for hunting, I believe."

"I have no idea. The guard dog occasion hasn't arisen yet," she said. "He only just realized he could bark. My almost ex-husband frowned on Mugs making noise, so a dog trainer trained him not to bark. But now that it's just us, he's found his voice again." She stroked his long silky ears and smiled at the bag-eyed dog. "Of course Goliath helps in that area too."

"Goliath can take care of himself, that's for sure," Nan said cheerfully. She looked at the teapot and poured another round of tea for all three of them. "Now Thaddeus, he's a different story."

"And why did you not tell me more about Goliath and Thaddeus, Nan?" Doreen asked. "It's one thing to leave me an independent monster-size cat, happy to be inside and outside, but to leave me Thaddeus?"

Nan's laughter trailed across the garden, making both Mack and Doreen smile. "Like we were just saying, Thaddeus is a gem."

On cue Thaddeus jumped up and landed on Nan's shoulder. In his soft crooning voice he said, "Thaddeus is here. Thaddeus is here."

And, in a moment of naked affection, the cat and the bird nestled in closer to Nan.

Doreen stared at the two pets, then shook her head. "How is it you could leave them?"

"I had little choice. Besides, Thaddeus is fickle, my dear. Right now he looks like he is my long-lost friend, and in truth, he is. But he could also be your long-lost friend in five minutes. And I can't have pets here. Thaddeus will outlive me, possibly all of us, so I had to make provisions for him anyway."

Doreen leaned forward. "But you didn't make provisions for him, Nan. You just left him and Goliath behind."

"Nonsense. You were arriving on a specific day. He and Goliath were fine until then as I went back and forth to feed them. And, if I had told you about them, you would have fretted over your delay."

Doreen sat back at that. Just because Nan was correct, it didn't mean Doreen felt like hearing it. Neither did she like to see the quirk of Mack's lips as he held back his smile.

She glared at him. "Didn't you have a reason for coming here?"

He put down his teacup and proceeded to ask Nan the exact same questions that Doreen had.

Nan laughed. "You really should hire Doreen as your assistant. You know that, don't you? She already asked me those same things."

Still, Nan went over the answers she'd given Doreen earlier.

Doreen was fascinated with the case. Quite a twist had been found here, and somehow Nan was involved. Doreen didn't think Nan had anything to do with either murder, so there had to be somebody else. There was really no other explanation.

Mack turned his attention to Doreen. "I had the powder analyzed. It was simple cornstarch. I suspect it was in the envelope to keep the photos from sticking together."

"Well... that mystery at least is solved. I'm glad it wasn't poison," she exclaimed. With a bright smile she finished the last of her tea and stood. She gave Nan a hug and kiss and said, "I'll stop by in another day or two." With Mugs at her side, Goliath at her feet, and Thaddeus now transferred to her shoulder, she turned to Mack. "I'm sure I'll see you again, Mr. Moreau."

In a gruff voice, he said, "I told you to call me Mack."

She smiled. "So you did. Have a good day, Mack, Nan." She walked away, hearing the two of them talking—and heard her name mentioned. Hopefully only good things were discussed because Doreen had been a laughingstock for a lot of people over the last few years. But she trusted Nan. She was the only other person in the world who cared what happened to Doreen, other than herself.

Her mind was consumed with the pictures of the dead man as she walked back to her house slowly.

A library was just around the corner—probably the only way to get the archives on the newspaper articles from thirty years ago—but she would have to leave Mugs, Goliath, and Thaddeus at home. She had the one article in mind, but that didn't mean other papers would have carried the same story.

What she really needed was more history on the death of the first man to die. And, for that, she should've asked Mack.

She pulled out her phone, hit his contact number, and smiled, loving that he'd stayed to visit with Nan after grilling her. When he answered, she asked without preamble, "Did you get any information on the man in the pictures?"

"I haven't gone to the office yet. I'll do that then."

She nodded and smiled at a neighbor, who gave her an odd look and hurried by. As Doreen approached her driveway, she spoke into her phone again. "Let me know what you find, please."

"It's a police matter," he said in exasperation. "I'm not checking in with you at every step."

"But it's probably better if you do," she said. "Otherwise I'll have to get that information myself. And you don't like me doing that." She hung up, cutting him off mid-sputter, and pocketed her phone with a chuckle.

Back at the house, the animals following her, she returned to the spare bedroom for another look around, seeing if she had possibly missed anything. She hadn't even begun to search the walls. Was that an odd thing to consider?

The walls were covered in wallpaper, but paneling appeared to be underneath as seen where the wallpaper had been torn. But how could she tell if something was hidden behind the actual walls? She guessed she wouldn't unless she tore off all the paneling to find the studs beneath. She didn't feel the need to do that. However, feeling foolish but unable to stop herself, she rapped on the nearest wall and continued around the room. It all sounded the same until she got to the closet. She studied the closet, stepped inside and looked around. In the ceiling was a trapdoor leading to the attic.

It appeared to be added to the house as an afterthought.

Just a small three-foot-square opening. From her first look, the cover was just propped there, to be pushed aside once she could reach that high. It wasn't a full-fledged attic access with a pull-down door that had a fold-up ladder affixed to it.

She stepped back out and stared around the room, walking out into the hallway and looking up. Every house had an attic, but wasn't the attic door usually located somewhere in the middle of the house? Where the roof pitch was the highest? That way, someone could stand up inside the attic. Also tradesmen would have access to wiring, piping, ductwork and whatnot strung throughout the attic, amid all the stuff people stored up there too.

Back in the spare bedroom, she eyed the night table but didn't think it would be tall enough for her purposes. Neither was a kitchen chair. Back downstairs, she found a big lantern flashlight. That would help. She clicked it on and off several times to make sure the battery worked. Then she located a small step stool. Its top riser was higher than the kitchen chair seat.

She dragged the light and the stool upstairs into the spare bedroom's closet. With the flashlight in hand, she slowly climbed up the step stool, setting aside the cover to the attic access. With her head and shoulders now popped through into the attic, she turned on the lantern light and slowly searched the space.

Initially it looked empty until she circled completely around and found several boxes. Easily six to eight boxes were stacked between where she was and the outside wall.

Once again, the hunt for treasure overtook her. Small sheets of plywood lay between the rafters to stop people from falling through as they got up here, but they would be a bit of a challenge to navigate. She would have to change clothes before she attempted that.

She walked into her bedroom, quickly put on a pair of her capri length jeans, some tennis shoes and an old T-shirt, courtesy of Nan's closet. Doreen suspected the attic would be full of spiderwebs.

She moved the stepladder closer to the edge of the attic opening and slowly climbed up. Using her arms, she pulled herself into the attic, sitting at the opening, her legs dangling below, and looked around. The attic was empty except for the stack of boxes she had spied earlier. She suspected the contents would be stupid things, like broken Christmas ornaments.

Carefully she crawled on the plywood sheets closer to the boxes. Two were stacked in front of her. She grabbed the bottom one and slowly tugged them both toward her.

Surprisingly heavy, she kept pulling. She needed to know what was in all these boxes. Shaking them first to check for breakables inside, but hearing nothing like that, she then dropped the first two boxes into the closet next to the step stool.

Joining the boxes on the closet floor, she inspected them in the light of the closet, finding no list of contents or other identification marked on any side of either box. She grabbed the corner of the tape sealing the top of the first box and pulled it off. The animals were curious too, as Mugs had joined her in the closet and milled around her feet, with Goliath on the bed glaring and an unusually quiet Thaddeus perched on the dresser.

She pulled out what appeared to be men's clothing. A charcoal gray suit. She shook her head. "Oh, Nan. Where the devil did these come from?"

Doreen searched the pockets of the jacket and pulled out

a twenty-dollar bill, almost proof that this was Nan's work, packing up these clothes in this box. But Nan never would have worn these clothes, so who the heck did they belong to? Inside the breast pocket, Doreen pulled out a business card. The name matched the name in the newspaper article.

Jeremy Feldspar.

She glanced over at Thaddeus. "What's the matter, Thaddeus? Don't have anything to say now?" Normally at moments like this, he had some catchy phrase of doom and gloom. But even now, Thaddeus just stared at her and the clothes and remained silent.

Somehow she found that even worse.

Chapter 21

F OR THE LIFE of her, Doreen couldn't understand why men's clothes were in Nan's attic. Old clothes too. Of course Doreen's mind associated these clothes with the dead man photographed in the spare bedroom. She couldn't be sure.

Doreen refused to believe Nan had anything to do with Jeremy's death.

Just then the doorbell rang. Doreen didn't want anybody to see this stuff, so she closed the bedroom door as she headed downstairs to the front entryway. She opened it to find a middle-aged couple beaming at her. Both were slightly overweight, in their early fifties and dressed like twins with pumpkin-colored T-shirts and khaki pants. She gave a hesitant smile and said, "Hello. May I help you?"

The woman grabbed Doreen's hand. "We're so delighted to meet you. And we're so sorry you've had such a nasty event upon your arrival."

Doreen tried to pull her hand back, but the woman wouldn't let it go. "Do I know you?"

The man gave a hearty laugh. "We're your neighbors to the right." He motioned to the house next door. "We were away the last two days, so we missed a lot of the commotion. But, when we heard, we wanted to come over and welcome you to the neighborhood."

Doreen's eyebrows lifted, and she studied the couple. "Oh, isn't that nice." Yet inside she wondered if that *was* a neighborly thing to do. It just seemed weird. When she was with her husband, nobody would ever do something like this. Of course they couldn't get past the security gates anyway.

The man thrust a tinfoil-covered pan into her free hand and said, "Here. We brought over a dish for you. It's one of our favorites."

She looked at the pan in surprise but felt she had no option but to accept it. "Thank you," she said quietly. "It smells wonderful. It's very kind of you." And it was. She'd seen little kindness these last few months.

He beamed at her. "Well, we're very kind people," he said.

The woman, still gripping Doreen's other hand, said, "Oh my, yes, we certainly are." She turned to look at her husband and added, "I'm sure you'll find everybody here is very friendly."

"So far, that hasn't been my experience," Doreen said in a dry tone. "Then again, it's not every day a dead body is found on your property."

Instantly the two visitors gasped.

"That must have been just terrible for you," the woman cried. At that she blushed, waved her hand, finally releasing Doreen's. "Oh, my dear, I'm so sorry. I'm Cindy. This is my husband, Josh."

Josh stuck out a big mitt to shake hers. "Pleased to meet you."

She nodded and tried to nicely free her hand from his. It was impolite to grab onto her hand and hold it so long. Still, they were being friendly, and she certainly hadn't seen many friendly faces since her arrival. "I'm Doreen," she said. "Nan is my grandmother."

The woman, slightly younger than her partner, clasped her hands in front of her and almost gave a little hop and skip, like a twelve-year-old. "Oh, my dear, that's lovely. Nan is such a sweetie."

At that Doreen smiled naturally for the first time. "She certainly is." She didn't know if she should invite them in, but for some reason, she was loath to do so. She turned to the man and asked, "How long have you lived here?"

"Oh, must be thirty years now, possibly more," he said with a beaming smile. "Best place to live. Nothing ever happens here. It's nice and peaceful."

She avoided pointing out that *something* had happened here and just nodded, figuring they were here when Jeremy Feldspar was in Nan's house. "Interesting. Was Nan here when you moved in?"

They both nodded. "She certainly was. What a colorful character. She was always out and about the city with the neighbors."

Doreen smiled. "I'm learning a lot about my grandmother since coming here. What you know about somebody on one level is a whole different thing when you step into their lives."

Cindy patted Doreen's shoulder. "We're so happy that Nan has you. She shouldn't be alone in the special years of her life."

"She won't be alone now." Doreen looked for a place to put the dish down, but Mugs, having completely inspected the front porch, was now sitting at her side, staring up at the couple. He wasn't being overly friendly, and if she wasn't mistaken, a slight growl came from the back of his throat.

She squatted down slightly and stroked his head. "This is Mugs."

The couple bent down to greet the dog with what must be their usual overexuberance. They must be exhausting to be around for very long. Who had the energy for all that ebullience?

"And what about Nan's other pets? Is Thaddeus still here?" Josh asked.

Instantly the bird was behind her, as if hearing his name. Thaddeus landed on her shoulder. She was startled for a moment but quickly adjusted.

The couple smiled. Josh gently stroked Thaddeus's neck.

"Thaddeus is here. Thaddeus is here."

The couple laughed gaily.

"Isn't he just wonderful?" Cindy said, beaming. "How lucky for Nan that you're here to look after her animals."

"Yes, how very lucky." Doreen tried hard to be polite, but something about these people made her depressed. Surely nobody was nice *all* the time.

Just then Goliath came up the front steps to weave his way through everybody and to join in the melee. Doreen glanced at him and then asked the couple, "Do you have any pets?"

Josh shook his head. "We had, but we lost them a couple years back, and it was just so traumatic we didn't feel we could go through that again."

Doreen nodded. *That* she understood. She wasn't sure what she would do when she lost Mugs.

Cindy stepped back and said, "We've taken up so much

of your time. So sorry if we were bothering you."

Doreen wondered if she had been unfriendly, if she should've invited them in. But they were already halfway down the steps, waving.

"Stop by anytime you want to visit," Josh said. "I work from home most days, so one of us is always around."

Cindy chuckled. "And thankfully I don't have to work. Josh looks after me very well," she said with a big smile. "If you're ever feeling friendly, or just don't want to be alone anymore, come over and have a cup of tea."

With a big wave, the two of them left.

Doreen stood in the front door, feeling like a fool. She'd been raised better than that. In the background she could hear Nan's voice in her head. *What was that all about, dear? Why didn't you invite those nice people in?*

And that was the crux of the problem. They were *too* nice. Maybe it was just her suspicious mind, but it did seem to her as if they had been fishing for information.

She didn't have any information to give them. The thing was, they would know when the house was empty. They would know when Nan was in or out, and if they had wanted to bury the body on the property, there was plenty of time for them to do so between Nan's exodus and Doreen's arrival. Still, these neighbors had come under Doreen's critical review just for being on the spot and having access. So chances were good they'd have moved the body elsewhere for just that reason. Unless of course, they couldn't carry him far or didn't want to get caught with a dead body in their vehicle. Both of which were very valid points too.

Still, she couldn't imagine trying to move a dead adult male body.

She gave herself a shake and walked back inside. "Come

on, Mugs. Let's go in."

With the dog and cat at her heels and Thaddeus on her shoulder, she slowly closed the door. As she did so, she caught sight of a woman on the other side of the cul-de-sac, staring at her. She gave her a half smile. The woman turned around and walked inside, slamming her door.

Well, not everybody was friendly apparently. What did Doreen expect? Since she'd arrived, there had been nothing but kerfuffles at her house. Anybody who wanted peace and quiet probably thought the neighborhood had gone to the dogs with Doreen's arrival.

Unable to help herself, she locked the front door behind her and headed to the kitchen. When she took the tinfoil off the pan, she found fresh-baked buns of some kind. She had to admit they smelled delicious. Were they homemade? Feeling much more endearing toward her neighbors, she picked one, ripped it in half, buttered it and took a big bite. In truth, it was very good.

That was exactly what she needed right now.

She made a cup of tea, buttered a second bun and then took both upstairs. The only reason she could think of for not inviting Josh and Cindy inside was because of the stuff she'd found in the attic. And, yes, she felt guilty now that she'd tasted the wonderful buns.

She still didn't want anybody to know what she'd found. Anyone but Mack. But, before she told him about her latest find, she had to go through all the boxes. Once he got here, he would likely take everything away. And then he wouldn't share any further information with her about them. Although she innately trusted Mack, for whatever reason, still the evidence found in these boxes could initially point more fingers in Nan's direction.

Chapter 22

UPSTAIRS DOREEN WENT back to the job of sorting through the boxes she'd found. Mugs lay contentedly at her side. Of Goliath there was no sign. Thaddeus had been on his roost in the living room as she'd walked through but she suspected he wouldn't be able to resist seeing what she was doing. She methodically went through every item of clothing, checking all the pockets for bits and pieces of paper, business cards, the odd candy and, of course, money. She shook her head to think that so many people left money in their pockets and wondered if she had done so too— *before*.

There was her life *before* the separation and then her life after the separation. She wished she'd saved some of the money that had passed into her hands *before*. But life was life, and it changed. When she'd gone through all the pockets of the men's clothing, she reloaded the two cardboard boxes, stacked them up again, repositioned the stepladder under the attic hatchway and climbed up again.

Carefully crawling on the plywood patches, she slowly dragged the rest of the boxes closer to the attic opening, dropping two more of them to the closet floor. The ones that she'd already repackaged, she had set off to the far side so she wouldn't get them mixed up. These next two boxes held more of the same, men's clothes. Still, if this represented the entirety of one person's life, not a ton was here.

Repackaged, she added these two boxes to the first two she'd gone through, and then brought down the rest of the boxes. It took her several trips because some of them were very heavy. She closed the attic access door and folded up the stepladder, just in case somebody came inside and wondered what she was up to.

"All done, Mugs."

Woof. Then he dropped his head back onto his paws and went to sleep.

She opened the flaps on all four boxes, found another one full of men's clothing and chose to go through that first. This one had outdoor coats, jackets and a sweater. Again a bit of money was in each pocket, plus a couple notes that made no sense and a key.

She stared at the key in amazement. A key to what? It was small, possibly a safe-deposit box key. Almost a mailbox-size key. Certainly not a house key.

She placed the key in the bowl with the money. When she was finished with that box, she closed it and moved it off to the side.

The next box was a little more interesting—books. So maybe these were his personal possessions. She carefully went through them all to find a motley selection of novels and hard-copy books. Everything from a Webster's dictionary to the latest *New York Times* best seller from thirty years earlier. Studying the collection, she frowned. She didn't understand why these had even been kept. She carefully opened and shook each book to make sure nothing important was inside any of them.

When she was done, she had a few more dollar bills, a couple bookmarks that appeared to be more like business cards and that was it. She repackaged the box and set it off to the side.

Now she was down to two boxes. She was hot and dusty and tired. But she knew she had to get through these, just in case somebody came by.

As she had that thought, the doorbell rang. Mugs barking like a loon skittered off the bed and around the corner. She went to the window and looked out to see who was on the front step.

She cautiously went back downstairs. Mugs stood at the front door, barking like a crazy man before she got there. "Mugs, please calm down."

For somebody who'd come here not expecting to know anyone, Doreen was getting way too much traffic through the place. She opened the door to find Mack standing on her front porch, his arms across his chest and a frown on his face. Mugs stopped barking and started whining instead. Somehow he'd taken a liking to the big detective.

"What took you so long?"

She frowned up at him. "I was busy," she retorted. "Sorry if it took me a moment or two to come downstairs."

He looked at her clothing and darned if he didn't hold back a grin.

She stared at her jeans; her trips to the attic had covered her in dust. And likely cobwebs. She brushed her hair back and groaned as her hands were covered in dirt too. "Crap."

"What have you been doing? Going into the attic or something?"

She swallowed her answer, not wanting him to know—

yet—what she had been doing. She opened the door wider. "What do you want now?"

He stepped across the threshold, taking her opening the door as an invitation, though her tone was much less than welcoming.

With a bright cheerful smile he said, "I came to ask a few more questions. But now I'm checking on what you're up to."

She glared at him, feeling her mouth pinch into the same expression after she'd sucked a lemon. "What I am doing is my business."

"Not if it pertains to the murder, or murders, that surround this property," he said with a hard glare. "So, you've been in the attic, from the evidence on your clothing. What have you found?"

She didn't even know how to begin. She wasn't sure she had a choice here. She upped the wattage of her glare. She only needed another hour, and then she'd be done. Darn him anyways.

He laughed.

"Do you have a warrant?" she argued but without any heat.

"Do I need one?" he asked, frustration rippling through his voice.

"I just figured I'd go through it all first. If I found something, I would let you know."

He grabbed her shoulder. "Stop." He gave her a little shake. "Just think about what you are doing. Remember this is a murder investigation? Everything you find concerning this case is information I need to know."

With the animals milling around their legs and generally getting in the way, she slammed the front door shut, put her hands on her hips and said, "I found some boxes in the attic. But I've barely looked through them all yet."

He snorted. "Oh, no. I want to see exactly what you found."

She ran to the staircase and stood on the bottom step, arms across her chest. "Only if I let you. You don't have the right to go upstairs and see what I found."

He picked her up at the waist, turned and put her down beside him. "I can get a warrant if you want. And that'll be nasty because then more officers will come through and make a mess of this place, and they won't care that it was Nan's special possessions or that anything here might be of value to you in one way or another. And the more you try to hide something from me, the more pissed off I get." He glared at her. "Do you understand me?"

She groaned, closed her eyes and said, "Why do you have such crappy timing? I was just getting to the good stuff." She snuck past him and ran up the stairs with him hard on her heels.

"What did you find?"

"Jeremy Feldspar's clothing."

"What?" he roared.

She laughed and darted toward the spare room almost tripping on Mugs as he tried to run past her. "They were all neatly folded and stored in boxes upstairs in the attic. And then I found a box of books with his name on the inside of each one, and I'm down to the last two boxes now."

"Anything interesting in the clothing?" he asked in a hard voice. "I want to see it all. Not just what you think I should see."

She shook her head. At the door to the spare bedroom, she stopped. "So far there hasn't been anything interesting, just little bits of money, little bits of paper, business cards. I went through the clothing pretty intently, and I didn't see anything that had any information pertaining to his death or his life." She pushed open the door, stepped inside and pointed to the boxes on the far side of the room that she had gone through and packed up again. Mugs took advantage of the wider doorway and jumped to retake his spot on the bed beside Goliath who opened one eye then closed it and continued his nap.

"Feel free to look. Everything here on the bed and in that small bowl is what I found in the pockets of his clothes." She turned and pointed to the dresser. "That bowl is tidbits from Nan's clothing. I kept it separate."

He studied the stack of packed-up boxes, turned to look at the bowl in the center of the bed, breezed through its contents—the couple of business cards and some coins—picked up the notepad and realized it was more a shopping list. "Are you sure you checked each item of clothing carefully?"

She nodded. "Those boxes against the wall are clothing, but feel free to help yourself. The last box was full of coats."

He walked over to them, opened the flaps on one of the boxes and pulled out a jacket. He held it up, looked at the style and said, "Definitely older-style clothing."

She nodded. "From the eighties maybe."

"How long has Nan lived here?"

"Since forever. She mentioned being here forty years. But I really don't know the exact year she bought this place. You'd have to ask her."

She watched as he pulled the pockets inside out, and then he did something unusual. He scrunched up the bottom of the jacket, as if looking for something inside the lining. He put the jacket down, pulled out another one and did the exact same thing.

She shrugged and opened the box in front of her. But then he walked over to the light of the window and held the jacket upside down. She walked closer and asked, "What did you find?"

"Something inside the lining."

He turned the jacket inside out and found the seam that had been opened and sewn shut again. He pulled a knife from his pants pocket, quickly cut the stitches, and reached inside.

When he pulled out a sheet of paper, she gasped and said, "Oh my. Somebody went to a lot of trouble to hide that."

He tossed her a hard gaze. "Most killers often do."

"That makes no sense. He was the victim. So why would he go through all the trouble to hide this?"

Mack carefully unfolded the paper. Together they could both see a simple number and also an address.

He glanced at her and she shook her head. "I don't know that address or the number."

He pulled out his phone, punched the address into Google Maps, and it instantly brought up the location—a building in downtown Kelowna. "It's a bank on Bernard Street. And that other number is likely to be his bank account number."

"Or somebody else's account number or a safe-deposit box," she said. "Oh, I found a key." She walked to the bowl and brought it and its contents back to where Mack stood at the window. The key sat among the coins. She picked it up and handed it to him.

He nodded, resting it firmly in his hand and said, "This

is where I'm heading first." He glanced at the box she'd just opened, stepped toward it, looked inside to see books and knickknacks. "I want you to stop right now. I want you to leave this room and not come back in here until I return." When she didn't answer, he added, "Do you hear me?" He glared at her.

She stuck her chin out at him and then considered his point. She'd tossed the suits off as not being of any more value, but he had found something epic that she'd missed.

Her shoulders sagged, and she nodded. "I'll wait for you to come back." She warned, "But I want to be here to go through this with you."

He smiled at her as they headed downstairs. "Put on a pot of coffee, and I'll be back in an hour." He walked out the front door. Mugs milled around on the porch then came inside to slump on the floor beside her.

She watched him get into his vehicle and drive away. Would Mack make it back in an hour? Didn't he need a warrant to access that safe-deposit box? Mack was a good ten minutes away from the bank. So twenty minutes to make the round trip alone. That left him forty minutes, including stopping off to get a warrant first, if needed, and then time at the bank.

If she stayed out of the spare room until Mack returned, he'd be more willing to share his findings with her. Yet, who knew what else she might find elsewhere upstairs while Mack was at the bank?

She walked into the kitchen, washed her hands and splashed some water on her face. Afterward she patted her face dry and wiped her hands on a small towel before putting on a pot of coffee. While he was gone, she made herself a quick sandwich. Her mind was consumed with what could possibly be inside Jeremy's safe-deposit box.

When the phone rang ten minutes later, she knew who it was. "I knew you wouldn't be back in an hour."

Mack's voice came through the phone, hard, clear, concise. "I won't be back for the rest of the afternoon. This led to something quite interesting, and I must chase it down. I'm calling to remind you that no way in hell are you to go back in that room. If you don't give me that promise right now, I will send over a series of officers to collect all that stuff."

She glared into the phone. "I already said I wouldn't." Her voice turned crafty. "Are you going to tell me what you found?

"No," he snapped. "At least not right now. I'll get there as soon as I can."

He hung up, and she put her cell phone on the kitchen table, finishing the rest of her sandwich while deep in thought. Nobody knew the man was actually dead, right? Not for sure. Unless it was the murderer. Not without a body, correct? He was deemed legally dead after he was missing for seven years. What did Jeremy Feldspar have to do with the man in the garden?

It made no sense.

She stood to pour herself a cup of coffee. Facing the table again, she saw Goliath walking along the tabletop, helping himself to the bits of ham and cheese there.

And Thaddeus was busy throwing crumbs to Mugs on the floor.

She smiled. Somehow her trio of furry, fluffy, and feathered friends had become a family.

And her sneaky family knew the exact second when she had turned her back on her food.

Chapter 23

NOT KNOWING HOW much time she had before Mack returned, she grabbed her coffee and led the way to the spare room, with her three-animal family following close behind. She stood in the doorway of the spare bedroom, remembering her promise. No matter how she looked at it, she couldn't go in there.

So the boxes would have to come out. Craftily, she studied the layout of the room, then went downstairs and outside to the back garden where she snatched up the hoe and raced back upstairs. Those last couple boxes were just close enough that she could snag them with the hoe and drag them over to the doorway.

"Ha," she cried out with the flush of success. Now she could go over the boxes' contents and not break her promise. Quickly she sorted through the remaining two boxes. They contained collections of souvenirs, photographs, books, even an odd pair of shoes tucked on top of everything else. As if there was no room for them anywhere else. The second box contained only shoes.

She went through each box, looking for something that would identify what had happened to Jeremy but found nothing here. At least nothing *she* could find. Mack might have an entirely different view on that. She put the photos off to one side and stacked the boxes together on another side.

She'd cleaned out the attic but maybe Mack would want to go up on his own, and that was fine with her. He might see something she'd missed.

Back downstairs again she looked at the photos under the bright kitchen light. Names and dates were on the back, like *Rose '79*, and *Jeremy and Tom '76*. All of them appeared to be in their forties back at the time these pictures were taken. Nothing was more recent than 1982, and she didn't recognize any of the people in the images, although the name *Jeremy* sure rang a bell. Possibly Tom and Rose were his siblings. Their approximate ages would seem appropriate for that.

And, if this Jeremy in the 1976 photo was the man who later disappeared in 1988, he would have been about fifty to sixty years old at the time he was last seen, or some eighty to ninety years old today. That put Jeremy roughly in the same age bracket as Nan.

There didn't appear to be any photos of Nan. Doreen didn't know if that was a good thing or a bad thing. She was rather desperate to clear Nan of all wrongdoings. But it was still a little hard to understand how all this stuff had come to be here.

She wanted to go to the library. She glanced at her watch. She wouldn't sit here and wait for Mack. He'd said he wouldn't make it back that afternoon anyway. Surely he would have no problem with her running to the library, looking up any information on this Jeremy Feldspar.

She snatched up her car keys and purse and ran outside,

locking the animals in. "I won't be long," she called out to Mugs.

She turned on the engine and quickly backed out the driveway. She still had boxes of clothes to drop off. She'd have to fit that into her day too. As she swept past the neighbor's house, she saw Cindy waving at her. She caught sight of her too late to react with a wave of her own, and she wasn't sure she wanted to either. Something was very odd about that couple. Was there such a thing as too much sunshine in someone's world?

With all the supposed neighbors forming a crowd in front of her house, few had introduced themselves to Doreen. Just the too-happy couple, Cindy and Josh. Oh, yeah, and Ella had earlier. But Doreen hadn't seen Ella since their first encounter. That was a shame because Ella was at least normal.

At the library, Doreen walked into the massive new-looking building, and, with the librarian's help, she was quickly set up, looking at the old records on microfiche. She went back to the early '70s, the same years as documented in the photos, searching for anything on Jeremy Feldspar in the newspapers.

Then she did a search for her grandmother, from approximately age twenty—her Nan wasn't exactly forthcoming about her actual age—until Jeremy went missing, so covering the thirty years from about 1958 to 1988. She found the odd mention of Nan, who was always very active in community events. So her name came up a couple times. But never in relation to Jeremy. The only time Doreen saw Jeremy's name was in an article about a court case, where he was suspected of killing his mother in the 70s, as mentioned in the newspaper clipping found in the envelope taped under the spare bed. She read this article thoroughly, just in case it had any additional information. But it appeared to be a rehash of the same material.

She searched other newspapers, hoping to find other mentions of him. But found very little. Back then the local newspaper ran more human-interest stories.

She looked through the rest of the years—the 1970s and early 1980s—but she didn't find anything more on Jeremy or her grandmother. Doreen closed down the machine, picked up her notepad and went to the librarian. "Excuse me. Are there any other resources that would allow me to track down somebody here?"

"Did you check the obituaries?" asked the librarian, Linda Linket, according to her name tag. "We do have a long list of those."

With the librarian's help, Doreen brought up the obituary list and checked through the late eighties and into the late nineties, but no mention of Jeremy was found anywhere.

After thanking the librarian, she got in her vehicle and returned home. As she pulled up, she saw Mack pounding on her front door.

She got out and said, "It's only common sense, but if my vehicle is not here, I'm not here." She climbed the front porch steps to join him.

He glared at her. "Why weren't you here?"

"Because I was at the library, looking for information on Jeremy Feldspar."

He fisted his hands on his hips, and his glare didn't diminish one bit.

She glared back as she unlocked her front door and let him inside. "You can rest easy," she said. "I didn't find anything. And how stupid is that?"

"What did you expect to find? A line saying, *Jeremy Feldspar was murdered by your neighbors?*"

She shot him a look and said in a dark voice, "You wouldn't joke about that if you had met them." She headed to the kitchen, scooping up Goliath as she went. She gave him a great big hug and a cuddle and placed him on the kitchen table. She had left the coffeemaker on. She stared at it and wondered if that was a fire hazard, then shrugged. She hadn't been killed by it yet. She refilled her coffee cup, filling one for Mack. She turned to look at him. "What did you find?"

In a cool voice he said, "Remember this is police business, and it's confidential?"

She stared at him in outrage. "If you want any information from me, I give it to you." In a casual movement, she tossed her notepad on top of the photographs on the table. If he wasn't sharing, well, neither was she.

But she had never been any good at lying.

"What did you find?" he snapped.

She gave him an innocent look and smiled. "What makes you think I found anything?"

He snorted and settled into his chair. "You look guilty as hell."

When Thaddeus hopped up on the kitchen table, Goliath jumped down and stalked off. She stroked Thaddeus's feathered neck, but he cocked an eye at her and said, "Liar. Liar."

She glared at the bird. "I don't need any comments from the peanut gallery, thank you very much."

Mack leaned forward and glared at her. "What did you find?"

She leaned forward and shoved her face into his. "None

of your business."

He let out an exasperated sigh. "Are we back to that again? You really want me to get a warrant, search this place from top to bottom?"

"It might be best," she said. "I keep finding stuff. I don't know if I found all of it or just part of it."

"What did you find? You went through the rest of those boxes, didn't you?" he roared. "After you promised not to go back in there."

She gave him a flat stare and said, "I didn't go in. I pulled the boxes out into the hallway."

He snorted.

She lifted her chin. "Besides, no harm done. They were mostly full of shoes."

"Both?"

"The other was mostly full of knickknacks."

"Anything else?" he asked suspiciously.

Just then Thaddeus walked between the two of them. He gave her that look again, as if waiting for her to open her mouth. She glared at the bird. "You don't know anything."

He made a funny cuckooing sound. She had never heard it come out of him before. Then he did it again. The bird constantly surprised her.

"If only that bird could really talk," Mack said, "I imagine he would have quite the story to tell."

"Especially since so many activities would've been done in and around him while he was here. He would've seen and known what was going on," she admitted.

"Like what you've done today?" Mack snapped. "So, give."

But he was still withholding anything about what he had found in Jeremy's safe-deposit box or about his account at the bank. She opened her mouth when Thaddeus fixed her with that odd glare of his. She raised both hands in surrender. "I can't keep any secrets from that dratted bird. He's against me."

She glared at the two of them, and both just stared back at her.

"Fine." She looked at the notepad and used it to push the photographs toward Mack. "These were inside the second box."

"Photographs," he noted. "Anything of value?"

"I was going to let you have them and decide."

He shot her a look that confirmed he understood her a little more than she liked. He spread out the images carefully, picking one up at a time, studying the features of the people in each photo. He read the names and dates on the back before placing each one down again.

"Before you ask, no, I don't know any of the faces, considering those photos were taken before I was born. And the only name I recognize is *Jeremy*, for obvious reasons."

He nodded. "What if Nan does?"

Doreen shrugged. "I don't know any of the landmarks in the images. For all I know, these could've been taken in Europe."

"I doubt it," he said. "Some of these are from the city beach in Kelowna."

"How can you tell? It could've been any beach anywhere as far as I'm concerned." She sat back and sipped her coffee. "By the way, did you check out my neighbors concerning the body in my back garden?"

He lifted his head and pierced her with that hard gaze of his. "What about your neighbors?"

"It's silly." She shrugged. "But that one couple is just so

dang happy."

That startled a grin out of him. "Is your world so dark you can't appreciate other people being happy?"

"No, they were *too* happy. *Too* bright. *Too* cheerful. *Too* ingratiating. It's not like they came by before, like the other lady—Ella, I believe her name was. She was at least normal."

"You've barely been here three days yet. Isn't there a rule about waiting at least seventy-two hours after a newcomer moves in before you welcome him to the neighborhood? So they have a chance to settle in, unpack some boxes?"

She shot him a flat stare. "I have no idea. Are there rules for things like this?"

"I wouldn't doubt it." He chuckled. "But just because they were extremely friendly, it doesn't make them killers."

"I know," she said morosely. "So far, they are the only ones who were over-the-top friendly."

"Were you friendly back? Did you bring them inside and have tea, spend an hour with them socializing?" He studied her and then shook his head. "Of course not. You probably stayed in the doorway, not even letting them get comfortable on the front porch."

"If I knew there were rules about things like that," she snapped, "then I might have. How was I supposed to know there was a right and wrong way to handle neighbors who were just too darn happy to be comfortable around?"

He stared at her, then despite himself, he laughed. "You might want to consider how that would've been a good way to get information from them. Information about whether Jeremy had ever been here. Information about strangers around the house lately." He settled back after looking at the last picture. "They might have answered your questions. When the police question the neighbors, the officers tend to get those lovely noncommittal kinds of answers. *But,* when a neighbor questions neighbors, well, that's a whole different story."

She stared at him in surprise and with a growing realization. "Well, consider me about to get friendly with my neighbors."

Thaddeus spoke up right then, once again repeating his earlier lines. "Liar. Liar."

It was a heck of a position to be in when even the bird knew her so well.

Chapter 24

Day 4, Saturday

THE NEXT MORNING, Doreen walked out to the garden, considering what to do next. Yesterday had been eventful, but she had just begun to dig into the Jeremy Feldspar case and didn't want to let it go. Checking out the neighbors should be high on her list. But how to approach the problem?

Thaddeus hadn't called her a liar again—then she hadn't lied to anyone since Mack left. It was stupid to let the bird motivate her actions since she was happy to convince herself she was doing this for Nan. Which she really was. The last thing Doreen wanted was to see her beautiful sweet grandmother accused of murder.

Doreen walked out to the garden, where she'd seen several decent flowers. With gloves on and clippers in hand, she carefully cut off a dozen blooms and walked around to the tulips and picked several long stems. She was delighted to see them still flowering.

When she had a collection of cut flowers, she went back inside, grabbed some of the ribbons she'd seen in her grandma's gardening cupboard and made several small bouquets. She planned to walk the neighborhood along the cul-de-sac and at least introduce herself and share some of Nan's garden flowers. Surely that couldn't go over wrong.

She collected the first bouquet and walked to the house on the left. She went up to the front door and knocked. Knowing not everyone loved animals she'd elected to leave the trio at home.

An older gentleman opened the front door and glared at her. "What the hell do you want?"

She studied his face and wondered if she'd seen him in the gawking crowd outside her place. He looked familiar. She glanced at the flowers in her hands. Maybe tulips weren't exactly the best thing to give to a single male. But she was already committed. In a cheerful voice she said, "I wanted to introduce myself. I'm Doreen. Nan is my grandmother, and I'm now living in her house, next door." She handed over the flowers. "These are for you. They are from Nan's garden."

He refused to take the flowers. Instead he crossed his arms, and his demeanor did not change in the least as he stared at her. "And why would I want anything to do with you? Since you moved into the neighborhood, it's gone to hell."

She tamped down her temper. "I hardly had anything to do with that, as I just arrived," she pointed out quietly. "And Nan hasn't been here either for the last few weeks."

"Still, all the police cars coming and going—this used to be a nice neighborhood."

With her hand still out, holding the flowers toward him, she felt foolish. But she still needed information. "Well, at least you could tell me your name, so I can recognize you in the future."

In a hesitant voice he said, "I'm Richard de Genaro."

"And you live here alone?" she prompted.

The wattage of his glare beefed up. "Not that it's any of your business, but my wife lives here with me."

"Oh, lovely. What's her name?" She wanted to back up and run away from the ire that he turned on her.

"Her name is Sicily," he said grudgingly.

She shoved the flowers against his hands and said, "Good. You can give these to Sicily." Figuring she had pushed her luck as far she could, she said, "It was nice to meet you, Richard." And she walked down the steps.

She could feel his eyes boring into her back as she walked to her front door. Inside, she slowly closed the door and leaned against it. "Mugs, if you think that was easy, it was not. Next time I have to visit him, I'm taking you. Surely everybody loves dogs."

She walked over to her notepad and wrote down Richard and Sicily de Genaro and their address. That was a hard mouthful. On the other hand, that should also make it easier to find more information about them online because their names were so unique, although each could have multiple spellings. But his attitude had been surly, and he certainly looked like he was quite happy to murder anybody who crossed him. She added Ella and Josh and Cindy to her sheet.

She tucked her little notepad and pencil into her pocket and grabbed the second bunch of flowers, knowing that the surly man would probably be watching her as she walked to the second house on the left. There were six houses in the cul-de-sac, and she planned to hit all of the ones whose owners she had yet to meet.

At the second door, she could hear dogs barking like

crazy inside. A young woman opened the door, looking harried and upset. Two small Maltese looking dogs ran around everyone in a frenzy of barking. The woman held a young child with a reddened scrunched—up face in her arm, which explained why the mother looked like she was having a bad day.

Doreen bent to say hi to the dogs. In a gentle voice, she introduced herself. "I'm the new neighbor. Doreen. Nan is my grandmother, and I moved into her house. I just wanted to stop by and say hi."

The young mother smiled nervously. She glanced outside, looked over at Nan's house and back again to her. "Nice to meet you. It's been so crazy here since you moved in."

Doreen placed her hand over her chest. "Oh, my goodness, has it ever. Who knew I'd move into my house and find a body in the backyard?"

The woman shook her head. In a gossipy manner, she leaned forward and said, "Do you know who it is?"

Doreen shook her head. "The police aren't talking. I imagine they've been around to talk to you already, but, outside of collecting as much evidence as they needed, I haven't gotten any information from them."

Disappointment settled on the young woman's face. "Same with me," she said. "I tried to ask them some questions when they came here, but they were pretty closemouthed about the whole issue."

Doreen laughed. "Which just means that everybody in the neighborhood knows already."

The young mother smiled. "Especially Ella Goldman. I'm Brenda, by the way. And this little one here, who's got a bit of a cold and is feeling pretty rough, is Cara. She'll feel better when her daddy gets home from running errands."

Much happier with this meeting, Doreen held out the flowers, letting Cara grab them. "These are from Nan's garden. I thought maybe you would appreciate some fresh—cut flowers."

Brenda smiled at the flowers, then back at Doreen. "Normally I'd invite you in, but she's having such a rough morning."

"Oh, dear, don't worry about it," Doreen said. "I'm just making the effort to introduce myself to everybody."

"You haven't seen my son, Travis, today, have you? I can't keep track of that boy."

Doreen shook her head, frowning.

"He said he met you Thursday. He was up a tree."

"Oh, yes, I did. But I haven't seen him yet today."

"He'll show up for meals. Is that Cindy in your side yard?" she asked, peering around the corner. "I thought I just saw her over on your place earlier." Then she laughed. "I thought I saw Richard, your other neighbor, in your yard a few days ago too. Although he might have been after the dog's ball again. You never see the dog, but Richard often throws the ball over his fence." She shrugged. "No clue what Cindy was doing back there, although Nan used to always share her perennials when it was time to divide them in the fall. She might have been looking to see what perennials Nan had…"

Doreen turned to check but didn't see anybody. "Really? Cindy? Richard?" She couldn't image why they'd be in Nan's yard. Still, there wasn't any problem with them being there, particularly if Brenda was right about their reasons.

"Ella lives in that far house, but she was looking along your back fence line. Not sure why she'd be there," Brenda said, pointing. "But it has been interesting around here, right?"

"It was pretty rough for my first three days here," Doreen admitted, peering into her side yard but couldn't see any sign of Ella. "I don't want people to get the wrong idea about me."

"Oh, my goodness, no. Although we're certainly very curious about what's going on."

As Doreen turned to go, she fostered a bright smile. "As am I." With a little wave at the sick girl, Doreen stepped down the stairs and called out, "Bye now. It was nice meeting you."

Brenda lifted the little girl's hand and waved. She called to the dogs, "Salt and Pepper, get back here. Come on inside."

Back at her house, Doreen sat and wrote down Brenda, Travis, and Cara. She hadn't gotten their last name, had no idea who the husband was, or what he did for a living. She frowned at that. How would she get a second excuse to find out more information? Public records most likely?

Still, she had gotten something, so, if Mack wanted to help, he could probably give her all that information too.

Determined to get this done, she grabbed her third bouquet and walked to the third house on the left. She knocked and waited. Not a sound inside, not a sound outside. The yard was pristine. Either the owners certainly spent a lot of time keeping their garden immaculate or they hired a company to do it. Doreen was impressed regardless.

When she rang the doorbell again, and there was still no answer so she walked back down the steps. Taking a chance, she crossed the cul-de-sac and went to the house at the far side. No point in going home with these flowers if she didn't need to.

It was Ella's house and a good way to see if she was home or skulking around in the back of Doreen's yard. Ella, she was lovely but chatty. As soon as she opened the door, she was off and running.

"Oh, my goodness, I'm delighted you stopped by. It's my day off," the woman gushed. "Nan was such sweetheart. I used to help her with her gardening all the time. I was over there a little bit ago, checking to see how bad it had gotten."

"Nan *is* a sweetheart," Doreen corrected, wondering if Brenda had been wrong about the identity of the person in the backyard. And did it even matter? "She's quite happy and healthy, living at the retirement home not too far from here."

"Oh, good. I should probably walk over and visit with her one day," Ella said. "She was always so full of stories and had such a great sense of humor. And, of course, she set up those betting pools." She shook her head and laughed. "My husband told me, after I lost ten dollars to her one day, to never sign up for one of them again." She held the door open wider. "Do you want to come in and have a nice cup of tea?"

Doreen hesitated and was tempted, but she wasn't exactly sure how that would fit in with her plans. Then she had no choice, as Ella grabbed her arm and tugged her forward.

"Don't be shy. This whole neighborhood is one big family."

And that gave Doreen an opportunity she hadn't expected. "I've been trying to meet a few of them. What can you tell me about the people here?"

Obviously that was the right question. Soon she was seated at the kitchen table, and Ella was bustling about, turning on the teakettle, making a pot of fresh tea. In the meantime, she talked. And talked. And talked.

Apparently Mr. de Genaro used to be in politics. He thought he was above everybody now, even though he was retired. But honestly, according to Ella, he'd been forced out of politics, with a little bit of a shady background in his history. His wife was a sweetheart though. How she ever got stuck with that old prude, Ella didn't know.

And then of course, there was Brenda and her baby. And she had a womanizing husband, Ned. Nasty old guy. Fifteen years her senior and she was his second wife. But Brenda was just a lovely little sweetheart.

The people on the far end were rich snobs. But they were okay when you got to know them. "In the meantime, don't expect them to be friendly," Ella cautioned her.

"So far, I haven't found too many people to be all that friendly," Doreen admitted. "Then again, the events after I arrived wouldn't exactly make anybody overjoyed."

Ella sat down, excitement lighting up her features. "Maybe. This place was boring until you showed up." She laughed.

"Unfortunately I found a finger on my first day here, just a few days ago," Doreen said. "I was supposed to be here earlier because Nan moved out three weeks ago."

Ella shook her head. "True. She was busy setting up her new life. So she wasn't here very much. This community needs somebody like Nan. And I must admit, the last year she hasn't been her usual self. She wasn't doing anywhere near the same amount of betting pools and didn't look as lively." Ella leaned back, her gaze studying Doreen, and added, "Honestly you injected some excitement to this place. And loads of fun."

Doreen silently questioned Ella's definition of *fun*.

Chapter 25

BY THE TIME Doreen finally freed herself from her chatty neighbor, Ella, and returned home, hours had passed, but Doreen definitely knew a lot more about the community. Still not anything pertinent to the case though. Unsettled and full of questions, she decided to walk to Nan's and ask her some more questions—especially about her betting activities. It was very convenient to have her grandmother just a few blocks away. Doreen had to admit to looking forward to the walk.

She put Mugs on a leash, admonished Goliath to get into no trouble while inside alone, then asked Thaddeus, "Do you want to go for a walk?"

Mugs started barking.

Thaddeus called out, "Walk. Walk." His head bobbed up and down and side to side. He jumped onto Mugs's back as she opened the door and locked it behind them.

Halfway to the retirement home, she realized she should probably call before visiting. Maybe Nan had company or had gone out shopping. Doreen quickly grabbed her phone from her purse and called her grandmother. "If you're not busy, I'm coming for tea."

Nan laughed. "Oh, I do like having you close by. I see more of you now than I think I've seen you in your entire lifetime."

Doreen winced. As a reminder of how little time she had spent with her grandmother overall, it was potent.

When she reached Nan's place, Doreen saw Nan carrying the teapot outside for them already. Nan straightened and waved. Doreen and her lively duo walked over and she took a seat at the little table. Mugs lay down at her feet. Thaddeus hopped onto the table and right up Nan's arm. He crooned and rubbed against her cheek.

Stroking his feathers, Nan beamed at her. "This is just lovely. After all the commotion this morning, this is exactly what I needed."

"What commotion?"

Nan shook her head. "Oh, I don't want to bother you."

"What commotion, Nan? I haven't heard anything about it yet." Doreen glanced around. "I thought I saw a cop car in the parking lot, but that could be for any number of reasons here."

"A man went for a walk and didn't come back," Nan said with relish.

"Oh, dear." Despite herself, Doreen winced. The last thing she wanted was the reminder of dead bodies. Her garden still looked like crap, compliments of the last officers who had come to her house. She glanced around. "Is he forgetful? Maybe he just got lost?"

"Around here, anything's possible." Nan patted her hand. "You're a sweetheart, but don't worry about him. He probably won't be back."

Doreen looked sharply at Nan. "What did you say?"

Nan looked confused for a moment, then added, "I'm

sure he'll be back."

Slightly unsettled because Doreen was darn sure that wasn't what Nan had said originally and not knowing why she had said it, Doreen sat back slightly and waited for her grandmother to talk. Perhaps her original wording was a simple mistake. She couldn't know that the old man wouldn't be home anymore.

Could she?

Still worried, Doreen asked carefully, "I presume a search party is out looking for him?"

"Oh, yes. The police are looking for him, and his family is looking too, I should imagine." And she gave Doreen the sweetest, blankest look ever.

Doreen frowned, a shudder rippling inside. Had Nan declined mentally all of a sudden, or was she just preoccupied? And how to tell? "What is his name? Was the man a resident?"

"Oh, no. Robert was a workman here. Nicest man. Always came in to talk to me. Had such lovely stories about the different places he worked in."

An ugly suspicion arose. "Did he mention your house, or ask you anything about what might be in your house?"

Nan looked at her in surprise. "Well, of course we talked about my house. It's not in the heritage zone of Kelowna, but my house has all kinds of unique things about it. Plus I'd lived there for so long."

Nan gave Doreen that breathtaking smile of innocence again that both made Doreen feel better and worse.

"Did he ever work on your deck or in the attic?"

Nan shrugged. "Not that I remember."

Doreen waited, but Nan added nothing further. So Doreen asked again, "But he worked on your deck?"

Nan paused, deep in thought. "He might have built the deck originally, but I don't remember for sure. Why?"

Doreen stared at the grass. Mugs slept at her feet while Thaddeus paced across the table, once again looking for scraps of things to eat. "No reason."

"We talked lots over the years. He's a very nice man."

Doreen nodded. "I'm sorry that he's missing."

Nan said in a very cheerful voice, "I'm sure he'll show up, or at least his body will in a few days."

"You think he's dead?" Doreen asked in a strangled voice.

"He's not here. He's not at home, and he didn't go to work." Nan shrugged. "Sounds like he might be dead."

Glumly Doreen had to admit her grandmother was right. That was often the case. "Well, if he's an older man, then that's possible," she said.

"Oh, dear. No, he's not old. Not even forty yet, I don't think."

Knowing she couldn't handle more of this conversation, Doreen determinedly shifted it to her discussion about the neighbors. "I went around to introduce myself to the neighbors today. Met three more people."

Nan beamed. "Aren't they lovely?"

"Some of them appear to be, yes. Some are talkative. Some are secretive. And some never seem to be home."

"That's people though. No matter where you go, you get a mix of them all." She picked up her tea and gave her granddaughter a sweet smile once again. "You'll fit right in."

"Finding a body didn't make for an easy introduction to the community," she admitted.

"Nonsense. The place is dull and boring. It added some excitement to the area."

"You sure you have no idea who killed him?"

Nan's gaze twinkled at Doreen over the teacup. "No, not at all." She leaned forward. "Do you?"

"No, of course not. I just got into the house. Nan, he was killed several days ago, if not weeks ago. He was killed while you were in the process of moving here, if not before."

"That's so sad." She sipped her tea again and put it back on the saucer. "I was very busy in the days and weeks before this move, and if I wasn't packing up things to bring with me here, I was in my front room watching the telly. Anything could've gone on in the backyard. I wouldn't have known about that."

"Or did you just not want to tell anybody about it?" Doreen leaned forward. "You do know that it's illegal to withhold any information from the police about a case? And it's also illegal to bury a body, even if you didn't kill the person?"

Nan's gaze widened. "Of course I didn't know that. Why would I know that? It's not like I have anything to do with dead bodies. Besides, sweetie, you were living at the house when the body was found." She shook her finger at Doreen. "Make sure you're not involved."

The conversation was making less and less sense and seemed to be sliding more and more off to the side of ridiculous. Doreen worried about her grandmother. "Have you made any friends here?" She was trying to be objective and to change the subject.

"Lots. Several of them are very interested in my hobby."

Doreen perked up. "Now that is good. What hobby are you talking about?"

She smirked. "You know what the hobby is. I had to stop for a long time. But I'm happy to say that I'm playing again."

Doreen cast her mind back and forth as she tried to remember any of Nan's hobbies from the last several decades. But she kept coming up blank. "Why was it you stopped again?"

Nan gave her a droll look. "The police didn't like it."

Doreen stared at her and then remembered Ella's recent words. Doreen closed her eyes and groaned. "Nan, you're gambling again?"

"No, of course not. It's just betting pools. Little stuff, you know? Fun stuff. It's not illegal. I already talked to the cops about it."

"Gambling is bad. Gambling is bad," Thaddeus intoned.

"Oh dear," Nan cried out staring at the now preening bird. "What are you teaching him?"

"Nothing. He picks stuff up all the time. Back to the point, it wasn't illegal before either, or so you told me, years ago I thought," Doreen said. "Why would you do this again?"

"I'm very good at it."

And again into such a bizarre conversation. Doreen leaned forward and asked, "Nan, what are you talking about? There was no need for the police to even know about your gambling before. Unless you were doing something illegal."

"I got in trouble because I was *disruptive* at the casino," she said. "I did have a temper back then, and everyone felt I had a problem. So I had to stop. I'm still not sorry I kicked that man though."

Doreen sat back in shock. "I don't think you ever told me the details about that."

"What can I say? He accused me of cheating, but he was the one cheating. You have to watch out for Walter White.

He owns the hardware store on Springfield. Definitely the sort to stay away from." Nan shrugged. "It's all good now. Besides, everybody should get arrested at least once in their life."

Doreen stared at Nan, shocked.

Her grandmother picked up a cookie from the plate on the table and broke off a piece then broke it again to place small pieces on the table. "Thaddeus here was a godsend. I got him soon after I was arrested. He made me realize just how much I had to change. But that was years ago, my dear. And the loan sharks were really very nice. One of them was sweet on me. Basil Champs. I do love that man."

Oh, my God. Nan had borrowed money from loan sharks? It was much worse than Doreen imagined. Nan's wording and that soft tone of hers had Doreen wondering at this new side to her Nan. She'd always seen her Nan as a sweet old lady. Now it seemed *sweet* wasn't as correct as maybe the term *colorful.* And did she go to the loan shark Basil out of need or out of want? Doreen wondered just how well she knew her grandmother.

"So, if all that was bad, why would you start gambling again now?"

"Well, because I'm not really gambling. It's just betting pools. It's fun."

"So, no real money is involved?" Doreen asked cautiously. "And what kind of stuff are you actually betting on?"

"How long before Robert's body shows up."

Doreen winced. How completely insensitive. "If the police hear about that, they might think you have some insider knowledge that he's dead."

"Of course they will." She gave a crafty grin, taking another piece of cookie and popping it into her mouth. "And the second betting pool is how long before the police solve the case."

"Oh, boy." Doreen shook her head. She stared at her grandmother in fascination. She was learning so much new information about her only living relative. Some of it was a little disturbing. But it *was* like Nan had a whole new lease on life. As if she figured she was too old to pay for the consequences and was just out to have fun. "It almost sounds like you're courting trouble, Nan."

"Not really. I'm harmless. Besides, nobody looks at us old people. Nobody thinks we're constructive or destructive elements. It's kind of irritating."

"I can imagine," Doreen said, her voice soft. "But still, do you want to spend the rest of your years in jail?"

Nan sat back with a thoughtful look on her face. "Only if it was in one of those nice jails. Of course most of them are nice. Especially in Canada. Now some of them in the States, that's a different story. Some of those are rough." She picked up her teacup again. "Would you still visit me there, my dear?"

"Yes, I would still visit, but I don't know how often. It's not like we have a jail close by."

"There is one a few hours away."

"How about you just don't get into trouble to that extent, and you can stay here and have fun with all your friends?"

"Oh, I intend to do just that." She held out a small piece of cookie in her hand. "Did you want some of this?"

Doreen looked at the big piece of cookie on her grandmother's plate and the tiny piece in her hand. "Just give that piece to Thaddeus."

Happily Nan obliged.

"Have you been eating well here?"

"I've been eating just wonderfully. These are Charlie's cookies." She leaned forward and whispered, "He put some of that green stuff in them, you know?"

Doreen's heart stopped and then raced ahead. "Green stuff?" she asked cautiously leaning forward to brush Thaddeus back from the crumbs he was inhaling.

"Yes, they're healthy cookies. He grows the green stuff in his backyard. I have to admit, when I eat them, I feel really good."

Doreen stared openmouthed as her grandmother snapped off another piece of the marijuana cookie and popped it into her mouth. Good Lord, what had gotten into her grandmother now that she lived at Rosemoor?

Chapter 26

HEADING BACK HOME again, Doreen took a different and longer route. Mugs could use the walk, and she could distract herself from her bizarre visit with Nan as Doreen's mind worried on all the little bits and pieces of seemingly unrelated information on the two dead men related to Nan's house that Doreen had gathered from her neighbors.

As for Nan's penchant for marijuana cookies, Doreen couldn't even begin to think about that and shoved it to the back recesses of her mind.

She also couldn't imagine Nan having anything to do with this murder mess, but unless some better evidence showed up, Nan was the most obvious suspect. How depressing was that?

And her two betting pools regarding the missing man, Robert, made her even more suspicious.

Doreen would normally have crossed the river on the small bridge, but she headed the other way, staying on the city-street blocks, going through town and then coming alongside the creek. It was a slow sojourn home letting Mugs happily sniff the trail to his heart's content.

Thaddeus sat on her shoulder suspiciously quiet. She gave him several cautious looks but he appeared to be swaying gently to every movement.

As she stood on the creek pathway, studying the backs of the houses, she realized that this was the same creek leading to the little bridge behind her place also. Farther up was where she'd seen Brenda's boy in the tree on Thursday. She walked the path, hoping she was heading toward home. If so, she'd see her house in a few minutes. It was such a beautiful walk here with the birds and the sunshine. Quiet and peaceful. Up ahead she could see the houses on the cul-de-sac beside her cul-de-sac.

She was almost home.

With Thaddeus giving a running commentary of oddball noises as he sat on her shoulder and Mugs wandering from place to place, Doreen slowly meandered home. It was a different life here. Despite all that had happened since her arrival three days earlier on Wednesday, it was a good life. At least she hoped it would be.

The creek drifted slowly beside her. The water levels were low, but overall enough water kept things flowing smoothly and curbed the smell of wet mud. She was only about ten or maybe fifteen minutes away from Nan's place right now by traveling this route.

She stopped and studied the water. They were coming up to her cul-de-sac, as far she could tell.

Hmm. A pretty place to walk—particularly if someone wanted to stay hidden. Could someone have carried a body that distance?

It would be a heavy load. But a wheelbarrow would make it easier. She studied the ground to find it relatively smooth, without big logs to cross over. But still, it would be taking a heck of a chance of being discovered by pushing a dead body along here in a wheelbarrow. Even though all the properties on her side of the creek had been fenced off from this creek, Travis had been playing on the far side. So there were people around regardless.

Although someone might be seen from the back of the houses across the creek, especially from a second-floor advantage, still any witnesses would have to be looking specifically at the creek path to see this hypothetical wheelbarrow transporting a dead body.

She'd never seen anybody walking back there. But then she'd never been looking. And she had only been here three days, and each one had been pretty time-consuming.

A log was up ahead. She walked over and sat down, happy to enjoy the view in the sunshine. Mugs sniffed around her feet and then lay down beside her. She scratched his back. "Hey, buddy."

He huffed heavily, gave a small bark, then dropped his head on her foot.

"Yeah, you get to roam about, get muddy. It's a good life."

She sat, talking with the animals, lightly stroking Thaddeus's feathers. "We should have brought Goliath with us."

Mugs gave an odd kind of a noise and bolted to his feet. His nose faced upstream, his nostrils flaring. Then he barked. At what, she didn't know. She stared at him. "What's the matter, boy?"

He raced off, pulling on his leash.

She held on tighter and stood. "Okay, let's see what's bothering you."

She didn't have to go very far when she caught sight of something that had her stomach dropping to her feet. She walked closer to make sure, her phone already in her hand. She hit Mack's speed-dial number and waited until he answered.

"What's the matter, Doreen?"

She took a shaky breath. "I found another body."

After a stark silence on the other end, he exploded, "What?"

"I'm at the creek about one hundred yards—maybe fifty yards—from my house. About ten to fifteen minutes away from Nan's retirement home. Apparently a man went missing from there. I think this is him." She took two steps closer. "He's lying in the water. He looks like he's been here for a little while."

"Did you touch the body?"

She shivered. "No. I presume he's dead. I've been sitting on a log here for at least five minutes."

"Sitting?" Mack asked in surprise.

"Not beside the body," she cried out. "That would be terrible… and so very gross." She shook her head. "I was sitting on a log a few yards down the creek when Mugs barked. So I checked it out. The man's wearing jeans and a hoodie jacket, from the looks of it. I don't know. Maybe it's a runner's jacket. He has running shoes on." She turned to stare up the creek, then down a ways. "Maybe it's somebody else. I don't know."

"Don't touch the body. Stay right there. If I come to your house and go through the back gate, will I see you?"

"If you come to my house, go through the back gate and take a left, then carry on down the path, you can't miss me."

"Be there in ten."

She could still hear him on the line.

In a much harder voice he added, "Don't move."

This time she heard the audible *click* as he hung up from the call. She stared at the bright blue sky and sunshine. "Why me?"

Mugs, now that he understood where the smell came from, laid down at her side and proceeded to fall asleep.

Thaddeus, on the other hand, had a whole different thing to say. He stared over her head and screeched at the top of his voice, "Murder in the water. Murder in the water."

"Stop, you silly old bird. You want all the neighbors to know somebody's out here?"

Thaddeus crooned a sorrowful song. Almost like a keening, wailing song that she knew some aboriginal tribes sang for their dead. She looked at him in wonder. "You have hidden depths, Thaddeus. But could you possibly keep it down?" She stood protectively beside the body. Although if anybody else came along, she would look darn suspicious.

With her phone, she took several pictures of the body in the water and the area around it. And, because she had to wait anyway, she looked for any signs of what might have happened to him. Surely Mack would understand that much.

The dirt was a little bit scuffed up at the pathway, although no marks resembled wheelbarrow tracks. She quickly stepped back, took a few more pictures of the scuffled area and searched for a murder weapon. For all she knew, the guy committed suicide, or maybe he'd been drunk and fell in the creek and drowned.

She didn't find anything of interest. But it didn't stop her from taking lots of pictures. She walked up the pathway and took some more pictures, walked to the other side and took even more. She had no idea what she was looking for but figured he'd be up on the matter a little later. Right now she was just protecting the crime scene.

And, for added measure, she took as many pictures of the creek as she could. And the houses on the far side. Who knew if anybody heard or saw anything? This cul-de-sac wasn't where her house was. This was the adjoining one. She hadn't met any of these people yet. Of course, once everyone heard she had found *this* body, there would be no end to the chaos in her world. And the added notoriety to her as the newcomer.

She waited ten minutes, which stretched to fifteen, then to twenty. Just when pulling out her phone on the half-hour mark to call Mack and to give him crap for being so late, she heard a noise on the far side of the creek. She waited, her heart racing. It could be the murderer coming back—if the body in the creek had been murdered.

That didn't stop the thoughts from going through her head.

She kept watch nervously.

Suddenly Mack appeared in front of her. He took one look at her and nodded. "Good. You're still here. Where is the body?"

"I said I'd be here," she snapped, relieved he'd finally arrived. "I kept my word. You, on the other hand, are late." She pointed wordlessly at the creek. "The poor man is there."

They both stared at the man, floating face mostly down with just enough of his face showing to see his open eye, the dirt and water in his mouth. He pivoted to look at her. "Did you touch him?"

She shook her head. "No, you told me not to."

"Have you been standing here in this vicinity for the last ten minutes?"

"*Thirty* minutes. That's how long since I called you. And, yes, I have been here, walking this pathway. I was afraid somebody else would come before you did."

He nodded, his attention returning to the area, then to the body. "I want you to go home, go inside your house, and stay there until I come." He glanced at Mugs and said, "Good job, Mugs."

Mugs barked, walked over to him, looking for a scratch. Mack bent down and gave Mugs what he wanted. Mack glanced at Thaddeus and said to Doreen, "I'm surprised he hasn't popped up with any comments."

She snorted. "He's been crooning some kind of death song for about ten minutes. And then before that, he called out, *Murder in the water. Murder in the water.*"

Mack nodded. "Go home with them both, please. And you're sure that Mugs didn't touch the body or pick up anything else either?"

"Not that I saw. He never went in the water or to the body, never touched or took a bite at anything," she said defensively.

Mack nodded. "I have to check. You know that."

She shrugged. "It'd be nice if you kept my name out of this."

He snorted. "Yeah, in your dreams."

She rolled her eyes at him. "I'll put coffee on. Make sure you get there before the pot turns off." She turned with her animals in tow and headed home.

Chapter 27

B ACK IN HER kitchen, Doreen put on the coffee as promised, noticing the dog food bowl was very low on kibble. She couldn't imagine Goliath eating it, but she wasn't about to make Mugs starve regardless. Then realized the cat bowl was empty too. She filled Goliath's bowl and gave both fresh water. Then checked on Thaddeus's food. It was fine thankfully. He was nodding off on his roost.

When the coffee finished, Doreen poured herself a cup and settled on a chair on the back veranda. What a day... That poor man... And what was going on in her world that she'd been the one to find the body?

That kind of stuff tended to stick to a person. She'd need to find a way to change this, or the neighborhood would label her as the village crazy lady who found dead people.

She stared at the old dilapidated fence that hid her view of the creek but also gave her a little bit of privacy from anybody walking on the far side. It also gave them cover from whatever secretive things they might be doing. The path hadn't been heavily used that she could see.

At least Nan shouldn't be a suspect in the latest death.

Right?

Except for her two damn betting pools. Crap.

The three deaths should all be unrelated... with Nan's house as the only tenuous connection.

Doreen sat for a long time when another thought entered her mind. What if the men were related? Maybe by a job, a common goal or having tripped over each other somewhere along the line? Or maybe being in the wrong place? What if the most recent deaths were people related to the dead man from thirty years ago? He would have been old enough to have a family. Any chance it was perhaps Jeremy's children? And the other two bodies were cousins or brothers? Not knowing the ages of the two latest dead bodies wasn't helping Doreen with her musings.

She pulled out her phone and quickly texted Mack. **I didn't see the man's face in the creek. And I don't know the physical features of the man found here on my property. Any chance the two men are related? And how old was each one?**

The response came back quickly. **This is Robert Delaney, general handyman, who worked at the old folks' home where Nan lives.**

Right. Something else to tie Nan into this.

But this man's last name, Delaney, and the dead body from Nan's garden, James Farley, plus the dead man depicted in the thirty-year-old pictures, Jeremy Feldspar, still meant nothing to Doreen. Yet, they didn't have to share the same last name to be related, to support this latest theory of hers. They could've been from the wife's side of the family, or they could've been cousins. They could've even been related on the mother's side—last names changed easier for women after they got married but also for a mom who remarried; her name would've changed too.

She quickly texted him again. **Don't let the names fool you. Make sure there is no blood between these two recently dead men, including any relationship to the man who went missing thirty years ago.**

We know how to do our job.

Short. Succinct… Right. Of course they did.

She had to be grateful for that little bit of sharing. Mack was the investigating detective, and she was somebody who tripped over bodies. Not necessarily a good thing.

Thaddeus crooned at her side. Goliath had somehow found her lap and had curled his not inconsiderable bulk into her arms. And to complete the picture, Mugs slept at her feet, stretched out on his belly froggy style.

"Thaddeus, if you're so smart, why can't you tell us something about these men who were murdered?"

With that thought, she pulled out her phone, shifted Goliath to lie beside her. Then she downloaded the images to her laptop that was parked on the coffee table for a closer look. Yes, she hadn't been mistaken. The man in the creek *had* been murdered, as evidenced by a hole in the side of his head that she could just barely see at the edge of his hoodie. She'd not looked too closely while he'd been stretched out in the water, but it showed up clearly in her photos. Looked like he'd been shot.

Speaking of images, she had none of the body found in her garden. She cringed at the thought of what a decaying body would look like.

But she had seen pictures of him from his insurance ads in the paper. She quickly did a Google search for James Farley and his company. And there was his photo. Then she searched Google for the man they'd just found, Robert

Delaney, bringing up his face on the monitor.

She studied the features of the two dead men, looking for something that would link them. They were both around the same age. She put them each in their forties. Possibly as old as mid-fifties. It was so hard to tell with some people. They were both sitting in the pictures, one heftier than the other. But then one had a more physical job—the handyman. No comparison for muscles and leanness. She kept searching and found profile pictures of both. They both had a bump in the center of their noses. When put side by side like that, there was definitely a resemblance. She saved both photos to show Mack.

And then she brought up the name of the man whose belongings she'd found upstairs—Jeremy Feldspar.

How was she to research wedding records, divorce records, or last known residences? She really needed Mack's help with this. Mack would probably say he needed her to stop interfering. Maybe he was right because, honestly, this was a bit beyond her investigative skills. She had to talk to somebody who had been around for a long time. So far Nan hadn't been a great—or reliable—source of information. Doreen considered her chatty neighbor, Ella. She had shared all about how she had lived in the Mission area for thirty or so years. Just not at the house in this neighborhood.

Then there was the retired guy who hadn't been friendly but was quite possibly someone who would know the old case. She didn't have his phone number, or she'd try calling. She wasn't sure what he'd say if she showed up at his door again. But she was willing to take a chance.

After another cup of coffee, she grabbed her notepad and got up the courage. She walked out her front door and down to the grumpy old man's house, leaving the animals behind.

She knocked on his door. He opened it as if he'd been standing at the front window, watching.

He growled. "What the hell do you want now?"

"I'm doing some research and was hoping you could help. Do you know any of these names or these faces?" She held up her laptop, sporting side-by-side full-face pictures of three men, beside her notepad with the names clearly written out in block printing: Jeremy Feldspar, James Farley, Robert Delaney.

Doreen watched Mr. de Genaro's face.

His gaze went from the pictures to the names and back again; then he stared at her. "Why do you want to know that?"

"Well, one of them is the man found buried in the back garden of my property, so I care. I was wondering if the men were related."

His eyebrows shot up. He shook his head, reached out and tapped one name on her notepad. "I knew this one. He went missing thirty years ago."

"In what way did you know him?"

He shrugged. "We were friends for a while. But he and his wife were into money scams. You know? Buy a property from him, then you find out there's no property to actually buy. The law was after them, as were a lot of angry people too. The fact that he disappeared was no surprise. I would have helped them on their way myself, but I couldn't find them. Jeremy cost me ten grand."

"Ouch. I'm sorry."

He nodded and said, "Jeremy was also accused of murdering his mother, but I never believed that." Frowning, he studied the pictures. "How are they all related?"

"Not sure yet. But I have profile pictures of two men,

one whose dead body was found recently, and they seem to share the same nose." She studied de Genaro's face, seeing the anger, resentment and pain from so long ago. "Can you tell me where Jeremy worked? Who his friends were? If any members of his family still live around here? What about his wife?"

His face twisted in disgust. "That was way back when. I have no idea where any of them are, except for his wife. Her name's Alice. I never could figure out if she was part of it or not. But she's living decent for somebody who never worked a day in her life."

Doreen didn't know if that was a diss on her too because she certainly hadn't worked a day in her life either, not a traditional job anyway. On the other hand, she wasn't living high on the hog now. She was living mostly on her grandmother's charity. And that did prick her pride a bit. "Do you know if she has the same last name?"

"Last I heard, she did. But not sure now. She'd be in her mid- to late seventies. She's living in the same retirement home as Nan."

Inside Doreen cringed. Of course she'd be living there. Everything kept circling back to Nan. An old-timer in this small town. But it'd be nice if one of the darn threads would go in the opposite direction. "Did they have any kids?"

He nodded. "Three or four of them, I think. They were young enough back then that the kids didn't really know what their parents were up to at the time. I don't think the kids were involved in the scams. They were in junior high or so back then."

"Outside of Jeremy just dropping off the earth, did you ever hear any more about what happened?"

Mr. de Genaro shook his head. At least this time his

tone was a whole lot more amiable when he said, "No, I haven't, but I sure would like to. Like I said, for a time, we were friends. If you find out anything, please let me know." On that note, he started to close the door.

She stepped back. "Likewise, if you hear of anything happening with these people, please let me know. I'm just trying to clear any suspicions regarding Nan in all this."

He stared at her for a long moment. "How can anybody possibly think Nan had something to do with this?"

"Oh, I agree. But, since the first body was found in her backyard..." She shrugged. "It does put her in a bad position."

"Fools. The whole lot of them." And the door closed with a bang.

She agreed and returned to her house. As she walked up the driveway, a vehicle came up behind her. She turned to see Mack, smiled and gave him a small wave.

He parked, got out, motioning at the notepad and her laptop in her hands. "Now what have you been up to?"

She gave him a look of complete innocence, but when he narrowed his gaze at her, she knew she had completely failed to convince him. She motioned to the neighboring house. "Richard de Genaro's been around for a long time. He's grumpy and angry, but I figured he might be a source of information."

"On who?"

She held up a photo of Jeremy Feldspar, the missing man from thirty years ago. "Him."

Mack stopped and stared at the photo. Then glanced at the neighbor's house. "Did he know him?"

She nodded. "Apparently Jeremy Feldspar and his wife were involved in a property development scam, and according to de Genaro, a lot of people wanted Feldspar dead."

Mack nodded.

She gasped. "You knew that already, didn't you?"

"I took a look at the old missing person's police file on Jeremy. It's a cold case with boxes of paperwork to go through. I haven't had time for that, but I read the brief on it." He shrugged. "Only so many hours in a day and, so far, you're doing a good job filling those hours with fresh bodies."

"Sorry about that." She winced. "It's not like I'm trying to find them. I'm just at the wrong place at the wrong time. Like moving into Nan's house. If I'd moved in right when she moved out, then likely the first body wouldn't have ended up on her property."

He stopped and grimaced. "Not necessarily."

She stared at the small circle of houses. "When Nan and I first talked about this change of residence, we didn't really lock down the dates. If we both had to live temporarily with each other in the house, we would have. No problem. And, if there was a gap between her moving out and me moving in, Nan was okay with that too."

Doreen spun to look at Mack. "I mean, Nan had been on a waiting list for Rosemoor, but usually someone has to die for a spot to open up at the retirement home. You can't exactly plan to give two weeks' notice for *that* event. Sure, sometimes a family caregiver will take a resident into their home and will give Rosemoor some notice. But those are rare events. So, when a *sudden* opening popped up, Nan took it rather than waiting for the next... opening."

He nodded. "And you got here as soon as you could."

"Something like that. It's not a good idea to leave a house empty for too long. But Nan wasn't all that worried.

Like she said, nothing happens around here, and I was trying to tie up something else before coming."

"The body had been here for at least a couple weeks."

She stared at him and swallowed. "Oh. So while Nan was in transition…"

He nodded. "So what's the chance that, even while Nan lived here, she had no clue?"

"It depends if she had her hearing aids in or not," Doreen explained. "Without them, she'd have heard nothing. And, if she was sleeping, then she really wouldn't have heard anything. Compound that with her moving to the retirement home and all the trips that would have entailed, plus she obviously never went into the backyard for quite a while…"

"So, of course, she had no idea. Likely the location was picked for just that reason."

Doreen froze and stared at the side-by-side pictures on her laptop in her hand. "Or for another more sinister reason?"

Now standing on the front doorstep, he put his hand on her shoulder. "What are you talking about?"

"I can't get past the idea that all the murders are related, that the victims might be related. But, what if the first man, who disappeared thirty years ago, is buried here too? And the body we found in the garden was his son? Maybe the killer wanted to bury him beside his father?" She shook her head and broke into maniacal laughter. "Can you imagine? That would make this property a family burial plot."

Chapter 28

"EASY, TAKE IT easy."

Her wild laughter morphed into sobs. She heard Mack's voice through her tears. She excused herself and ducked into the bathroom while Mugs greeted the newcomer. There she turned on the cold water and splashed her face, patting down the tears. When she was composed enough to face him, she walked into the kitchen, sat down and very quietly said, "I'm sorry."

Mugs nudged his nose against her leg. She reached down to stroke his big ears wondering what Mack must think of her.

He looked at her in surprise. "Why? You've come across two dead bodies, one in your own backyard, and may have found a conspiracy involving the third, all within your first four days here in Mission." He shook his head. "Anybody who's not in law enforcement or the medical profession would have the same kind of reaction."

She nodded, but it didn't help very much. She didn't want to be just anybody. She craved to be somebody special, to be somebody different. She'd been *just a wife* for so long, and now she was an individual person, in her own space. But what did that mean? Who was she? She wasn't sure what to do now in her life. She felt lost in the brand-new scheme of things as her daily events unfolded here in Mission. She could only hope she'd find out who she was soon enough.

She picked up the coffee cup Mack had filled for her and took a big drink. Then she hugged the cup with both hands. "Did you find any connection between the men?"

"Not yet, but if it's there, I'll find it. We do take murder very seriously here."

She nodded. "Mr. de Genaro said Alice Feldspar, Jeremy's wife, is a resident at Rosemoor. Maybe I should ask around at the retirement home or speak to her directly."

"No." He glared at her. "I'll take care of that. What is your problem? Just leave it alone, please."

Doreen glared back. At least she no longer felt like crying. "How can I just sit here and do nothing? The least I can do is talk to people, find out information, and feed it to you. Unless you want me to go off and find the killer myself."

"You just did find out info and feed it to me. The Alice Feldspar lead. And, hell no, I don't want you to go off and find the killer yourself. How would you even know who the killer is at this point? And what would you do? Just walk up to some suspect and ask him if he committed two murders recently? You realize somebody has killed two men in two weeks, possibly the third from as many decades ago.

"If it wasn't you, and it wasn't Nan, chances are it'll be somebody who Nan knows, possibly very well. It could even be somebody who you know. This is a small-town community. Sure, the city itself is big, but this area that we live in, it's small, it's tight, and everybody knows each other. You can't take the chance of pissing off the wrong person. Neither can you take the chance of tipping off the person who did this."

She sat back, disgruntled. Mugs looked up at her from his spot on the floor then dropped his head down again Doreen finally nodded. "Okay."

He stared at her as if waiting to see if she really understood. "Now let's get your police statement started." He pulled out his notepad and pen but also set a handheld tape recorder on the kitchen table and hit the Record button. "What made you go in that direction coming home?"

She frowned at him. "I was just looking for a path along the creek. It's pretty back there. I wasn't looking for the missing man."

"How did you know he was missing?" he asked, a hint of suspicion in his voice.

She gave him a drawn look. "I didn't kill him."

He rolled his eyes. "Just answer the question please."

She nodded. "Nan told me about it."

"And by sheer accident you went in that direction? Just a coincidence that you stumbled over the second body?"

"Absolutely." It sounded a little thin to her ears too.

He studied her for a long moment and then nodded. "Okay, so you went directly from the retirement home toward this creek path?"

She shook her head. She gave him as many of the details as she could remember about the convoluted way she came home. "I was just walking aimlessly, exploring. I don't know the area. I thought I'd walk around and see something new about the town. I came upon the creek, crossed it and kept going. I figured I would end up at home if I kept walking in this direction. I saw the cul-de-sac beside ours." She nodded toward the houses she could see out the back window. The two cul-de-sacs were kind of in a cloverleaf pattern. "I knew I wasn't very far away from home."

"How did you recognize the cul-de-sacs?"

"Only one house in both of these cul-de-sacs has those big Spanish tiles on the roof," she said quietly. "I do observe things, you know."

He wrote down some notes. "So what made you see him in the first place?"

"Mugs."

"Right, the dog."

"But not right away."

He raised his head and looked at her again. "Why not right away?"

"We were sitting on a log maybe ten yards from where the body was. I was enjoying the rest, thinking how beautiful the spot was and how absolutely lovely the town is to live in. That Nan had made a wonderful decision in spending as much of her life here as she had."

"Mugs wasn't bothered?"

Mugs lifted his head at the sound of his name. She stroked his body with her foot and shook her head. "There had been a nice breeze up until then. It came more from across the river. But when a big gust of wind came downriver, then Mugs barked like crazy. Up until then I think he was just tired and sleeping."

"And then what did you do?"

She looked at Mack in surprise. "I stood, and the three of us walked the creek toward home. Mugs was still barking like crazy, and he didn't stop until we approached the body. I could see that the man was dead, just lying there in the water."

Mack finished writing down another note, looked back at her and said, "And then what?"

She raised both hands in frustration. "What do you

mean, *And then what?* I called you. That's what."

"You didn't check out the man's pockets? Did you move him? Touch the man in anyway? Check to see if he was alive?"

She stared at Mack in horror. "He was in the water. Facedown but slightly twisted to the side. Dirt was in his mouth from the water washing around his face. His eyes were open. I didn't think there was any chance he was still alive. And, no, I did not touch him. I did not go through his pockets." She still stared at Mack. "I can't believe you'd ask me that. Check my shoes. They are dry."

Upset, but not letting him get to her any further, she continued, "And then I walked back and forth. I felt like I was being watched, just kind of an odd feeling, like I had to be protective of the body, and I was afraid that somebody would come along before you got there. I had been in that area on Thursday. I had actually found the same path but starting from the house. A boy had climbed one of the big trees. I didn't want him to come along today and see the body." She glared at Mack. "And you said you'd be there in ten minutes. But you were thirty minutes getting there."

It was his turn to roll his eyes at her. "Sorry. I came as fast as I could."

"Yeah, right. What? A dead body wasn't priority enough?"

"I was getting a team together so I wasn't the only one arriving. Also, I had to figure out exactly where you were. Your general directions were not very good." He reached over and shut off the recorder.

"Whatever." She finished her coffee, rising to pick up the pot. "This is becoming quite a habit."

"One I hope you will break."

She froze, coffeepot in hand, and stared at him. "What are you talking about?"

"Your habit of finding dead bodies."

"Oh." Relief washed over her. She waved the coffeepot around slightly. "I was talking about you coming here for coffee is becoming a habit. *A good one to break.*"

He grinned, chuckled and then laughed a great big belly laugh that roared through the kitchen.

She filled his coffee cup. "It's not that funny."

He gasped and tried to regain his breath. "Actually, yes, it is pretty funny. I intended to cut back on my coffee habit. But it's worse now because I'm always here."

"That's not my fault," she protested, but it was hard not to grin. "How about you just solve these murders? That would make my life a lot easier. Although I do have a theory, if you want to hear it?"

"What is it?"

She broached the subject carefully, leaning forward. "You know? I've been giving this a lot of thought. I was thinking about the man who disappeared decades ago. I think somebody in this area probably murdered him, and I think the recently murdered two men were related to him. They were probably looking for his killer."

"Wow. That's quite a theory. Any evidence to back that up?" he asked in a mocking tone but with a smile on his face, letting her know that it wasn't a taunt, more like a casual teasing remark.

"I'm not into conspiracy theories," she said. "Honest. It just seems like all this has to be related. And I thought I saw a family resemblance." She glanced over at her laptop and then back at him. "I have some photos." At his headshake, she got mad. "I did this before you arrived, so you can't get upset with me."

Mugs sat up and woofed.

"It's okay, boy, he's just being difficult."

He glared at her.

She sighed. "Okay. I also sent them to you. Did you get them?"

"No, I didn't. However, I have a lot of messages here. Some of us work for a living, you know?"

"Some of us are trying to find a job so we can make a living, you know?" She grabbed her laptop and brought up the pictures of Robert and James that she had put side by side, in profile. "This is what I found. Do you see the resemblance in these?"

He leaned forward and studied the images. "You know something? You could be right." He glanced at her in surprise.

She beamed. "So I'm not such a foolish old lady after all."

"You're not old at all."

Pleased, she brushed past how he failed to say she wasn't foolish either and said, "What I need is a photo of the man who went missing decades ago. Something in profile that might show features to match these two men."

"There should be some in the archives," he said. "Send those to my email again. I'll check for myself."

She brought up her email program, typed in his email address and sent off the photos as an attachment. When she was done, she sat back. "Can you send me the other photo when you find it?" She added the last bit hurriedly.

He gave her that long stare. "Remember? It's official business."

She gave him a long stare right back. "Remember? I'm

not a suspect."

He chuckled.

"You have to admit I've been some help, haven't I?"

"Maybe. Or maybe you're taking up a lot of official resources, sending me off on a wild goose chase. Maybe you're a Photoshop magician and just made these photos look like this."

She stared at him in shock. "Why would I possibly do that?" She looked at the photos. "Can people do that?"

"Way too often people do that." He glanced at her. "You don't actually think those models on the magazine covers look like that, do you?"

She considered the question. "I never really gave that much thought. But I know my husband believed them to look just like that."

"Ouch. That would be a hard thing to live up to, because it's *not* something you *can* live up to. Those photos aren't real. All those images have been fixed to make the women look better."

She studied him. "But who determines what is *better*?"

He grinned. "Exactly the problem."

Chapter 29

LATER THAT NIGHT she struggled to fall asleep. Goliath was curled up at her side and Mugs at her feet. Thaddeus roosted happily at the end of her bed. She lay in bed and stared at the ceiling—the ceiling that hid where all the clothing had been kept in boxes. She couldn't ignore the idea that another man might be buried close by. Why else would all his belongings be stored in the attic?

The last thing she needed was to find yet another body. But she couldn't forget the notion. Plus she was learning she didn't like to wait. Especially for answers. And the fact that she was waiting on other people made it much worse. Why couldn't Mack hand over information to her?

"Because he doesn't have any yet, idiot."

She shook her head. She was tempted to go back to her chatty neighbor and ask more questions tomorrow. She sat up in bed and turned on her lamp, then reached for her laptop. She'd searched earlier, looking for a connection between the two men. It'd be easy enough for one to have had a different father with a different surname. But it still didn't answer what the potential connection was to the first man who had gone missing. And she hadn't found very much under his name anywhere.

Theoretically any one of them could have owned property on this cul-de-sac too. And maybe there were more relatives than just the two men. With that thought, she searched for the family of the first dead man found, James Farley, to see if he had any sisters or somebody still living.

She couldn't find anything, but when she searched for family members of the man who she had just found—Robert Delaney—he had an adopted sister, although their parents were both dead.

That was interesting too. But she needed more family information. Stuff that Mack hadn't shared with her.

Frustrated, she finally put everything away and lay down on her bed again. Wide awake.

Mugs was so laid-back that he lay there with his feet in the air, snoozing away. She'd love to sleep a deep sleep like that. But this bed was more conducive to wakefulness than sleepfulness.

Her phone rang just then. Startled, she reached for it and checked the caller ID, surprised to find it was Nan. She glanced at the clock. It was late. "Nan, are you all right?"

"Yes, dear. I just needed to hear your voice."

Doreen didn't know what to say about that. "Well, I'm glad you called. I'm just lying here, unable to go to sleep."

"Well, rumors are circulating here, something about you finding yet another body?"

Doreen winced. "Oh, dear, I was hoping you wouldn't hear about that."

"It's true?" Nan's voice rose in shock. "Doreen!"

"I didn't mean to," she said hurriedly. "After visiting you, I went a different way home, and I found a body in the creek."

"Whose body?" Nan asked suspiciously. "This really isn't helping your reputation in the town, you know, my dear?"

Doreen rolled her eyes. "Nan, I didn't do it on purpose." She could hear Nan's heavy sigh come through the phone.

"No, of course you didn't. I'm sorry, dear. Could you tell me what time it was you found the body?"

Doreen stared at her phone, nonplussed. "Nan, you want the exact time?"

"Yes. We had a pool on how long before the body was found. Some of the bets are really close. I need to know who the winner is."

Doreen rested her back against the headboard. "Nan, I thought you were teasing when you first told me that." Besides, she had been really gobbling up those marijuana cookies at the time too. "You didn't really have a betting pool on when somebody would find the body, did you? That's morbid."

"Well, we didn't know for sure he would be dead when he was found. And you found him, didn't you?"

"Yes." She frowned. "Nan, how do you know I found the missing handyman?"

"You just said so, dear."

Yes, just now. But Doreen cast her mind back on their conversations to remember if she had mentioned the handyman specifically earlier.

"Not that it matters, dear. Everyone is talking about it." Nan went gaily onto the next subject, completely unrelated. "How's Thaddeus?"

Doreen brushed her hair off her face, wondering just what kind of marijuana-induced haze Nan was in. "Thaddeus is fine, Nan." She stared at the bird perched at the end of the bed. "Why?"

"Well, he does have a good nose. So, if you had him with you, it's no surprise that you found our missing person." Her voice perked up as she added, "Oh, my goodness, it's actually a great thing. Maybe we can use you and Thaddeus and Mugs to hunt down lost people."

"No," Doreen cried out. "No, Nan. Stop. That's really not how I want people to look at me."

"Well, it's better than people thinking you murdered all these men."

Nan was nothing if not blunt.

"You could put yourself in my position and realize they might think *you* murdered all these men," Doreen said slowly. "Nan, I found the bodies. I didn't turn them into bodies."

Nan laughed. "Of course not, dear. I was just teasing. So back to when you found him again. Can you remember exactly what time it was?"

"I phoned the authorities. I probably have a record of the call, so hold on." Doreen looked back at her recent phone calls to when she had contacted Mack. When she came back on the phone, she said, "I think it was around 3:15."

"You *think*? You do understand that it's kind of important to know these things. People get quite irate if we don't have exact information."

"I *know* it was around 3:15," Doreen snapped. She couldn't believe Nan was doing this. "Nan, would you please stop betting on things like this? It's very upsetting."

"Well, we need something to do. Rosemoor's a small place where nothing much happens, and we have lots of time on our hands. We bet on lots of things. It just happened to be that Robert Delaney's disappearance was one somebody suggested. We didn't know he would end up dead, did we?" Nan paused for a moment and said, "Doreen, I hate to say it, but you sound awfully tired. You really should go to sleep. It's after eleven, my dear."

On that note she hung up, leaving Doreen to stare at her phone in surprise.

"And how am I supposed to sleep now?" she asked of the empty room. "Nan's setting up a betting pool as to when a dead person is to be found?" She shook her head. "Oh, I feel like I fell down the rabbit hole."

Thaddeus straightened a bit. "Body in a rabbit hole. Body in a rabbit hole."

She glared at the bird as Goliath rolled out and used his claws on her belly to get comfortable and Mugs kicked out at her feet to make more room. "No, there is no body in the rabbit hole."

He cocked his head at her and squawked, "Are you sure? Are you sure?"

She groaned, lying down in her bed, pulling the covers over her head. She just wanted this to be all over.

Chapter 30

Day 5, Sunday

WHEN SHE WOKE the next morning, she was surprisingly rested and in a relaxed state of mind. She sat up and stretched. Mugs wasn't on the bed—he was lying in the open doorway to her bedroom, stretched out on his back with his feet in the air again.

She smiled. "Mugs, are you still alive?"

He rolled over, his tongue flopping with his movement. But he didn't bark. There was no sign of Goliath or Thaddeus.

She hopped out of bed and headed to the shower. When she dried off and dressed for the day, she went downstairs to start her coffee and to feed her furry and feathered family. Waiting for the pot to finish dripping, she sat at the kitchen table and opened her laptop to check her email. She found an email from Mack, which made her brighten. When she clicked on it, she read, *No news yet. Still working.*

Her shoulders slumped. She had been so sure some good news would appear somewhere along the line. At least he had responded. It was always worse waiting.

With her first cup of coffee and her animals in tow, she

stepped onto the back veranda and surveyed the massive garden. Now that the dead body was gone, she really needed to get something done out here. With all the chaos going on, Mack had postponed any work in his mother's garden. But there was no reason Doreen couldn't get started on Nan's garden.

She walked through the backyard while Thaddeus strutted behind her, thankfully silent. Mugs was rolling in something. Too late to stop him now. With a groan, Doreen expected that he'd probably need a bath afterward. Surprisingly Goliath was acting well behaved and calm.

The weeds were *heavily* overgrown here in the backyard. Doreen shook her head. Even the *planned* additions to the garden had gone awry. Irises had grown into massive clumps, and other bulbs were mixed in with each other. The hyacinths were done, and the tulips were almost done. There could be bulbs planted all throughout the place. Nan had been nothing if not passionate about bulbs. Doreen would have to sit down, draw out her plan for the garden, so she could relocate a lot of these bulbs. That way, they'd have more room to grow.

A whole bed designated for the bulbs would be nice, especially if she could coordinate the colors, putting in summer-blooming shrubs for when the bulbs were done. As she looked at the yard, she realized there'd once been grass in the middle. It needed either new sod or some topsoil and seed.

As she walked along, she thought maybe just an application of nitrogen would help it. Most of the garden could be salvaged, but it would take a massive amount of labor. *Her* labor.

With her now empty coffee cup in her hand, she walked

around to the front yard, drawing the animals with her. A few hours a day would bring this garden back into shape. Nan had poured her love into the small front garden, and it showed.

Out of the corner of her eye, she thought she saw a woman at the side of her house. Wondering if it could be that nosy Ella, Doreen headed that way, where mostly moss and ferns grew in the shade. She didn't see anybody there but found the ground was spongy. Soft. She wondered if there was a water leak in the area. It seemed really damp. But then she spied the neighbors' hose, dripping steadily in a stream toward her place.

That explained that. She tossed the end of the hose back on the neighbors' lawn and then returned to her backyard for one last look—finding no sign of Ella—and Doreen decided that she'd get started on her gardens today. She went inside, made some toast, and ate it as she formulated a plan for her morning.

She went upstairs to put on her work jeans—the comfy and durable ones from Nan's closet that looked like capri pants on her since she was a good five inches taller than Nan. Afterward she grabbed a pair of Nan's garden gloves off the back veranda. With what tools she could find, she headed out to the front garden. Less work to be done here. Then she'd work in the back garden a little bit too.

She happily got down on her knees in the dirt and grass and quickly pulled up the weeds out front, waving at several of the neighbors who appeared outside for no other purpose than to see what she was doing. To Mugs she said, "They're probably looking to see if I find another body."

Mugs barked, then gave her an open-mouthed tongue-licking grin.

She glared at him. "That wasn't meant to be funny."

With Thaddeus settled on the front porch railing and Goliath asleep on one of the porch steps, Doreen spent the next couple hours pulling weeds, trimming shrubs and generally getting a handle on Nan's front garden. Doreen glanced up to see her chatty neighbor walking toward her. Ella had a smile on her face. Doreen settled back on her heels and smiled. "Good morning, Ella."

Ella's smile widened. "Good morning. I see you're cleaning up Nan's garden."

Doreen wanted to make a snide comment about that being obvious but held back. She was just hot and cranky. Then Mugs growled low in the back of his throat. "Hush, it's fine, Mugs." He sat down beside her but didn't relax. He really was taking to the guard dog role. Even Thaddeus flew onto a rock at Mugs side. And as if to not be outdone, Goliath stretched out on the grass, his tail twitching in short sharp snaps.

As the neighbor woman approached, Ella said, "I heard you found another dead body."

Something was off in her tone. Doreen studied her and gave a small nod. "I did, indeed. But don't make it sound like I do this as a habit. I'd be happy to never find another one ever."

Immediately Ella made a sympathetic face. And yet, again, something was off.

Doreen lowered her head, spotted some lady's mantle and gave it a yank. The herb was helpful in some cases but had a tendency to take over if given half a chance.

"Some people are just unlucky," Ella said cheerfully.

"Yes, like these two men apparently." Doreen studied Ella's face. "Maybe you knew him?" She watched carefully as she mentioned Robert Delaney's name. And caught a flicker in that steady gaze of Ella's.

Ella made a mock shudder and shook her head. "No. Thankfully I didn't."

Doreen nodded but didn't believe Ella's carefully schooled expression. "He worked at the retirement home," Doreen said. "Actually he worked several places as a bit of a handyman. I've been looking into his life and finding out all kinds of things." She shouldn't say things like that, but she couldn't help it. Something about this woman made her want to prick that complacent expression on Ella's face.

"Oh, dear. I'm sorry to hear that. It couldn't be pleasant to have been the one to find him." She gave another physical shudder. "I won't take that path again."

Doreen looked at the garden again, her mind caught on the fact that Ella knew where the man had been found. "Do you go down there often? Maybe you saw something that would be helpful to the police."

"Oh, I couldn't talk to the police," Ella cried out in horror. "That's just too unnerving."

"I talk to them all the time." Doreen studied Ella's face for a moment. "I didn't tell you that he was found in the creek."

Ella stopped and stared. "Didn't you? Well, somebody did. It's all over town." Ella stepped backward, her nervous gaze zipping from Doreen to the garden and back. "That's another reason I couldn't possibly talk to the police. I'm always spitting out the wrong information because I don't hear quite as well as I used to." She apologized, backing up several more steps.

Doreen watched as Ella retreated again. "Who were you talking to about it?"

Ella stopped—something about her gaze hardened. She snapped, "I'm sure I don't remember. People like to gossip. Nobody can resist a chance to spread the news." And she stormed off.

"I just bet they do," Doreen said to the animals that all watched the woman rush away. She pulled out her phone and dialed Mack's number, watching as Ella reached her house.

"Yes, Doreen," he said cautiously.

She frowned into the phone. "Is that any way to talk to me? I am trying to help, you know?"

After a short silence, he exploded, "What have you done now?"

She gasped. "That's so unfair. I didn't do anything."

"Then why are you calling?"

"I just spoke with Ella, my chatty neighbor. She already knew that the body was found in the creek by my house. How does everybody know so fast?"

"One of the greatest mysteries of life is how fast gossip travels," he said drily. "Remember how you were behind other houses? Somebody may have seen you."

"She didn't tell me who she heard it from."

Mack's end of the phone went silent.

She pressed further. "She's acting really nervous. I think she knows a whole lot more than she's telling." Doreen sat back on her haunches as something occurred to her. "And something's familiar about her face. Maybe she's related to the two men."

"Now hold on a minute," Mack protested. "We don't even know if the men are related yet."

"Well, get on it," she moaned. "Her name would be different because she is married. She could be the sister. I'm working in the front garden right now, so why don't you come by in a couple hours? You can go over and talk to her then."

"I'm running an investigation here. Stop interfering," he retorted.

"Fine." She smiled. "I'll see if she does anything suspicious."

"No," he said, alarm in his voice. "Leave her alone. I don't want her to get any more suspicious, just in case she is involved. Back away until I can talk to her. I need you to butt out of my case and stay out." When she didn't respond, he added, "We are trained to deal with murderers. You are not."

She didn't like it, but it made sense. "Okay, fine."

"I mean it."

"I heard you," she said in exasperation. She ended the call and finished weeding the flower bed. Yet, her mind was consumed. Now she wanted to research this lovely chatty neighbor of hers and see what she had been up to. Because Doreen was sure Ella was up to something. Now to figure out what.

Unable to leave it another second, she hurried inside, the animals excited at the change of pace. After washing her hands, she put on a cup of tea, sat down at the table and turned on her laptop, grabbing her notepad of information on the case so far. Thank God, she had had the foresight to make notes of all her conversations with the neighbors. She typed in her chatty neighbor's name—Ella Goldman, per Brenda—and brought up as much of her history as she could locate on Google.

What did people do to get information in the old days?

Instantly pages popped up. "There she is," Doreen said

aloud.

Sipping her tea, Doreen read through the various articles. The first revealed when Ella got married, another one when her mother had died. Somewhere in the obscure paragraphs of still another article about some charity work Ella had done was a mention that she was adopted.

Doreen sat back and studied that for a long moment. *Adopted.* She went back to the article and read it again. It didn't say by who or when. Doreen knew those distinctions mattered because she herself had been adopted by her mother's second husband.

He'd been a good man with strong beliefs about right and wrong.

There was no way for Doreen to determine the circumstances surrounding Ella's knowledge of the latest dead man. Maybe it was just a fluke. Or maybe Ella was a liar.

Looking through various articles, Doreen learned Ella had lived in Kelowna all her life. Another said she'd been married twice. Her first husband had died from a heart attack a few years after they were married. To Doreen, that alone was suspicious. Of course, she was *looking* for reasons to be suspicious. "A heart attack? How old a man was he?" It had been her first husband after all. He could have been too young to have a heart attack.

Ella had ended up with the house, vehicles and whatever money her first husband had left behind, as was normal in most marriages. She'd done very well for herself in the end. That in itself didn't mean she'd done something to him. It could mean that she just had some compensation to help her deal with the loss.

Mugs barked. Doreen stood, grabbed her tea and walked to the front room. Someone was at the front door, but no one had knocked. Doreen walked over to the living room window in time to see her neighbor Ella walk across her front yard.

Was her neighbor going for a walk? Why would she be at the front door and not knock? Doreen wasn't sure *what* was wrong, but things felt all kinds of wrong.

Hidden behind the curtains, she watched what her neighbor would do. Ella was up to something, most likely seeing if Doreen was home. They had just spoken to each other earlier this morning. And Doreen's car remained out front. Why wouldn't Doreen be home? On a hunch she waited and watched as her neighbor walked up Doreen's driveway and around the side of her house. Ella's hands were empty, and she was smiling. What was Ella up to?

Doreen picked up her phone and called Mack.

"Now what?" he said in exasperation.

"It's the same neighbor. She's back in my yard, walking about, acting weird. I think she's trying to figure out if I'm home, which of course, I am since my car is here."

Silence followed on the other end.

He was still there from the staticky sounds, like she was losing the connection. "I'm not making this up."

Resigned, he said, "No, it's too crazy for you to have made it up."

Just then she heard the doorknob on the front door turn. "Somebody's trying to open the front door," she whispered.

"What?" he asked in alarm. "Are you sure?"

"Yes, I'm sure. I have to go." She ended the call, pocketed it and watched as Mugs, barking, ran toward the front door. Using his commotion to distract the woman, Doreen headed up the stairs to the first landing on the staircase. From there she waited, listening to find out what the woman would do.

Ella entered Doreen's house. "Nice dog. Aren't you a nice dog?"

Mugs wasn't having anything to do with Ella. He barked and barked and barked.

There was no sign of Goliath. But that was fairly typical. If there was work to be done, Goliath was gone.

Thaddeus, on the other hand, screeched.

The woman cried out. "Oh, my God! She has a zoo in here."

The woman raced throughout the living room, and Doreen could hear sounds of drawers opening. The only thing in the living room with a drawer was the coffee table. What was Ella searching for? Doreen's laptop and handwritten notes were on the kitchen table. She wondered if she should grab them. If Ella opened the laptop, she would see what Doreen had been looking at—Ella's history. And that wasn't anything Doreen wanted her chatty and possibly insane neighbor to know about.

However, while the woman was in the living room, Doreen could sneak into the kitchen. Taking a chance, she quietly took the stairs, thankful she was barefoot. In the kitchen, she snagged her laptop, turned. And stopped.

Her neighbor faced her with a feral smile, raising her hand.

Doreen's jaw dropped. "Is that a gun?" Her gaze locked on the barrel pointed in her direction.

"Oh, my God!" Ella yelled. "Are you that stupid? You really are the typical dumb blonde, aren't you? Of course it's a gun."

Doreen raised her gaze, seeing the anger and determination in the woman's eyes. "Why do you have a gun? And why are you pointing it at me? What are you doing in my kitchen? That's breaking and entering."

"No, it isn't. The door wasn't locked," she said. "Idiot. This may be entering illegally, but I didn't break in."

Doreen stared at her, stood stock-still, her mind racing to pull the pieces together. And then it clicked. "You shot the man in my garden."

"I didn't shoot anyone," the woman snapped.

But Ella wasn't anywhere near as convincing now as she had been earlier. Doreen shook her head. "What did he ever do to you? That man was harmless."

"He was my brother. He was also an asshole."

"Oh, my God! You killed your own brother?" Doreen gasped. "He was family."

Ella glared at her. "No, I didn't kill him. My brother did."

"What?" Doreen was too shocked to make sense of that. "So how did he end up in Nan's garden?"

"I told him to get rid of the body. But he's an idiot and buried it on your property."

Doreen felt shaky. Her legs had turned to rubber. "Why did he kill him?" she asked in a faint voice. This was too bizarre.

"It was an accident. They had a fight over a woman they both wanted. Robert punched James hard in the nose, and it killed him. Shoved his nose right into his brain. Robert came to me afterward for help, and we worked out what to do. But, instead of burying him out in the woods, like I suggested, he said he knew a place that had been recently turned over."

"Of course… He's a handyman. It wasn't by chance that he asked Nan if she wanted him to do some gardening work in the backyard. Put in a small extension to the deck so she could walk down easier. It's been a huge mess, and he knew it was bothering her."

Ella nodded. "She told him that she wouldn't bother as you'd be coming soon, and you'd take care of it. He'd seen her digging a few months ago though and figured it would be the easiest place to hide the body, but he was an idiot. You have to bury a body way deeper than that."

"Six feet," Doreen said. "Six feet to stop the dogs from smelling it."

"Well, my brother was lazy. He's always been lazy." Ella shook her head. "Now I have to do everything myself to fix this."

Doreen looked at her. "Well, you didn't bury your brother six feet deep either. How can you blame Robert for being lazy when you did the same thing? Hell, you didn't even bury him. You left him to rot in the creek." She paused and fixed Ella with a direct question. "You did kill him, right?"

The woman waved her gun hand, brushing away the question, as if taking a life was just that simple. "It doesn't matter. What matters right now is that I need your notes, and I need to know who you may have said something to."

"Why would you want my notes?"

The woman shot her a look. "Oh, for the love of God. Are you really that stupid?"

Doreen bristled. "Are you really that crazy to keep insulting me? I put up with that crap from my husband for a long time," she snapped. "I don't have to take it from you too."

"I can't imagine why he stayed married to you." She snorted, waving her gun around. "Then I read about the divorce online. Saw pictures of him and his new much younger girlfriend. You should have realized what was happening. Once you hit forty, you're automatically replaced."

Doreen glared at her. "I'm not forty."

The woman smirked. "Okay, so in your case, thirty-five, and he was done early. How is that any better?"

"This is a ridiculous conversation. You can't shoot me. How would you explain my death? And, if the same gun was used to shoot your brother, the police will connect all the murders," she said, hoping to keep Ella talking long enough to give Mack time to get here.

"Of course it won't be related. I'll shoot you in such a way that it looks like you shot yourself." Ella's gaze turned crafty. "Overwhelmed with guilt for having shot my brother."

Doreen's jaw dropped. "I didn't kill your brother."

Ella rolled her eyes. "No, but the cops don't know that. See? They'll get all the evidence together, proving that you shot him, and then you came home and shot yourself. After all, you're depressed and despondent about losing your lifestyle and your husband."

Glumly Doreen wondered if that would work. Surely Mack would see she had no motivation for these killings. Would Mack fight for her cause? Would he understand she wasn't that stupid and how he had been tipped off that Doreen was suspicious of Ella first? Or would he not care, as it would nicely close several cases for him?

Hopefully he was already on his way here right now.

Suddenly she remembered the insurance office. "Was that you making a mess at James Farley's insurance office too?"

"No, that was my stupid brother. Tried to make it look like a robbery and kidnapping or some such thing."

Mugs sniffed around the woman's legs. Thaddeus was in the corner of the kitchen. Doreen could see him walking back and forth in obvious distress, his head bobbing up and down, his wings flapping as he looked around. Somewhere in the mix was Goliath. What Doreen really needed was a sneak attack from Mugs or Goliath or Thaddeus or all three. Something to distract this woman so Doreen could grab the gun.

She looked down at Mugs and said in a determined voice, "Attack, Mugs."

Mugs jumped toward Doreen, barking.

"Not me, Mugs, her."

Ella chuckled. "You're such a mess. Your dog doesn't know what that means."

But a streak of orange flew into the kitchen as Goliath raced forward, dodging between Ella's legs. Ella shrieked, stumbling a bit, and grabbed the doorjamb to stop herself from falling.

Mugs turned, barking at Goliath, chasing him back out of the room again. Both of them bumped into Ella as she tried to right herself and to also get out of the way of the animals.

It gave Doreen her chance. She stepped forward and kicked the crazy woman's legs out from under her. As she went down, Doreen knocked the gun out of Ella's hand and smacked her hard across the face with her closed fist. It wasn't really a punch, but considering she still had rings on her fingers, it would do major damage to the woman's cheek, and that wasn't all bad in this particular situation.

With Ella down on the hallway floor just outside the

kitchen, Doreen sat on her. She looked around for something to hold her here but found nothing to use.

Ella arched her back and tried to dislodge Doreen. When that didn't work, Ella scratched Doreen's arms and screamed, "Get off me."

Meanwhile Mugs barked like crazy, Goliath howled and Thaddeus flew about the kitchen.

Doreen shook her head and grabbed one of the great big books sitting in a stack on the floor off to the side—another of Nan's perpetual collection of useless things, *until now*— and smacked Ella over the head with it. It shouldn't have been a hard blow, but her eyeballs rolled into the back of her head, and she collapsed, unconscious.

Just then both the front and back doors burst open, and cops streamed toward her. She held up her hands and pointed at the floor where Ella's gun had landed. Mack picked up the gun and asked, "What just happened?"

Slowly, as the cops holstered their guns, Doreen stood. "The man in the creek was her brother. She shot him, as far as I can tell, because he didn't bury their other brother deep enough in Nan's garden." The cops looked at her, then at the woman unconscious on the floor and back at Doreen. "If you can believe anything Ella says, Robert Delaney accidentally killed James Farley. Then Ella killed Robert Delaney because he messed up the burying part of James's body." Doreen smirked. "Talk about family love."

Mack shook his head. "Can't you stay out of trouble for five minutes?"

She glared at him. "I'd be happy to."

"So there is no connection with these recent murders to the things found upstairs?" Mack asked, frowning.

"I didn't really get a chance to ask her about the rest, but

I think these three siblings were Jeremy Feldspar's children."

"You think they killed him?" Mack asked, raising his eyebrows.

One of the policemen had Ella's arms behind her back, cuffing them together. She opened her eyes while still on the floor. "No, our mother did."

Doreen crouched beside her. "Why?"

"Because he was having an affair with Nan. Mother and Father had had a fight. When Father came to stay at Nan's house, Mother came over and killed him while he was sleeping."

"And where is the body?"

Ella just stared at her.

Doreen looked at the back garden, particularly the vibrant long patch of azaleas. "Never mind. I think I know where he is."

Tears came to Ella's eyes. "I've lived with that for so long. And everything we've done since then just seemed to make it worse. All we could do to protect Mother was hide the body. So when Robert buried James here, probably to be close to our father, I knew that the earlier murder would come out. I was so mad at him. At his stupidity. I couldn't let that happen."

"You didn't have to shoot me," Doreen protested. "I didn't have anything to do with this mess."

"I was so frustrated about everything going wrong that I didn't know what else to do. You seemed to be everywhere all the time. Digging into stuff that you shouldn't be into. Then you found my brothers' bodies. James's first and Robert's shortly afterward. I figured, if I could make it look like you killed Robert, you'd be the prime suspect for James's death."

Doreen said, "So you hid all your father's clothing in the attic here? Was that to point fingers at Nan? Did she even know about that?"

Ella shrugged. "I've no idea. I don't know what she thought when he left her house and never returned."

Doreen shook her head. "For all I know, Nan had no interactions with Jeremy Feldspar. He may have even been in her house without Nan's knowledge or permission."

"Mother was sure they were having an affair. She found him sleeping here."

"*Here*, yes. But in the spare bedroom."

Ella's gaze widened. She stared at Doreen in horror.

Doreen nodded. "He was probably just taking time away from your mother while going through a tough spot in their relationship. For years, when Nan was younger, she came and went on a regular basis, traveling a lot around the world. He probably knew she wasn't home most of the time. Maybe he was even looking after the place for her. I do know that he was in the spare room. He wasn't in Nan's bedroom."

At that Ella burst into tears.

Doreen stood and walked to the kitchen table and collapsed in a chair. She stared at her now cold tea. "All this death for nothing."

One of the cops beside her said, "So often we find that is the case."

She turned back to Ella. "How did your mother kill him?"

Ella was still sobbing as the men hauled her to her feet. "She poisoned him. She came over here, supposedly to tell him that they could work things out, and she put arsenic in his tea."

"And his mother? Your grandmother? Did your father

kill her?"

That sent Ella's sobs to a louder pitch. Finally she sniffled back the tears enough to answer. "That's why Mother chose arsenic. He'd killed his own mother that way." Her sobbing resumed.

Doreen watched from the front porch as the police led Ella to the waiting cop car.

At her side, Mack said, "That's what we found in the safe-deposit box at the bank. A signed confession from Jeremy. He said he'd hated her all those years ago for the way she'd treated his father. He'd idealized the man and his mother ran around on him constantly. He'd watched his father take it for as long as he could then he took his own life. Jeremy then took her life. He'd written the confession and saved it all these years. Maybe to clear his conscience or maybe waiting for a time for his conscious to bug him enough to give it to someone. But we found it, and now we can close four cases at the same time."

The satisfaction in his voice made her laugh. "See? I wasn't such a hindrance after all." Doreen pointed at the look on his face. "Maybe it's time for a good cup of coffee."

"Maybe you would prefer tea?" Mack asked with a wicked grin.

Doreen shuddered. "Maybe never again. Jeremy's tea was poisoned, and his wife buries him in the azaleas and tosses the empty arsenic bottle in there with him."

Mack laughed. "Murder is often a simple affair."

"Arsenic in the azaleas." She shook her head. "What a way for the story to end."

Epilogue

In the Mission, Kelowna, BC
Thursday, Not Quite One Week Later …

DOREEN MONTGOMERY STOOD in the open doorway to her kitchen. *Her kitchen.* There was just something about settling into this house finally, with the chaos under control and something like normality entering her life … Well, as long as "normality" could include her three very unique and personable pets. It was weird, but the phrase, *settling into this house,* to her, meant having a cup of coffee or tea whenever she wanted it, going to bed when she was ready, and sitting in the garden because she wanted to. And, boy, did she want all that. Even better, somedays she could take a step out her front door without being accosted by somebody wanting more details on the recently solved murders.

Somehow she'd become a celebrity in the small town of Kelowna. But she really didn't want that role. At least it took the townsfolk's focus off her status as a penniless thirty-five-year-old *almost* divorcée, living in her grandmother's home.

Yet Doreen was determined to handle her new life, sans chefs and gardeners and maids and chauffeurs. Doreen could handle most of that herself, except for one thing. Doreen couldn't cook. Which was why she had to face down this most terrifying thing of all things in her kitchen. She strode forward to fill Nan's teakettle and placed it on *the stove*—the appliance she had a hate-hate relationship with. She turned the dial to light the gas, but, of course, there was no blue flame. However, immediately she could smell gas wafting toward her nose.

She snapped off the dial and glared. "You're not a stove. You're a diabolical demon. I don't understand how you work, what makes you work, and why the hell anybody would want something like you in the house," she announced to anyone nearby. The only ones listening were Mugs, her pedigreed basset hound—content to lay on the floor out of the way—and Thaddeus, Nan's huge beautiful blue-gray parrot with long red tail feathers, currently walking on the kitchen table, hoping for food scraps. "I've already fed you this morning, Thaddeus." Doreen shook her head. She should have never let him eat there. Now she'd never be able to keep him off her breakfast table.

Goliath took that moment of calm to appear, racing around the kitchen, through Doreen's legs, and out again into the living room area.

"Goliath!" Doreen yelled, righting herself. "Stop doing that, or you'll end up hurting me and you too." Goliath was the gigantic golden Maine coon cat—the size of a bobcat— that came with the house. Goliath, being Goliath, was disruptive, picking any inopportune moment he could possibly find, yet sleeping the rest of the time. Initially Doreen had considered Goliath's races through the house were in pursuit of a mouse—heaven forbid—but Doreen had never seen one or any evidence of one inside. She decided this was Goliath's "normal" behavior.

Sighing, Doreen glared again at her stove. *Is it too much to ask for hot water for my tea?* Other people managed to produce incredible meals by using one of these things.

And then there was Doreen.

Her stove was a black gas-powered devil. Yet she was determined to not let it get the better of her. Again she reached forward to turn on the gas and then froze. She couldn't do it. What if something was wrong with the gas line? What if something really was broken? At least that gave her an excuse to stop her half-assed attempts at cooking. She grinned at that thought.

Feeling like it was a cop-out but grateful nonetheless, she picked up the electric teakettle she'd found in the back of Nan's pantry when Doreen had first arrived, filled it with water, and plugged it in. Then she pushed the button on its side and waited for the water to heat up. *That's the best way to make tea anyway.* She comforted herself with that thought as her gaze returned to the stove. "Damn thing."

Right behind her popped up a voice. "Damn thing. Damn thing."

Talking parrots should require an owner's manual—and circumspect owners. She turned and shook her finger at Thaddeus. "Don't you repeat that."

"Damn thing. Damn thing. Damn thing."

She stared at the African Grey parrot with her hands on her hips, worried that now Thaddeus would swear at the most awkward moments. Like with every other terrible thing he'd learned to say since she'd arrived.

Another *first.* Doreen was free to swear now. Free to say anything she wanted. Throwing off the shackles of her marriage had also freed her tongue. Maybe not such a good thing. She did have an image to uphold. She wasn't exactly sure what that image was yet, but it was here somewhere, and she was supposed to uphold it. Nan's image had been tarnished for a little bit with the recent murder cases. But Doreen had cleared Nan's name, and that was what counted.

Such a sense of peace flowed through Doreen now, as if she'd somehow successfully passed a major test, probably one of many as she made this major life transition.

Mugs waddled over and rubbed against her thigh, giving a bark.

"I haven't forgotten you, you silly boy." Doreen bent to give him a quick ear rub. When he barked again, now sitting at her feet, giving her that woeful look, she reminded him, "I've already fed you too."

As the teakettle bubbled beside her, she opened the kitchen's back door and stepped onto the long flowing veranda along the rear of the house. The dark slash beside the second set of veranda steps at the far end, where one of the bodies had been dug out, was still a raw insult to the garden that should have been here. And, of course, the rest of the garden was even worse. She wanted to wander and plan and design how and what she could do with this space, but, since she had no money, it was hard to imagine any workable options at this time. At least she had no pressure to do all of it now.

That brought back memories—when she had been only a decoration on a rich man's arm—how she'd directed gardeners to do what she wanted, regardless of the cost. As she stared at her massive backyard space, nonstop ideas filtered in. She smiled with delight, then walked back inside, grabbed her pad of paper and a pencil, and was about to step outside again when she realized the teakettle was still on.

That had never bothered her before, but now she

couldn't leave the house while any appliance was running. The thought of having this house—her home—burn to the ground was too unnerving. She'd only recently settled into having something of *her* own and couldn't bear to lose it.

Making tea for herself over the past couple days had been an eye-opening experience. She used to get fancy lattes with beautiful patterns on the top without realizing they came from a five-thousand-dollar machine and a skilled barista. What she could do with five thousand dollars right now. ... She cringed every time she thought about the seemingly insignificant cost of one of those fancy lattes that she'd consumed on a daily basis when married. A humble cup of home-brewed tea was a simple pleasure now, those fancy coffees an indulgence. Something she could no longer afford.

She waited until the teakettle fully boiled, then dropped a tea bag into a large chipped mug Nan had left behind and poured the boiling water atop it. Checking the fridge, she was relieved to find a little bit of milk left inside an open carton.

She opened the top, took a whiff, and grinned. It was still sweet. She poured a splash into her tea, put the carton back into the fridge, picked up her cup, and said to Mugs, "Are you ready to go outside?"

Mugs barked joyfully at the trigger word.

The door was already open, but she propped it to stay that way with one of the chairs off the veranda. Mugs ran forward, his great big saggy facial jowls wobbling and shaking with every step. Thaddeus flew overhead—although how the bird could fly, Doreen didn't know. When she had first arrived, he didn't fly much. Now he did a half-soaring and half–free fall to the ground. But he did it very elegantly.

Or at least it would be elegant if the words pouring out of his mouth weren't "Damn thing. Damn thing."

Why did he have to repeat himself? She had heard him the first time ... unfortunately.

Goliath raced past again, his tail in the air.

Apparently this was a family outing.

She chuckled. It was a beautiful day, and everything felt ... right.

She wandered the far back area of the property, her entourage in tow. The paperwork still had to be processed to legally transfer the house, compliments of her grandmother, into Doreen's name. Nan had chosen to move into a nearby seniors' home and had left her house to Doreen. She'd been absolutely stunned and heartened by Nan's generosity at a time when Doreen had been desperately in need of a place to call home and a pillow to lay her head on at night.

Thaddeus flew down and landed on her shoulder. Doreen stroked the beautiful bird's head. "Good bird." But Thaddeus didn't repeat that. *Figures.*

Now she wandered the backyard, taking delight in the garden, knowing it was hers forever. Even though overwhelmed with weeds, the garden held so much potential. Seeing several small trees in the mix, Doreen walked closer and gasped. "Fruit trees," she cried out in joy. Bending down to avoid the unruly branches, she studied the leaves and identified an Italian plum, maybe an apricot too, and one she wasn't sure of—possibly a cherry tree.

Fruit trees were a delightful addition to her garden. This place could shine with a little effort—everything outside came alive in her mind as she contemplated the improvements she could make.

Doreen heard muffled grunts and stopped to see what

Mugs was digging up. Thankfully it was just dirt this time.

Gardening was Doreen's one and only talent. But designing a garden that *somebody else* would implement was a whole different story than making it happen by her own elbow grease. She didn't know the last time she'd held a shovel in her hand. She wasn't at all sure how much physical strength would be required to clean up this backyard. Plus she'd signed on to do some gardening for Mack's mother, hopefully for some much-needed money. Just the reminder of the local detective who'd helped her navigate the nightmare of finding several bodies in her garden last week made her chuckle.

He was a very interesting man ...

And likely thought she was nuts. Then it had been a crazy week, her first week living in one of the oldest neighborhoods in Kelowna Mission, so she could hardly blame him.

Mack had helped her through this trying time. He had been a godsend when the bodies had showed up at her place. Not that the dead bodies were her fault by any means, but somehow she happened to trip over them. Or maybe she should blame Goliath. Or Mugs. They had both helped ... or hindered. Then there was Thaddeus ...

She frowned as she watched her brood, especially the dog sniffing deep into the brush. "Mugs, don't you dare find any more bodies," she warned. "We've had more than enough corpses in our world."

Mugs gave a heavy *woof* and continued to waddle forward, the grass splitting wide to let his girth through. She grinned. He had been with her for five years already. She had inherited both Goliath and Thaddeus from Nan, as part and parcel with her house. Goliath had an attitude. He came and went on his own and still demanded that she look after him when he did show up. Kind of like her soon-to-be ex-husband. Only Goliath had had his tomcat ways fixed, and her almost ex-husband had not.

She chuckled at that. "That's what we should have done. We should have had him fixed. Then he wouldn't have brought home another arm ornament and booted me out."

Regardless, she was better off without him. Now all she had to do was figure out how to make money. At least enough to keep the electricity on in the house and food in the fridge. It was proving to be a bigger challenge than she'd realized.

But that wasn't today's problem. She walked over to the dilapidated fence, built out of several different materials, each of them finding their own unique way of partially crumbling to the ground. It might keep out some people, but it sure as hell wouldn't keep out anybody who didn't want to stay out.

She wished she could afford brand-new fencing all the way around the property because that would be the place to start. Structural work first, then do the prettier stuff. In this case, she wasn't sure how to do the structural stuff, especially on a shoestring budget.

She walked to the rickety, now-broken gate—Mugs behind her, Thaddeus still on her shoulder, Goliath off somewhere—unlooped the wire from the post, and pulled it open. She stepped outside to the path and the pretty creek that ran behind her property. She didn't want the fence along here at all. Most of it was past saving anyway.

About 140 feet of the creek's footage area was a beautiful sight to see from her backyard, much more so than a dilapidated fence. She looked closer at the creek, not sure to call it a creek or a river. Right now it was more of a babbling brook. But she imagined, later this spring, it could get a little bit uglier. Still, the creek's bank had a decent slope, so flooding shouldn't be much of a problem. She spotted a place where she could set up a little flagstone patio to sit and to enjoy the water.

Thaddeus flew from her shoulder to land near the water, strutting around, looking hopefully for fish and bugs.

No defined pathway was on this side of the creek, and everybody else's property was fenced off from the creek too. She thought that was such a shame. The creek offered a beautiful, peaceful view.

She walked back to her rearmost fence, put her pad of paper and teacup down on a rock, then grasped a fence post and shook it to see how strong it was. Instantly the fence made a low groaning sound and bent over sideways. She jumped back, crying out, "Oh, no."

But whatever she'd done had been too much for the old wood. Several of the fence panels toppled to the side, creating a bigger mess than she'd intended. Mugs came closer, but she shooed him away. "No, Mugs. Stay back. You could hurt yourself on a nail."

As she retreated into her backyard, coaxing Mugs with her, and stared toward the babbling brook, she laughed. "It might not be the way I had planned to do this, Mugs, but the end result is beautiful. It really opened up the view." She took Mugs's silence to be acquiescence.

Some really nice overhanging willows were on the far side of the brook, and her property had other trees dotted along the remains of her back fence. She had a small bridge just at the other end of the property that she could access. In fact, it was a beautiful scene.

Enthused by what she'd accidentally started, she returned to the remainder of her fence and gave it a shake.

And, sure enough, three-quarters of the rest of the creekside fence fell to the ground, almost grateful to give up the effort to stand any longer.

With a big smile, she walked to the last piece of this section, all wire fencing with iron rods deep into the ground. She pushed and pulled on the first iron rod, hoping it would be loose too. The first one was, but the second one wasn't. She managed to lift up one and watched as most of the wire fencing fell into a big snarly mess around the next pole still standing. What she really needed was a handyman to finish pulling out the fence and to haul it off, but she didn't have one. That brought back unwanted memories of last week's events. The only handyman she had known of in town had been murdered.

With a shake of her head, she returned to the problem at hand. She wasn't sure how much yard debris she could transport in her small Honda. A truck would be helpful to make a trip to the dump. She wondered what it would take to get somebody big and strong to come give her a hand.

On that thought, Mack came to mind. Again. The detective was well over six foot—his shoulders were almost as broad as he was tall. He was a big mountain of a man. But, so far, he'd been very gentle and kind to her. Although she exasperated him more than anything.

But all for the right reasons ...

UNFORTUNATELY DOREEN WASN'T sure Mack believed that though. Nor had he believed her at first about the dead bodies. It took closing an old cold case and several more current cases before he did. So, all in all, Mack should be thanking her. Maybe he should even be paying her for her assistance. She brightened for a moment, contemplating the idea of a fat check coming from the local Royal Canadian Mounted Police and then shook her head.

"Not going to happen."

She shrugged. It was her current reality. And, for whatever it was worth, she was a whole lot happier now than when she had been a plastic Barbie who never worried about money.

She stared at the scratch on her palm, blood already welling up. She should have worn gardening gloves. No point looking at her damaged nails. Besides, she couldn't see them for the dirt.

"Doreen?"

She spun around and yelled, "I'm in the back!" She turned toward the felled wire fence and sighed. This would make a mess of her hands. And possibly her back. She headed to her teacup, scooped it off the rock, and took a sip. When she heard footsteps, she pivoted to see Mack walking toward her, holding Goliath while scratching his furry head, and talking to Mugs who had run to greet him. She set down her cup and beamed. There was just something about Mack …

Mack grinned, setting the cat free on the grass, giving Mugs a smile and a quick ear rub. "Leave you alone for a week and look at you. You're ripping apart the place."

She laughed. "Well, someone had to," she said with a smile.

Thaddeus decided to join them now, landing inside the backyard.

"Hey, boy," Mack said, waiting for the bird to walk to him for a quick pat on the head.

All three animals clustered nearby to watch the big man.

"What brings you by?" Doreen asked.

He pointed to the front of the house. "Is that crowd bothering you?"

She shrugged. "The notoriety is definitely different. Can't say I'm accustomed to it. However, the stress is easing slightly."

"Well, you are accustomed to notoriety, just not necessarily at this level."

She winced at the reminder of her wealthy now-estranged husband and the number of times she'd been photographed as his partner at one do or another. She nodded. "Point to you. Doesn't necessarily mean I like the sensationalism though."

He motioned to the fence. "Did you mean to take that down?"

She glared at him. "Does it look like I did it by accident?"

He laughed. "With you, anything's possible." He walked over and tested the corner post. "This won't stand for long either." He looked at the long and rambling busted-up fence on the side edge of her property shared with one neighbor and the big fancy fence butted up against it that was her neighbor's. "Are you going to remove this side too?"

"Is there any reason I can't and just use the neighbor's fence?"

He shrugged. "That's what I'd do."

With a big fat smile, she asked, "Can you pull out the last of those posts?" She was almost rubbing her hands together in joy at the thought of getting rid of this huge eyesore. Having this much of the ragtag fencing down had opened up so much of the creek's natural beauty that she couldn't wait to get rid of the rest of her creekside fence.

It seemingly took him nothing but the same effort to lift a cup of coffee, and he had the huge iron post up and out of the ground.

She couldn't even rock the pole slightly.

"It's a big mess back here," Mack said. "For now, the only good place to drag this old fencing is in the middle of the backyard. It'll take some of this plant stuff here with it."

"That *plant stuff* you're talking about happens to be perennial bushes that I would like to keep."

He glared at her but twisted so he had the post with both hands, pulled it higher over his head, and dragged what he could toward the center of her backyard where it ended up in a big heap on the lawn. "You'll need some good wire cutters to clip this into manageable pieces."

"What I need is a truck to make a trip to the dump," she announced. "I can't get very much in my car at one time."

"After you work on Mom's garden project, we'll probably make a trip to the dump, depending on how much yard waste we need to get rid of at Mom's house and how much new compost we may need to add. We can always take some of your yard debris at the same time."

She beamed. "Now that would be lovely." Then she frowned. "I don't think I have any tools that will cut up this wire fencing."

"I don't know. Nan had a whole pile of them in the hall closet."

Doreen glanced at him in surprise and then remembered the hall closet full of an odd assortment of things. "You could be right. I'll go check." She started toward the house before suddenly turning and calling out, "Careful! Don't hurt those plants!"

He shot her a look but continued to struggle with the posts.

Leaving him standing there, tugging at more fencing, trying to pull it up without damaging the plants, she headed inside to the closet. Once there, she wasn't exactly sure what wire cutters looked like. She found a hammer though—she needed that to pull out the nails in the wooden boards on the fallen pieces of fencing.

She grabbed what looked like two pairs of something—possibly what she needed—and, with the hammer, raced back outside. As she reached Mack, she held them up and said, "Ta-da."

He took one look, and his smile fell away. He started to laugh.

"What's wrong with that?"

He pointed to one and said, "Those are fancy toenail clippers for a dog."

She stared at them and then over at Mugs, who gave her a look that could have said, "Don't you dare."

She shook her head. "I've never seen any like this."

"It certainly won't cut wire. Now these, on the other hand," he said, taking the other pair that looked like weird shears to her, "will probably do it." He tested them on the center post he had pulled out. Instantly the wire snapped under his grip. He went to the main rod, cutting the wire off there and said, "Now do that to every one of those posts and separate the wire so you can roll it into a bundle."

She nodded eagerly. "I can do that." While she'd been searching for tools, he'd pulled out the rest of the main posts. Some of the plants were likely damaged, but she would spend the afternoon cutting this fencing monstrosity into something easier to handle. She smiled. "You can see how much better it looks already."

He turned and studied her massive backyard all the way to the creek and nodded. "You're right. Just getting rid of that ugly nightmare has opened it up beautifully. But you don't want a fence at the back?"

She shook her head. "No, I want to see the creek. It's beautiful." She led him to where she'd been standing earlier. "I think I would put a patio in here."

"Don't let the government know about that," he warned. "This is a riparian zone. You're not allowed to do anything without a mess of permits."

She lifted her eyebrows. "Permits? It's my land. Why can't I put down some flagstones?"

He shrugged. "All I can tell you is, you'll probably need a permit to do even that much."

She frowned, disgruntled. The last thing she wanted was anybody to stop her gardening fun. "I can just make it gravel then. I don't know. That's not a top priority. I have this lovely bank and a small path and the bridge. Although old, it's solid." Except for where she'd put her foot through one of the boards last week.

The bridge theoretically could be used by anyone, but she'd never seen anybody walking that creekside path, as it was quite overgrown and not very popular. But, for Mugs, it was a great way to get exercise. He could use it.

Just then Thaddeus hopped onto the pad of paper on the rock, sending it and her pencil flying into her teacup. The teacup fell with a crash to the rocks below, and Thaddeus hopped farther away from the damage. But, of course, in his high piercing voice, he called out, "Damn thing. Damn thing."

"Oh, Thaddeus, why do you say that?" She walked over, collected the busted pieces of china and the pad of paper, now covered in tea. It was her fault. She shouldn't have put it here. But she had no table or outdoor chairs at this spot that she could have otherwise used.

"I see you're teaching him more words." Mack kept his voice carefully bland.

She sent him a suspicious look. "Not intentionally."

He chuckled. "I'm pretty sure that damn bird will pick up everything you don't want him to."

Thaddeus looked at Mack with beady eyes, tilted his head to one side, and said, "Damn bird. Damn bird. Damn bird."

She groaned. "Watch what you say around him."

Mack held out his hands. "Me? I'm not the one who taught him the first phrase."

"But now you have taught him the second one," she snapped. "Before we know it, he'll know all the curse words and shock the neighbors."

"I think you've already shocked the neighbors," Mack said with a grin. "Finding bodies, capturing a murderer, and solving a case that has been cold for a long time all definitely counts as shocking the neighbors."

She blushed at the admiration in his tone. "Well, I did my best. Besides, you needed my help."

"I did *not* need your help," he blustered. "I have been a detective for a long time, solving crimes well before you ever came here."

"Yes, but you didn't solve this one, did you?" She couldn't help teasing him.

"Well, how was I to know you had a body hidden on your property?"

She shrugged. "At least *we* solved it," she said, magnanimously adding, "the two of us together."

He hesitated, tilted his head in her direction. "Okay, I'll give you that. We did that one together."

She beamed. "Now that Thaddeus has emptied my tea and broken my cup, do you want to go inside and have a cup of tea?"

He shook his head. "I'll take a rain check on that. I

stopped by to ask if you could come to my mother's house. She's got a patch of begonias she's fretting about. I don't know if you can fix them. But, while we're there, we could discuss what to do and when."

Doreen donned her expert gardener face. "Of course I know how to deal with ailing begonias. I have begonias here that need to get into the ground. They were dug out when your department came and removed the body. The first one."

He nodded. "And since I mentioned that begonias had been pulled out here, my mother has been fretting over the begonias in her garden."

"When do you want to go?"

He hesitated. "I don't want her to worry, so would you mind coming with me now, just to take a quick look? We'll come up with a plan on what we can do with them."

Excited, Doreen said, "Absolutely. Let's go."

They walked around to the driveway. Ignoring the people standing and staring outside her house, not saying a word to anyone, Doreen hopped into his truck, Mugs trying to follow her. "Okay if Mugs rides with us?"

Only it wasn't just Mugs as Goliath raced toward them, Thaddeus squawking from the porch before soaring in their direction.

"Everyone? Really?" Mack sighed and allowed time for Doreen to pick up her menagerie. When they were all in the vehicle, he reversed out of her driveway and drove the five minutes to his mother's house. It was close enough to walk, but then they would have been accosted by all the curious onlookers.

As they got out of his vehicle, he said, "She should be napping still. I left her ready to go to sleep and came straight to your place." They slipped around to the back, and he pointed out a large patch that wasn't doing very well.

Doreen sighed. "If these are begonias, they've definitely seen better days." She wandered the large six-foot-plus patch and then bent down on her hands and knees, plunging her fingers into the dirt, checking and testing the soil. "I'm not exactly sure what's wrong with them. Is there a shovel handy?"

He brought over a small spade. She dug in close to the roots on the first bush, pulling up some of the dirt so she could see the root system. After scooping away several spades full, she stopped, brushed off some of the dirt against the tubers, and took a closer look. "They're definitely not happy. How often are they getting water?"

"There are sprinklers and soaker hoses on timers. So they should be getting plenty."

She nodded and shifted her spade back a little bit, so she could pull out more dirt. Some perlite was all around the base of the plant, but the black dirt was decent. Although plenty of clay was here too, it appeared to be absorbing enough water. As she pulled up another handful, she froze.

Mack bent down beside her. "What's the matter?"

She plucked up something white, dropping it in his hand. She turned to look at him. "Is this what I think it is?"

He frowned, shook his head, but his mouth opened, and then he froze. "I sure as hell hope not."

"It would be fitting," she said in a dark tone.

"How?" he barked, his gaze on what was in his hand.

She snickered. "Bones in the begonias, anyone?"

This concludes Book 1 of Lovely Lethal Gardens:
Arsenic in the Azaleas.
Read about Bones in the Begonias:
Lovely Lethal Gardens, Book 2

Lovely Lethal Gardens: Bones in the Begonias (Book #2)

A new cozy mystery series from USA Today best-selling author Dale Mayer. Follow gardener and amateur sleuth Doreen Montgomery—and her amusing and mostly lovable cat, dog, and parrot—as they catch murderers and solve crimes in lovely Kelowna, British Columbia.

Riches to rags. ... Chaos continues. ... Murders abound. ... Honestly?

Doreen Montgomery's new life in Kelowna was supposed to be a fresh start after a nasty split from her husband of fourteen years, plus a chance to get her bearings and her life back on track. Instead her first week in her new hometown was spent digging up dead bodies, chasing clues, and getting in Corporal Mack Moreau's way.

But now that the old cold case has been solved, and the murderer brought to justice, Doreen believes things might go her way this week. When Mack hires her to whip his mother's garden into shape, it seems like a second chance, both for Doreen's new beginning in Kelowna and for her budding relationship with Mack.

But, instead of digging up Mrs. Moreau's struggling begonias and planting them in a better location, Doreen discovers another set of bones ... and another mystery to solve. As the clues pile up, Mack makes it abundantly clear that he doesn't want or need her help, but Doreen can't resist the lure of another whodunit. As she and Mack butt heads and chase red herrings, Doreen's grandmother, Nan, sets odds and places bets on who solves the crime first.

All while a murderer is watching ...

Book 2 is available now!
To find out more visit Dale Mayer's website.
http://smarturl.it/BonesDMUniversal

Lovely Lethal Gardens: Corpse in the Carnations (Book #3)

A new cozy mystery series from USA Today best-selling author Dale Mayer. Follow gardener and amateur sleuth Doreen Montgomery—and her amusing and mostly lovable cat, dog, and parrot—as they catch murderers and solve crimes in lovely Kelowna, British Columbia.

Riches to rags. … Chaos calms. … Crime quiets. … But does it really?

After getting involved in two murder cases in the short time she's lived in picturesque Kelowna, divorcee and gardener Doreen Montgomery has developed a reputation almost as notorious as her Nan's. The only way to stop people from speculating, is to live a life of unrelieved boredom until the media and the neighbors forget about her. And Doreen aims to do just that with a tour of Kelowna's famed Carnation Gardens. Plants, more plants, and nothing whatsoever that anyone could object to.

But when she sees a fight between a beautiful young woman and her boyfriend, she can't help but be concerned. Concerned enough that she follows the couple out of the parking lot and through town. And when gunshots interrupt the placid afternoon, it's too late to worry about how her nemesis, Corporal Mack Moreau, will feel about her getting involved in yet another of his cases.

With bodies turning up in the carnations, and a connection to a cold case of a missing child from long ago, Doreen has her hands full, not least with trying to keep her involvement in the investigations a secret from her Nan, Mack Moreau, and especially the media. But someone's keeping up with Doreen's doings… and that someone can't afford for her to find the answers to the questions she's asking.

Book 3 is available now!
To find out more visit Dale Mayer's website.
http://smarturl.it/CorpseDMUniversal

Author's Note

Thank you for reading Arsenic in the Azaleas: Lovely Lethal Gardens, Book 1! If you enjoyed the book, please take a moment and leave a short review.

Dear reader,

I love to hear from readers, and you can contact me at my website: www.dalemayer.com or at my Facebook author page. To be informed of new releases and special offers, sign up for my newsletter or follow me on BookBub. And if you are interested in joining Dale Mayer's Reader Group, here is the Facebook sign up page.
facebook.com/groups/402384989872660

Cheers,
Dale Mayer

About the Author

Dale Mayer is a USA Today bestselling author best known for her Psychic Visions and Family Blood Ties series. Her contemporary romances are raw and full of passion and emotion (Second Chances, SKIN), her thrillers will keep you guessing (By Death series), and her romantic comedies will keep you giggling (It's a Dog's Life and Charmin Marvin Romantic Comedy series).

She honors the stories that come to her – and some of them are crazy and break all the rules and cross multiple genres!

To go with her fiction, she also writes nonfiction in many different fields with books available on resume writing, companion gardening and the US mortgage system. She has recently published her Career Essentials Series. All her books are available in print and ebook format.

Connect with Dale Mayer Online

Dale's Website – www.dalemayer.com
Twitter – @DaleMayer
Facebook – dalemayer.com/fb
BookBub – bookbub.com/authors/dale-mayer

Also by Dale Mayer

Published Adult Books:

Lovely Lethal Gardens
Arsenic in the Azaleas, Book 1
Bones in the Begonias, Book 2
Corpse in the Carnations, Book 3
Daggers in the Dahlias, Book 4
Evidence in the Echinacea, Book 5
Footprints in the Ferns, Book 6

Psychic Vision Series
Tuesday's Child
Hide 'n Go Seek
Maddy's Floor
Garden of Sorrow
Knock Knock...
Rare Find
Eyes to the Soul
Now You See Her
Shattered
Into the Abyss
Seeds of Malice
Eye of the Falcon
Itsy-Bitsy Spider
Unmasked
Deep Beneath

Psychic Visions Books 1–3
Psychic Visions Books 4–6
Psychic Visions Books 7–9

By Death Series
Touched by Death
Haunted by Death
Chilled by Death
By Death Books 1–3

Broken Protocols – Romantic Comedy Series
Cat's Meow
Cat's Pajamas
Cat's Cradle
Cat's Claus
Broken Protocols 1-4

Broken and... Mending
Skin
Scars
Scales (of Justice)
Broken but… Mending 1-3

Glory
Genesis
Tori
Celeste
Glory Trilogy

Biker Blues
Morgan: Biker Blues, Volume 1
Cash: Biker Blues, Volume 2

SEALs of Honor

Heroes for Hire

SEALs of Steel

Collections

RomanceX3

Standalone Novellas
It's a Dog's Life
Riana's Revenge
Second Chances

Published Young Adult Books:

Family Blood Ties Series
Vampire in Denial
Vampire in Distress
Vampire in Design
Vampire in Deceit
Vampire in Defiance
Vampire in Conflict
Vampire in Chaos
Vampire in Crisis
Vampire in Control
Vampire in Charge
Family Blood Ties Set 1–3
Family Blood Ties Set 1–5
Family Blood Ties Set 4–6
Family Blood Ties Set 7–9
Sian's Solution, A Family Blood Ties Series Prequel
    Novelette

Design series
Dangerous Designs
Deadly Designs
Darkest Designs
Design Series Trilogy

Standalone
In Cassie's Corner
Gem Stone (a Gemma Stone Mystery)
Time Thieves

Published Non-Fiction Books:

Career Essentials
Career Essentials: The Résumé
Career Essentials: The Cover Letter
Career Essentials: The Interview
Career Essentials: 3 in 1

42700165R00163

Made in the USA
Middletown, DE
17 April 2019